John Ski never dreamed of being a writer but one day, on a drive to the Lake District, he was inspired to write this story and he never looked back. Married with two children and living in a small village in Scotland, John is loving the quiet life and watching his children grow up.

To my wife, Caitlin. Without you I wouldn't have managed to complete this book. Your belief in me and your support all the way through this process from start to finish was unwavering and completely amazing. You had full faith in me and in my story and I love you with all my heart. Thank you for everything.

John Ski

SETH BRONX AND THE COATHANGER KILLER

AUSTIN MACAULEY PUBLISHERS™

LONDON * CAMBRIDGE * NEW YORK * SHARJAH

A CIP catalogue record for this title is available from the British Library.

ISBN 9781398425675 (Paperback)
ISBN 9781398425682 (ePub e-book)

www.austinmacauley.com

First Published 2022
Austin Macauley Publishers Ltd®
1 Canada Square
Canary Wharf
London
E14 5AA

Chapter One

June 7th

Exactly one year to this very day, saw the most brutal and noteworthy moment in the history of a small town of Kentsville. Seth, having just awoken, got up from his bed and made the short walk into the bathroom across the hall. Looking in the mirror, he saw a tall, well-built man with striking blue eyes staring back at him. He focused on his reflection for a few moments, lost in his thoughts of this day and what it meant to him. Eleandra Jacobson, the 22-year-old music teacher, whose life was unfortunately taken in this brutality, was none other than his cousin, his family. Seth being seven years older and having lost both his parents in a car crash when he was twelve had grown up living with Eleandra and her mother, his aunty Dorothy. Seth and Eleandra had a very close relationship, a connection like that of siblings. His bright blue eyes shared an uncanny similarity to his younger cousin, and even in the barely lit bathroom, he could see her eyes through his own. With the mirror doing its best to taunt him, Seth moved his gaze away and turned on the tap in front of him, splashing cold water onto his face to shake himself from the dazed memory of her. Clutching onto the edge of the sink, Seth exhaled a large breath of air. "I will do this no matter what it takes. I'll do this for you, Eleandra."

Leaving the bathroom, he glanced at the small picture frame hanging on his wall in the hallway. It was a moment in time when he and his buddies from the local fire station were smiling all too brightly at the camera, mere minutes after completing what was once his first, real rescue. Pausing briefly, Seth reminisced about his days in the forty-eighth division of the Kentsville Fire and rescue team. Joining the force as an 18-year-old, fresh-faced teenager who was eager to serve and impress, Seth made this his sole purpose, his career. His decision to leave the forty-eighth division came with a heavy heart, however, he knew that in order to find out the truth about Eleandra's death, he must dedicate his time and efforts solely to her case. Seth and his aunty both strongly believed that Clarke Richards, the accused killer, was framed or was somehow an unknowing accomplice to another who is still out there. The supposed evidence that was presented just didn't add up for Seth and he knew in his heart that something wasn't right. No matter what the explanation, Seth was determined to find the real killer; he was aiming for justice.

"I will do this for you, Eleandra."

He repeated this before walking away from the picture and down the hallway, Seth stopped in the doorway of his large open space living room, which happened to be the biggest room in his two-bedroom cottage. Nothing adorned the plain coloured walls in the main living area, no family photos or much of anything really. Seth had what he needed but didn't really have many of what some would deem lavish or materialistic belongings; that one photo in the hallway was probably the only captured memory that Seth allowed in his home. He used to have about twenty-five photos and memories of him, Eleandra, his best friend Cassie and his aunty Dorothy hung here but not anymore, all of that had changed over the past year. Walking through the open space towards the table in the kitchen, Seth removed a black shirt which was situated on one of the four wooden chairs, and proceeded to put it on, dark grey trousers followed suit. He then reached to the chair directly to the left grasping his dark grey jacket. Seth fastened up two buttons and in moments, had gone from a half-naked man to the perfect businessman. He made his way back through the hallway to the bathroom and grabbed some socks from the overcrowded clothing airer. Sitting on the toilet seat, he battled with his balance to put them on. Standing once again in front of the mirror, Seth ran some gel through his short brown hair, styling his quiff to perfection. Giving himself a nod of approval and a final smug wink, he washed the gel off his hands and brushed his teeth, leaving for the living room once more. Grabbing his shoes and bag from beside the door, Seth rushed to put them on. Collecting his keys from the hook and phone from the table, he stuffed them into his pockets and was ready to go. Having a swift look around to make sure he had everything he would need for the day, he assured himself that he was good to go and turned to leave the house. One hand on the door, ready to exit into the cold morning air, Seth stopped, hearing a loud ring coming from his jacket pocket. Looking at the digital clock on the small hallway unit, he had just walked up and down; he noticed that the time was 8:03 AM. He wasn't expecting a call this early in the morning but decided to answer as he was already leaving three minutes later than planned anyway. Hesitating in case it was the pests of the phone industry calling, he pressed the green 'accept' button to answer.

"If this is PPI or about an accident that I definitely haven't been involved in, then save your breath because I will be hanging up. If this is about changing my energy supplier, then no need to speak either, just hit the end call button as I'm happy with what I have."

After a few seconds of silence, Seth removed the phone from his ear and glanced at the screen, thinking that the caller had just hung up like he suggested. This was proved wrong when a voice that he could only just make out, buzzed through the phone's speaker. Slapping the phone quickly back to his ear, Seth listened eagerly to what was being said.

"If you want information with regards to the murder of Eleandra, then meet me at the old paper mill at 3 PM. And please come alone. I repeat, please come alone."

The call ended abruptly before Seth could reply. Stunned into a moment of silence, Seth's mind instantly became bombarded with the need for answers. Who was that? How did they get my number? Was it genuine? Why the old Paper Mill? It was common knowledge in the town that today marked the one-year death anniversary of Eleandra. The local paper had already sent out an article a few days prior, however, it wasn't meant to be common knowledge that he was investigating her death. Seth understood that today was the talk of the town and therefore, he was under the impression that the phone call he had just received was not a coincidence. Seth lowered the silent mobile from his ear and returned it to his left jacket pocket. Swinging open the front door and slamming it behind him, he walked in a trance like state towards his car. This was an intriguing start to the day indeed. It was Seth's first proper day investigating this case and all of a sudden someone wants to give him information. Although, he was questioning whether or not this was a trap, it was a good place for him to start as he knew he could use all the help he could get. Stopping in front of his car, he reached for his keys and pressed the button to unlock it, continuing to saunter around the other side and placing his bag in the front passenger side. Seth walked back around to the driver's side of the car and climbed in. Resting himself in the driver's seat, he took out a photo from his inside jacket pocket. The familiar soft features that stared back at him in the bathroom mirror were the same as in this photo. The beautiful blonde girl tugged at his heart, and the image of the all too familiar Giraffe pendant resting around her neck pulled at them even more. Seth had bought this for her birthday, the year before last. He had a real sadness in his eyes whilst looking at the creased image and a lump once again formed in his throat for what would be the hundredth time of him looking at it. The photo was of Eleandra, one that he had taken the very day before she died. It was the last photo anyone ever took of her, as far as he knew and it meant the world to him. Even though it made him tear up almost every time he looked at, Seth couldn't help the small smile that came upon his stoic face as he reminisced about that particular day, their last day. Placing the photo back in his pocket, he turned on the car, and with a newfound roar of determination, headed towards his first destination. The sky above was shining bright, as confident a person as Seth normally was, he knew that he was also a tad nervous as he was putting a lot of pressure on himself to solve this alone. He headed towards his new office, where he would pick up the keys and finally be able to settle himself in. He had already signed the paperwork for the office a few days before but he had asked to collect the keys today; a good first distraction from the harsh reality of what this day represented. He collected his keys and then discarded boxes onto his desk from the trunk of his car, ready to be unpacked at a later time, Seth took a moment to stop and survey his surroundings. It wasn't much but Seth never really was one for over the top, material items. A wooden desk was perched under a small, rectangular window and two grey filing cabinets stood against opposite walls from each other. As Seth was the only person who would be using this space, it was more than enough for him. Side glancing at the unpacked boxes once more, Seth moved towards the door, stepping out to lock it and he then proceeded to head to his next stop. Next up for Seth was the hardware store. He was nearly there when a potential accident almost occurred with him and another car. Taking the corner too fast, the other car nearly came barrelling into Seth but thankfully, neither car took any damage and nor did the drivers. However, Seth flipping the driver off in his rear-view mirror let whoever it was, know that he wasn't impressed. Upon arrival at the hardware store, Seth parked up out front, managing to take up one of the six spaces with ease due to the little custom at this particular time of the morning. Walking inside the store, he selected only the items which were on his short list; cable ties, A2 flip chart, a stand and small black bin bags. Seth exchanged pleasantries with the owner of the store, Jerry. Jerry was a short, stocky man, who had short grey hair, a long drawn-out face and a grey moustache. He had owned this hardware store since before Seth was born and was therefore accustomed to Seth and his family. He knew Seth's parents well, especially his dad, as they both attended poker nights together years ago before their tragic car accident. Losing them was the hardest thing he ever had to experience and then he lost Eleandra too. Seth always made time for Jerry and his selfless, kind personality. Jerry would always go out of his way to help others and Seth feared that his kindness was often taken advantage of. After the items were purchased and the conversation with Jerry was done, he wished him a good day and got in his car, speeding off towards his next place of interest, the most important stop of his day so far, a place to really kickstart his search for the truth. For many weeks, Seth had been pondering about where to initially start his investigation, and he went back and forth in his mind. He didn't really have a great place to start and the stress of this decision took a great toll on him. Not knowing where to start was proving to be really difficult for him, this eventually led him to the decision that the first port of call was going to be to visit Mrs Richards, Clarke's wife. The only person who knew about this decision was his aunty, who had attempted to talk him out of it. Disagreeing with her negativity on this idea, Seth was eventually more than adamant that it was the place to start. After all, other than himself and his aunty, Clarke's wife was probably next in line for wanting to know the truth of that day, to finally clear her husband's name of these horrible accusations. Seth also decided against pre-warning Mrs Richards of his imminent arrival, and although he did actually question that decision more than once, he knew that had he announced his desire to talk face to face, she may have probably refused. Standing outside the Richards residence, he paused and waited for a few moments, closely observing the main window to see if he could spot any movement or sign that someone was home. There was a car in the driveway which hopefully meant she was present inside. Seth knew that theoretically her two boys should have been at school and glancing down at his wristwatch understood that school run time was over. Staring into the window once more, Seth could see no movements or indication that anyone was home. However, with a deep breath, he approached the front door and knocked anyway. It didn't take long before he heard movement from the other side of the door. The echoing of a chain being removed from the latch forced Seth to straighten up and then to hear the latch put on again made him unsure what the person behind the door would do. After a short pause, they opened the letterbox and a female spoke to him. He stepped back and crouched down, looking into the brown eyes of an unknown female. With a short pause, she finally spoke in a small and timid voice, "I...I...I know who you are, I remember seeing you on the television a lot over the last year. What do you want from me? I'm sorry for what happened to your cousin, I truly am but we have suffered enough, please just leave us alone."

Her pleading and desperate tone encouraged Seth to quickly react.

"Mrs Richards, it is correct that I have come here to speak of what happened with my cousin Eleandra, however, I have not come to cause you any stress or grief. I strongly believe your husband was innocent in the partaking of my cousin's death or at least an unknowing accomplice. I believe him to be a victim, an innocent bystander who was framed. I don't think he killed anybody; I don't think he killed Eleandra."

From the moment Seth stopped talking, he could hear her sobbing behind the door, giving her some time to get out some tears, he proceeded to talk once again.

"Mrs Richards, I aim to prove his innocence but I need your help to do so. Please, will you help me? Help me clear your husband's name and help me get some truth and justice for Eleandra and in turn, for Clarke."

Seth could hear her large gulp of breath before she opened the door slightly and spoke.

"How can I help you?"

"I just need to sit down with you and talk. I have some questions that I would be grateful if you could answer. Sometimes, we know more than we realise we do."

The following silence, which coincided with her decision to stop the sobbing, still didn't get her to answer right away. Seth was going to speak again when the door slowly opened much wider than before, revealing the tear-stained face of Clarke's widow. Unwilling to spook her, Seth held his tongue momentarily as he observed her timid features, then he asked his next question.

"May I please come in?"

Again there was no verbal response, however, she nodded to indicate he could, even going as far as opening the door more for him and gesturing towards the inside with a wave of her arm. Slowly stepping forward, Seth observed as she moved back slightly to give more room to enter through the doorway where she stood a few feet in front of him. Stepping through the doorway, he could see lots of family photos hanging on the hallway walls; photos of Mr and Mrs Richards, the children and photos of them altogether. Closing the door softly, Mrs Richards led Seth into a fairly big, cosy living room. Sitting on a plush pink sofa, Seth couldn't help but feel sad for the timid woman. Just like himself, she had suffered a great loss, and so had her young children. The loss of a husband is hard but the loss of a father would no doubt have a long-lasting effect on the children, Seth had first-hand experience of that. Even after all of this, if somehow Seth was wrong and Clarke was the real killer, he would still feel this anguish for the children. They had done nothing wrong; they were innocent, no matter what the outcome. Looking around, Seth spotted a large family portrait, printed on a canvas, situated in the middle of the living room. The smiling faces gave Seth the feeling that this was once a happy family home, and in the spur of the moment, it made Seth think of how this could potentially be him one day. *Was this something he wanted,* he thought.

"How old are your children, Mrs Richards?"

"They're ten and seven."

"Oh, that's a good age."

Seth had no idea if this was true or not, he had just heard people say it in the past and it seemed to always go down well as a quick and standard response.

"Seth, what is it you think I may know? I don't mean to come across as rude or ungrateful but if you think you can clear Clarke's name, I would like to hear how I can be of assistance."

Her long puffy face was pulled into an unnatural frown, which made her look older than her actual age but it was the determined tone of her voice that took Seth by surprise. Pulling out a small notepad and the picture of Eleandra from his inside jacket pocket, Seth delicately presented it to her.

"I keep this photo with me to remind me of her and to remind me of why I'm doing this and what she means to me. My cousin had her whole life ahead of her and someone decided to take that away in mere moments. Your husband didn't kill her, I'm sure of it, and I know I'm asking a lot of you here but please trust me. I'll go as far as to say I promise you he didn't kill Eleandra. Do you have any photos of Clarke you keep with you?"

"I used too but we've had a whole year of abuse, both verbal and physical. My boys have had to change school, I've had to change jobs twice; it's been hell. It made me stop carrying them around, not because I stopped loving him, not for the fact I didn't believe his innocence but because it was one less way of people finding out that he was my husband or the boy's father. We've been through enough; I need to protect them in any way I can."

"I can't say I know how that feels but I understand that must be incredibly hard to go through, another reason to let me help you, by you helping me." With steady hands, Seth put Eleandra's photo on the table in front of him and retrieved a pen out of the same jacket pocket the photo was in.

"Excuse my lack of manners, I seem to have forgotten myself for a moment, can I get you a drink?"

"Yes please, that would be nice," he said.

"Hot or cold?"

"A nice hot chocolate would be great if you have one, please, if not then a glass of water would be a good way to go too."

"I'm afraid we only have a milky way hot chocolate; it's the boys' favourite and we always stock up on it. Sorry, I mean I always stock up on it."

"That sounds delicious, sign me up."

She was gone for just over a couple of minutes before returning with a cup in each hand and a biscuit tin under her left arm.

"The kettle had actually just finished boiling when you arrived and please, help yourself to a biscuit," she said pushing the tin across the table towards him.

Seth didn't want to overstep his welcome but he thought it rude to refuse her hospitality, so reached forward and embraced the goodness of a chocolate digestive. Once he had finished his biscuit, Seth wiped his hands on his trousers and proceeded to pick his notepad up from the table, wasting no time with the questions.

"Mrs Richards, did you or Clarke ever have any money troubles?"

"Seth please, call me Monica. And no, to my knowledge we didn't."

Monica had perked up a fair bit now and Seth imagined this was what she was like on a normal day. She wasn't swinging from the ceiling or shouting from the rooftops but a few sips of tea and the idea of her husband's name being cleared had obviously helped her cheer up a tad.

"Did he have any enemies or anyone who had any resentment towards him?"

"One guy he worked with wasn't happy because he got a few complaints and their boss made him switch shifts with Clarke, that's about it, no one else I can think of."

"I'll speak to his boss to be safe but I doubt that would make anyone angry enough to kill him and then frame him for Eleandra's murder."

"Did he have any lads' nights out on a regular basis?"

"Yes, actually he did, the first Saturday of every month; there was a poker night at his friend Peter's house. Peter Head, he lives six doors down."

"I know of Peter, my dad used to play poker with him when I was a boy, he used to say that Peter Head was as decent a man as anyone you could ever wish to meet."

In his mind, Seth reminisced of stories his father told him when he was small and couldn't help but smile. He eventually snapped out of it and continued his questions when he noticed Monica staring at him.

"This one's a bit more personal Monica but I need to cover all the angles. Did you ever suspect Clarke of having an affair at any point?" Much to Seth's surprise, she let out a small giggle before composing herself.

"I don't mean to laugh but Clarke, have an affair? Please, no one else would have him."

They both smiled and Seth continued.

"Any issues with neighbours or family members?"

"No. We are a quite small family, and everyone is harmonious with each other except during the football anyway." Seth was scratching his head, figuratively speaking, he thought there would be at least some small detail he would get from Monica that would help but apparently it was not to be, so far, he had reached a dead end.

"Monica, what shifts was your husband working leading up to that day?"

"He worked the same shifts he normally did; he started at eight in the morning and he was due to finish at four in the afternoon. He did do some overtime every now and then but it wasn't very frequent."

"What time did he normally leave the house for work?"

"He normally left about 7:30 so he could go to the locker storage near to the office. Afterwards, he would go to the taxi bays which are a five-minute drive from there."

"He was here with you before that? He never left the house until 7:30?"

Seth thought about this carefully. Eleandra's body was pronounced dead sometime between 7 and 9 AM. That meant Clarke left home at 7:30 and got to the office just before eight after visiting the storage unit, he would have had to pick up Eleandra, kill her and display her body in that inhumane way, all in the space of an hour.

"Actually Seth, Clarke left late that day. I'd say about seven fifty as the car wouldn't start at first, so he came back into the house and woke me up to jump-start it with mine."

"Did you tell the police that?"

Monica nodded her head to indicate she did. Seth sat silently for a moment and calculated all the details up in his head. He turned to face Monica and with a small smile relayed everything back to her to double-check it. At first, she was confused but eventually seemed to come up to speed with what Seth was trying to say. Wide-eyed, she gasped, "So are you saying this proves he didn't do it?"

"It's not undeniable in a court of law, a good lawyer could still argue it but I believe this means exactly that Monica. I believe that this proves Clarke is innocent."

Chapter Two

Monica jumped out of her chair so fast, that had Seth not been paying attention, he would have been flattened by her sheer physicality as she flung herself at him. Embracing him in a hug, Seth felt almost suffocated, like a small animal trapped in the hold of a deadly anaconda waiting to squeeze the life out of its prey, yet he also had a small amount of comfort building inside of him. Feeling her body shake against his, Seth could tell that she had started to sob again. Hearing her tears of joy this time, he imagined she hadn't been this happy in a long time but he did not want her to get her hopes up in case this newfound information didn't clear her husband of anything.

"Monica, I cannot guarantee that this will prove anything, so please don't get too carried away. It would be best if you keep what we have discussed to yourself, and I'll do the best I can with what I have going forward."

Composing herself, Monica nodded and began to clear the empty cups and biscuit tin to the kitchen. Upon her return, Seth explained he needed to head off so she escorted him towards the front door, saying her farewells once there. Stepping out into the cold, Seth turned towards Monica with one last wave and proceeded to get into his car. The news station was the next destination that Seth had in mind. A few hours into the first day of the investigation and it had already been an eye-opener. Seth knew that it wasn't always going to be as easy and smooth sailing as this but he had high hopes that he would make fast progress with this case. He was meant to be meeting his best friend since early childhood, Cassie Bowl. They had been friends since they were three and had attended school together, walked dogs together at school for extra money, and had seen each other through the good times and the rough times too. Cassie was his rock and Seth couldn't have wished for a better friend. Seth arrived at the news station and parked opposite the main revolving doors to the entrance. Getting out of his car, he walked through the doors and approached the reception area, coming face to face with a petit, brunette lady. She raised a pointed eyebrow at him from the other side of her glasses, obviously waiting for him to state his business. He felt a bit like he was on trial but with a silent gulp, Seth informed the woman that he was there to see Cassie. Much to his surprise, the woman cracked a small smile and informed him that she would give Cassie a call but not before pointing Seth in the direction of the seating area and telling him to wait there until she was ready. Seth took a seat as prompted and waited patiently for Cassie to arrive. He hoped he wouldn't be waiting too long as he was eager to tell her all about his morning adventures and converse over the segment she would be reading tonight on the six o'clock news. He waited for more than ten minutes without a single word from the receptionist, so he made the decision to go back over and speak to her again.

"Hello again, any idea how long she will be?"

"I'm sorry, who were you here to see?"

"Cassie Bowl, I have been waiting for over ten minutes and need to speak to her urgently."

"Oh yes, let me ring her now and see if she's coming down."

Seth frowned at the woman's response. He was confused, had she not rung or messaged her already? Was she forgetful or just incompetent at her job? He didn't sit back down in the seating area instead he decided to linger by the desk in hopes of speeding up the process. The lady picked up the phone and punched in some numbers, her blank expression indicating that she was waiting for an answer. Seth hoped she was actually ringing Cassie and not just wasting his time. He breathed a sigh of relief as she began to speak to the person on the other side.

"There is a gentleman here to see you. Oh his name, erm I never asked, one moment, please. Sorry, what was your name?" she said addressing him.

"Tell her it's Seth Bronx."

"He said his name is Derrick Socks but he looks more like an Abraham to me."

Seth was flabbergasted, taking a few steps back to put some distance between him and the woman, he couldn't decide if she was extremely dense, hard of hearing or just very rude. After the call ended, she turned to an annoyed Seth (Who had no words to describe how badly he thought this woman needed a new profession) and mentioned that someone was on their way down. Thankfully, Seth had only just sat back down when a tall, thin man with a smile like a Cheshire cat, approached him. The man extended his hand forward, grabbing Seth's; he started to shake it vigorously.

"You must be Seth," he said while still shaking his hand.

"I am and you're most definitely not Cassie."

"Good observation. My name is Roy and I am the station's managing director. I would like to have a chat in my office before you speak to Cassie, if that would be alright?"

"Regarding what exactly?"

"All will become apparent soon, shall we?"

Seth hesitated for a few seconds, looking at Roy's outstretched hand which was pointing towards the inner part of the building.

"Sure, after you," he said but he wasn't entirely comfortable with this idea. Roy led the way around the back of reception and towards the lifts. There were no words spoken between them; it was dead silent. Seth was taking this time to size Roy up. He wasn't usually one to judge a book by its cover but on this occasion, he felt he knew his type. From just their brief interaction, he seemed a cocky, entitled man who looked down on anyone he thought less important than himself. Seth already wasn't a fan. As they were going up in the lift, both men kept their silence, not intentionally at first but as time went on neither man dared to break it; it would probably make it more awkward than it was already. For this Seth was thankful, he already had bad vibes from the man next to him and didn't want to encourage unnecessary interaction. The lift stopped at the sixth floor, which also happened to be the very top floor of the building. The men waited as the doors opened for them but they were only able to take a few steps forward, as there was another set of doors parallel to them. Taking a key card out from his suit pocket, Roy swiped it against the electronic lock to the right of him and stepped into his modern office, motioning for Seth to follow after him.

"Here we are then, my office."

Roy spread his arms out around him in some grand gesture as if Seth was supposed to be pleased or even impressed at the sight in front of him.

"Please come and have a look at this view, I had a private garden put in for the staff to enjoy their lunch, when the weather is allowing."

He ushered Seth past his pristine white desk, towards a big bay window at the far left of his office. Although, Seth didn't want to admit his adorance towards the view, he couldn't believe his eyes when he looked out the window. It was both vast and breath-taking; there was a pond beautifully littered with different types of fish, a majestic fountain that stood proudly at the end of a marbled archway and a cosy outdoor seating area that was surrounded by a few wickered garden swings. Seth was very impressed; he never knew about this part of the building and Cassie never mentioned it but his lack of knowledge on this wasn't much of a surprise considering this was actually the first time he had been to the news studios. He turned to Roy and decided to express how impressed he was with the view even though he didn't want to, however, he motioned towards the desk, eager for whatever was to be discussed, to be over.

"Shall we get started?" said Roy, taking Seth's initiative and trying to make it his own.

"Let's."

"First you should order food, Cassie and I have already sent ours down to the chef, he is sensational, what would you like?"

Seth was thinking about meatballs when Roy made a recommendation.

"I'm having lobster and some shrimp cocktail, you'll love it, it's fantastic."

Seth was definitely not about to order lobster, his dislike for seafood made that decision easy for him. Lobster was not up his street at all and he honestly knew he would prefer meatballs; he was craving them in fact.

"Thank you for your recommendation, however, I am not really a lover of lobster. I am really in the mood for some meatballs if that is an option."

"Of course, I'll call down now and add that to our order."

Roy was placing Seth's order for meatballs when Seth had a sudden change of mind. Interrupting Roy's conversation with the Chef, Seth asked Roy if he could change his order. Sensing Roy's frustration, Seth watched as the man placed the phone on the desk and put it on loudspeaker. Roy raised an eyebrow at Seth and directed him to speak.

"Is there any chance you could make me a sandwich instead please?"

There was a slight pause before an Italian male voice replied sounding completely out of sorts. "You want me to make a sandwich? I make ze most amazing culinary delights and you want me to make a sandwich?"

"Yes please," Seth replied slowly in an unsure tone.

"I will do this for you because in my kitchen, even a simple sandwich is a work of art. What would you like in between ze bread?"

"My favourite, corned beef and banana please. Oh and no butter."

"What did you just say? That sounds like a monstrosity."

"Corned beef cut thin if it's not sliced, then the banana sliced into 12 equal pieces spread out on top. No butter, that's important, not a great lover of butter."

"Fine, az you wish. I will prepare zis disaster sandwich for you but you tell no one, it didn't come from my kitchen. I don't want zis to haunt me or my menu if anyone gets hold of zis story."

Roy put his hand up to ask Seth to not respond, he instead spoke to the chef.

"Once again Antonio you are the best, thank you in advance for the scrumptious meal you are preparing."

"You are welcome, ze food shall be sent up to you in a short while."

Roy ended the call and displayed his pearly whites towards Seth, which made him feel somewhat uncomfortable and nauseated.

"Now Seth, I know it was planned for you and Cassie to have a little chit chat about the unfortunate passing of Eleandra, then she would deliver a small piece about it on the news tonight. However, I've had a brain wave, a splendid idea in fact."

"Well, the worst I can say is no, so please continue Roy," said Seth.

Although Seth's reply made it seem like he was open to this newfound brain wave, he wasn't, he usually wasn't the type to support spontaneity once something was already set. Nonetheless, he decided to at least hear him out on what he had to say, maybe it would be a grand idea after all.

"Consider this, Cassie could interview you tonight live on the six o'clock show. You could present to the town exactly what it is you are doing and why you are doing it, which then leaves room for us to be able to open up an anonymous tip line for anyone who may have valuable intel on the issue but may be too scared to approach you in person. This is a great way to gain the attention of the correct people and may even become a part of a massive breakthrough for you."

Seth was stunned, he wasn't sure what shocked him more, the fact that Roy's idea was good, no, fantastic! Or that it was Roy who came up with the notion in the first place. Unwilling to show his initial excitement or that he was actually on board with the idea from the moment it left Roy's mouth, Seth approached his response with caution, after all he didn't want Roy to start making demands of what was said in the interview. Instead, he opted for a moment of silence; face blank and void of any emotion, which allowed enough time to make Roy sweat a little. Prolonging the suspense, Seth rose from his seat and walked towards the window, leaning down and gripping at the frame, he sighed very loudly for Roy to hear. He stood up straight and rubbed a hand over his face before making his way back over to his chair and sitting back down. Roy himself made no effort to speak again or break the silence instead he observed Seth's movements and sat patiently waiting for a response as the man in front of him stared him dead in the eye. Much to Roy's annoyance, Seth made no attempt to move, however, he abruptly reached over and shook his hand cordially just as Roy had enough of Seth's time-wasting and was about to impatiently break the deafening silence.

"I accept this proposal of yours and would like to go ahead with it, with a few provisos of course."

"Of course, Seth, we can discuss that with…"

He was cut short by a soft rapping on the door and Cassie entering the room.

"With Cassie, when she arrives," he continued as she started walking towards them.

"Speak of the devil and she shall appear." Seth chuckled.

"Me, the devil, never," she responded with a glowing smile.

She approached Seth with urgent strides, and once he stood up in front of her, began to embrace him in a friendly hug.

"You look great Cassie, as always, of course. How are you?"

"Thank you, Seth, I am doing well. You are looking quite sharp yourself, I must say I don't think I've seen you in a suit in about what, eight, maybe nine months."

"Yes, it's something like that."

"So boys, what did I miss?" she said.

Her question addressed them both and it was Roy that answered.

"I was just asking Seth if he would be up for a live interview on the six o'clock show tonight. It will be a great opportunity to progress his investigation."

She turned to look at Seth.

"And?"

"After listening to Roy's offer, I decided to partake in a bit of live news action tonight."

"I'm delighted to hear that, Seth. When Roy mentioned it to me on the way down to meet you, I wasn't sure if you'd actually go through with it or think it was a good idea. I am thrilled to be wrong for once."

"For once? I remember you being wrong many times, Cassie." He joked.

"Seth, you know I'm normally always right," she said with a smirk.

"We shall agree to disagree."

Observing the exchange, Roy felt as though he was interrupting something private between the two, almost third-wheeling. He made a small, awkward cough in order to snap them out of the flirtatious exchange and back to the matter at hand.

"In all seriousness, Cassie you must discuss with Seth about his investigation and conjure up some questions in order to make a spectacular interview. I shall email over any input or questions that I think may make a key part in the interview. Seth, any of those provisos you want, just clear them with Cassie. I trust she will do what's best for all parties."

Roy stood from his chair and swiftly left the room.

"Before you say what you are about to say, just let me mention that I know how he can come across but give him a chance. I promise he's not all bad, just a little rough around the edges, and there is a reason he gets paid big money to do what he's doing. He is a genius at his job, no one else comes close. Yes, I know he can be cocky, pompous and self-assured but he is also very intelligent, ahead of the curve and downright amazing with his ideas and suggestions, and it makes my job easier and a lot better with him on my side. Anyways, he is right, this would be the best way to get as many people to potentially help and share information as possible."

"I agree, however, the verdict will remain out on Roy I'm afraid but if you vouch for him though it's good enough for me, for now, so I'll trust him to do what's best for Eleandra."

"Thank you, Seth."

Another abrupt knock on the door interrupted the exchange between the two. Walking over to the door and pulling it open, Cassie was met with the familiar tanned face of the studio's chef. He nodded at her and proceeded to push the silver food trolley into the centre of the room, stopping once he noticed it was just the two of them in the room. With a frustrated sigh, he raised an expectant eyebrow at Cassie.

"I'm sorry chef but Roy had to take his leave and therefore won't need his lobster. Neither of us eats seafood so it will be better if it goes back to the kitchen for his return later."

The pair watched on as the man's soft features turned hard and with a dramatic stomp of his foot, picked up Roy's food and rudely left the room, slamming the door on his way out. Exasperated, Seth turned to Cassie and motioned for her to sit down. He walked over to the trolley and picked up both their dishes before placing her's in front of her.

"Well, he's a bit emotional, isn't he? Shall we eat and chat about what happened today, I have a couple of things to fill you in on."

"Sure," said Cassie.

Seth rambled on about his morning before he came to the studios. He was sure to fill her in about the random phone call he received before leaving his house and left no detail untouched as he reminisced about his visit to Mrs Richards and the information that she shared with him about the timings of events on that morning. Cassie was almost as excited as Monica and had some theories of her own that she wanted to voice.

"So this is a step to prove that he didn't kill Eleandra but it doesn't prove anything in the eyes of the law, especially not with the local authorities, the police chief is adamant. It also doesn't explain how he ended up there after the murder, I guess maybe he accidentally witnessed what was taking place and had to be silenced?"

"I was thinking the same thing myself. There are plenty of details that still aren't making sense and a fair few dots that need to be connected but at least I know I was right, Eleandra didn't die at the hands of Clarke Richards."

"I can't believe you started your investigation with his wife. That was a ballsy move even for you and completely out of the box thinking. I think we should team up; my journalism has allowed me to obtain some pretty good investigation skills; we'd be amazing together, unstoppable even."

"I agree, we would indeed be unstoppable. Something for us to think about after our interview, Seth Bronx and his trusted sidekick Cassie, taking on the evil of the world, well, Kentsville to start with."

They both chuckled and started tucking into the food. Cassie gave Seth some of her carbonara, as she knew he too liked the flavoursome pasta dish, and in return, Seth shared with her his sandwich. Cassie wasn't a big fan, however, accepted his offer to share in hopes of not hurting his feelings. She always said yes, at first, she was interested in what it would taste like, now every time he made it when they were in each other's company, she had a bite or two. It has a unique taste just not her taste. Finishing up their food, they decided to make a start on a rough run-through of the interview in which they would be partaking in a few short hours.

"So I'll start off with a brief introduction of whom I am speaking with, which will obviously be you, then I will ask you a few questions in regard to why I am interviewing you. The more information you can give to us, the better. We will then end with me asking you to make any final comments and then I'll thank the audience for tuning in and wish them goodnight. If I overstep or you feel uncomfortable, just stop me. I just want to make sure all or as many bases are covered as possible, that will give us the best chance in getting justice for Eleandra."

Seth nodded and then indicated he was ready to start.

"I understand, let's proceed," he said.

"Seth, why don't you tell us in your own words what happened on the day which led to the brutal and unjust loss of life to your dear cousin, Eleandra."

"Well Cassie, it's no secret that one year ago today, we lost a beautiful soul to the darkness of this world. My cousin, Eleandra, was taken from us in an inhumane murder which this town has never seen before. The police investigation said it was an open and shut case. Eleandra's body was discovered on the floor, empty of all major organs, displayed like trophies on coat hangers. Hanging next to her, was a body of a male with a full written confession in his limp hand. I feel that it's not that simple. I feel like there is more and I am going to prove it. I'm going to find out what really happened that day."

"The police seemed very confident with their findings Seth, what makes you disagree that all aspects were covered and that Clarke Richards did not in fact commit this crime?"

"A guy murders a girl, a girl he has never met before. This guy has no known previous history of violence or of any aggressive tendencies. He is a man with a beautiful family, a family in which he is loved and adored, and he just so happens to have a full, written confession in his hand. It's never that simple, there is so much that just doesn't connect and I know in my heart that something is not right."

"Do you currently have any evidence as proof to substantiate your claims?"

"I currently have two very strong leads, one which nearly proves it wasn't Clarke, and the other will hopefully lead me to the real killer."

"Seth, interview aside, that's not entirely true, is it?"

"No it's not but I want people to think that, I want the real killer to sweat."

"You want to make him nervous, that's not an entirely bad call on your part. Moving on then. You and Eleandra were very close, like brother and sister, how did her sudden death affect you?"

"I'm the same as everyone watching and I feel what others who have suffered this before have felt."

"I understand but how did it affect you in particular, Seth?"

Taking a deep breath, Seth knew this was a question he couldn't ignore, especially if it was going to potentially touch the hearts of millions of people watching the show. For the first time since she had died, he finally opened up to Cassie, not as much as she had hoped but enough to make a small breakthrough.

"The death of a loved one is one of the hardest things you will experience in life. It's never easy to accept, even now. Eleandra was so young and so full of life and I question how anyone could do this to her, how they could take her life away just like that and in the way that they had done so. It was so evil and so dark; I will never understand the psyche of the person who was able to commit such an act. It really messed me up inside, it still does. On the outside, I appeared sadder but was more or less the same person but inside I was crushed. Living a life that only lets me reveal a false impression of my real feelings because I didn't want my colleagues or those closest to me to know how I felt. I don't like to discuss any feelings with anyone, I never have but in reality, I miss her face, her smile, her impressions that she always did of me. She would make me sound like anyone from Mr Bean to Elvis and I will never get that back, I will never hear that again. I tell the worst jokes but she always laughed at them, always, even the real bad ones, the real dad jokes and it hits me every day that her laugh will never again be heard aloud. What if one day I forget what she sounds like? She was the warmest and kindest person you could ever meet, she had so much life to her and she was taken away before her time. It hurts, it really, really hurts, kind of like a dagger to the chest. One that never stops slicing, never stops inflicting pain."

If Cassie looked closely enough, she would be able to observe that Seth looked like he would cry at any moment. Instead, he cleared the lump from his throat and continued.

"I think I needed to say all of that Cassie, not for the viewers later but for me."

"I'm glad I was the person to hear it, Seth."

Seth smiled long and hard at Cassie, she meant the world to him. She was the one constant in his life that had never changed and managed to give his world some normalcy. He badly wanted to take her for dinner but couldn't muster up the courage to ask. She interrupted his thoughts asking if he wanted to continue.

"Sorry, yes I'm good."

He smiled in order to convince her of this, however, in his head, he knew he wasn't. He was now thinking about his feelings for Cassie, which proved to be a good distraction from his sadness of Eleandra. Well, for a few fleeting seconds that is.

"Next question Cassie."

"How do you feel now, Seth?"

"Now I feel focused. Every ounce of my feelings, my grief, my anger and my longing to see Eleandra again, is channelled into determination to catch the real killer and get justice."

"How is your aunty Dorothy?"

"Do we have to bring her up? I know she will come up at some point but I haven't spoken to her about this interview yet. I mean I didn't really have any forewarning of this and I'm not entirely sure of how she would feel."

"Seth, I would never do anything that would hurt you or your aunty but the more we talk about this and the more emotions the viewers see, the more chance we have of people calling in to help. I get that you want to portray the hero but they don't want to see a hero, they want to see a man who will go to any lengths to help his family. They want to see a human being and his pain, not a robot. Therefore, I want everyone to know how much you are both hurting, which in result will make a bigger connection between you and them. We will just mention her and then move on."

Seth nodded his head in understanding.

"Seth, how is your aunty?"

"She is doing well, as well as you can expect. Most of her time is taken up with volunteer work as she left her job after Eleandra's death. Unfortunately, she couldn't be around children at the time of losing her own even though Eleandra was grown up. My aunt is a positive person just like her daughter was. Some days can be a struggle for her but with that same positivity she tries to make the best of every day. It goes without saying but no parent should ever have to bury their child. It was so cruel on her and I understand that my sufferings are nowhere near as bad as hers. She lost her daughter and had to say goodbye, I couldn't imagine being strong enough to do that, she is the strongest person I know. Her main goal in life is to live on for Eleandra and do great things to honour her memory."

"Seth, I'd really like to hear your insight into the murder and I'm sure everyone at home watching would too."

"Firstly, as I briefly touched on earlier, I have to say Clarke is innocent and soon I will prove that to everyone. His family is also innocent and have been suffering just as much as we have and I send my condolences to them. I am positive it wouldn't have been easy for them after all that's happened and they have become victims just as much as anyone else affected by this. The police made the call to close the case as they felt this was the correct thing to do given the evidence they were presented with. However, I know there is more evidence out there and I am going to find out what it is so that I can provide a different result."

"Seth, thank you for coming in and talking to me today, what would be your final message to the people who are watching?"

"Parents, grandparents, aunties, uncles, siblings, neighbours, friends and work colleagues out there, imagine this was someone you knew, someone who meant the world to you, how would you feel? How would your lives change? Think about how your families would be affected, how you would be affected. With these thoughts in your head, I implore you, please, if you know anything that could even remotely help me find the real killer, anything that you think would benefit me in my investigation, no matter how little, then please make contact and help me. Help a mother get solace in the fact her daughter's real killer has been found. Help me get some justice for Eleandra who was like a sister to me, help make our streets safer for our families and friends, for our children. And please do what is right for an amazing young woman, whose light was extinguished too early in life."

"Thank you for sharing with us today, Seth. I know these things aren't easy to talk about at home let alone on TV. Please, if anyone believes that they know something, anything, then please contact the number now showing on the bottom of the screen: 0800 000880 and our anonymous line will be open twenty-four hours a day. Remember, the smallest news could have the biggest impact. Thank you for being with us today, I'm Cassie Bowl wishing you all a safe and pleasant evening."

"That's done I guess?" said Seth.

"Yes, pretty much. One of the crew will say we're off and then we will be done."

Seth looked at his watch completely forgetting his limit of time; he needed to be at the paper mill at three o'clock.

"I am going to have to make a move. I need to meet this mystery caller at three and I want to be a little early to prepare for any unexpected turn of events."

"Please be careful. I know you'll say you will but I also know you'd do anything to find the truth, so I reiterate, please be careful."

"I will Cassie, I promise you."

He had a very sincere look on his face and he meant every word. The feelings he had earlier that he tried to suppress were coming back ten times stronger. He had never felt like this before, especially towards Cassie. They had been friends for over twenty years, why did he suddenly now have feelings of something other than friendship building up inside him? Seth moved closer to her; his heart was pounding in his chest. He was in uncharted waters but didn't want to show this to Cassie as he was sure these feelings were not mutual. He leant in for a hug and he was shocked when she kissed him on the cheek, close to his mouth too. She had never done this before and Seth couldn't work out if he was overthinking or maybe if she actually shared some of the same feelings towards him as he did her. He decided to leave, this wasn't the right time to bring this up and no matter how confused this made him or how much he wanted to discuss this with her, the investigation must come before anything else.

"Goodbye Cassie, I will see you again in a few hours."

"See you then, Seth, thanks for the sandwich."

He waved her goodbye as he stepped into the lift and let out a breath of relief that he didn't mess up that situation once the door he had opened to the lift closed behind him. As the lift descended, his heart ascended. It hit him like a flying brick to the face, he was in love with Cassie and he always had been.

Chapter Three

Seth's day was getting more intriguing by the hour. So much had happened and yet he still had to get to the paper mill to meet his mystery caller. For his first day on the investigation, Seth was impressed with the progression of the case and how much he had already fit in. From arranging a live TV interview to a personal meeting with Monica, and now off to meet someone else. Seth was sure of one thing, that it was about to become more intense. Moments away from pulling up at the paper mill, he slowed down and decided to drive around the road that goes past the car park to see if any other vehicles were there. Completing his lap with a steady pace, Seth observed that there were no other cars parked here in any of the spaces or anyone who stood near the entrance. Making his way through the emptiness, Seth parked his car right in the middle of the wide-open space to ensure that he was visible to anyone who was around. Either the person he was meeting wasn't here or maybe they were hiding inside and laying wait for him. Ensuring his own safety, Seth reached over to the glove compartment and weighed up his options, handgun or flash-bang grenade? He opted for the flash-bang, no need for the gun at this point, he figured that if things went wrong, he could still stun them and make a speedy exit. Glancing at the time, Seth decided he had a few minutes to spare so decided to call his aunt. He thought it wise that someone other than Cassie knows of his whereabouts, precautions needed to be made in case this went south.

"Hello, Seth," she said.

"Just a quick call to tell you there has been a slight change of plans. I'm going live on the six o'clock news this evening to be interviewed about my investigation. I thought it best to let you know as they will mention you briefly and I didn't want you to see it before you had heard it from me. I'm also meeting someone at the paper mill in a minute, if you for any reason don't see me on the news and don't hear from me, then please let the authorities know of my location and why I was here."

"I think that is a marvellous idea. I will tune in to the six o'clock news but Seth, please be careful at the paper mill and I will speak to you later. Thank you for letting me know."

Saying his goodbyes, Seth got out of the car and headed towards the abandoned building, a feeling of nervous excitement overcoming him as he walked into the unknown. He entered the building through the main door and was graced with faint memories from his time here a few years prior. Although somewhat familiar, Seth couldn't completely comprehend the full layout of the building, and therefore knew that the main entrance was his best route to take. He entered dark room after dark room; broken desks, smashed windows, graffitied walls and caved-in ceilings now all over the floor were his main view. The place was a mess, in his opinion it needed knocking down and rebuilding again. After five or six dark rooms, Seth finally entered a well-lit one that contained one glass ceiling panel, as the rest were all smashed on the floor mirroring the previous rooms. The bright light streaking out of it was a major contrast to the rest of the building. A light so needed; Seth couldn't understand why the place was shut down with all the employees making a run for the hills years back. Although a sight for sore eyes, this room and the structure had vast space which could be used for so many things. His impatience was now starting to get the best of him, he began to think this was a set-up as it was ten minutes past the meeting time and still no one was here. Slightly disheartened and ready to leave, Seth paused when he heard the faint noise of footsteps hitting the floor. He ducked behind a metal filing cabinet next to the door and waited for the footsteps to get closer, finally watching as a small, scruffy boy walked past him. His cautious movements made him seem very timid and the slight shaking of his body did not help to lessen this impression. Seth didn't know if this was the mystery caller or some kid playing around but he decided to take affirmative action just in case he was the caller and decided to make a run for it. Seth slowly approached the individual, gently taking hold of him and spun him around to face him, tightly holding him in place.

"You look familiar, who are you?"

At first, Seth was met with silence before the boy quickly began to mutter quietly. "Speak up lad, I'm not going to hurt you."

"My name is Bruce, I met you when you picked Eleandra up from school a few years back," he said shakily.

"You are too young to have been at school with Eleandra."

"Eleandra was three years above me sir, I've just turned 19."

"Then how did you know her?"

At first, he was silent, again, but then Bruce mustered a bit of courage, at least enough to speak.

"I never had a lot of friends at school, it was tough but I got through it unscathed in my first year. However, the second year wasn't so easy as I was getting bullied every day and I was too scared to speak out. That's until Eleandra saw a group beating me up one day and she managed to stop it. I couldn't believe it, no one had ever paid any mind to what was going on or even attempted to try and help me, yet here she was acting like my own personal superhero. One lad tried to punch her but she got him first, then another one lunged at her and she kneed him in the stomach and head-butted him just above his ear, it was enough to send him a clear message. The other two ran and from that day, they never bothered me again. I think they were worried that people would find out that a girl beat them up. From then on, she was so selfless, always made sure to check on me and made sure no one was bothering me, she was the nicest person I ever met. She could have just told a teacher but she knew I didn't want that so she kept quiet. She was so brave and fearless and in that one moment, she managed to stop nearly 8 months of bullying, something that the school had no interest in doing. I owe her everything, so now I want to help you to help her."

"Bruce, thank you for reminding me what an unbelievable young woman Eleandra was. But now I need to know what it is that you know."

He took a couple of deep breaths, inhaling and exhaling like he was breathing for the first time in months.

"The day before she was killed, she had a fight with a girl named Chelsea Chive in the field behind my house. No one else was there, just the two of them and they were very angry with each other, it was way past the point of being heated. I was walking my dog but they were so engrossed in their anger that they didn't even take notice of me, so I picked her up and rushed off. I don't do well with confrontation as you can probably tell, so I didn't want them to think I was listening in and get angry at me."

"Bruce, you look very pale are you alright? Do you need to sit down?"

"Probably a good idea, my legs feel all wobbly." Seth kicked some rubble out the way and helped Bruce sit down on the floor against the wall.

"Carry on Bruce, if you can?" Bruce nodded that he could and continued.

"Chelsea went to school with Eleandra and it was actually her ex-boyfriend that was one of my bullies. I don't think that has anything to do with the murder but the pair arguing the day before sure is suspicious, even more so given that they weren't friends and didn't do anything that connects them socially. I hope she wasn't involved; I'll never forgive myself if she was and I was too scared to tell the police this information a year ago."

"Bruce, the main thing is you are telling me now but I do have a few questions. How did you know I was investigating her murder? And how on earth did you get my phone number? Why are we meeting here of all places?"

"She was the only person who ever stood up for me at school and I have to be brave like she was, I have to help if I can. I got the phone number from my uncle's phone, Duncan Fairview, you two used to work together at the fire station."

"Duncan is a good man and I'm sure he won't be mad, what you did was for a good reason. So why here?"

"Eleandra used to bring me here and teach me how to defend myself against anyone who wished to harm me, so I know no one ever comes here, not even to graffiti anymore. I walk my dog here sometimes and talk to her, I know it sounds silly but it helps me to cope. She was the only person I really talked to, I couldn't talk to my parents, I still can't."

"I understand Bruce. I talk to her too sometimes."

"I hope this will help you, Seth."

"I'm sure it will. Thank you, Bruce, I will go and speak to her tomorrow. Do you need a lift home?"

"NO!" he said abruptly.

"No, thank you for the offer but I will walk, I like to walk and I don't want anyone to see us together."

"Take care of yourself, Bruce."

Seth helped him up, shook his hand and left the way he came in, through all the dark rooms. He looked around outside and still no one was there. Checking his watch once more, it was clear time was getting on. He had best get back to the station and get ready for his first-ever live interview. Taking his notepad and a pen out of his pocket, he wrote the name Chelsea Chive under another that was on the paper already, Mr Quinton Forsythe. He placed the items back in his pocket and headed back towards his car, ready for the short drive back to the station. On arrival, Seth was hit by a wave of emotions ranging from stress to nerves. You see, running into fires didn't faze him, looking for a murderer didn't faze him but what did faze him, was going on live TV for the first time ever. Seth was never really good at public speaking in front of any crowd, and even though he wouldn't see the faces of millions staring back at him, he would be fully aware of just how many were watching and that was enough to make his stomach churn. Nothing would prepare him for this, not even the comfort that Cassie was close by but he managed to soak up his nervousness and buried it deep inside and for the second time that day, headed towards the entrance of the studios. The same woman he had to suffer through earlier was situated in the same spot behind the desk, had she even moved? Seth hoped that this encounter would be different from their first one earlier and the process of seeing Cassie would be quicker. Sadly, he was wrong; she seems to have forgotten him as quickly as she'd frustrated him.

"Hello again, I am back to see Cassie."

"Cassie who?" Seth really couldn't believe her stupidity.

"Cassie Bowl! I was here a few hours ago, you sent me off with the studio's manager, Roy."

"Oh Cassie Bowl, I'll ring her for you. Please take a seat in the waiting area and I'll let you know when she is ready for you."

Seth didn't respond, he didn't see the point. He sat down on one of the solid chairs in the waiting area and got his phone out, proceeding to message his aunt to let her know all was good. After that, he sent a message to Cassie, informing her that he was waiting for her downstairs, as he didn't trust the competence of the receptionist who so rudely forgot about him earlier that day. Cassie's response was almost instant. She let Seth know that she was finishing up and that she would be down soon. Shortly after, Cassie, true to her word, walked into Seth's line of sight and greeted him with a huge smile, showing off her perfect teeth and small dimples by the edge of her cheeks. Seth replied with a smile of his own, however, he was unsure if it was because he was happy to see her and her smile, he did like that smile or if it was because it was actually her and not Roy meeting him. Cassie closed the distance between them with a friendly hug but it was her tense shoulders and deep sigh that caught Seth's attention.

"You seem worried, what's wrong?"

"I'll tell you in the lift where there are no prying eyes or listening ears."

"That doesn't sound like good news." Stepping into the lift, Cassie turned to look at Seth and unleashed the source of her worry.

"It seems someone else wants to meet you."

Seth stayed quiet, allowing her time to continue.

"Ted Stevens, the man who owns this news station. He has a few things he would like for me to ask you during the interview and he wants us to allow time for viewers to call and ask questions."

"Does he now? Well, let's meet this Ted Stevens and see what he's all about."

"You aren't mad? I thought you'd be a little mad."

"I'm not mad. I'll see how I feel once we've exchanged words but for now, I'm intrigued."

"Oh, I don't like the sound of that. Seth please be calm and think thoroughly before you decide to speak or take action."

"I will Cassie, I wouldn't jeopardise you or your career."

Cassie gave an uneasy smile once the lift stopped and the doors opened. Leading the way, she knocked on the door to Roy's office, entering once there was a mumbled "come in" from the other side.

"Hello again, Seth, hope you are ready for the main event," said Roy greeting them with that Cheshire cat-like smile.

"I believe so."

"Good, good. This is our owner, Ted Stevens; he has been eager to meet you after hearing about what we had planned for tonight's news."

"It's a pleasure to meet you, Ted."

"The pleasure is mine Seth; however, this isn't a social meeting it's a business one."

Seth paused momentarily as he observed the short, stocky man. It was apparent that the man prided himself on his appearance as he wore a crisp black suit with a burgundy tie. His face was perfectly shaven, making it difficult to hide the small beads of sweat on his upper lip. Seth would say the man was in his mid-forties, however, he was never really good at the whole age guessing thing.

"Oh really, well please go on," Seth replied with a wave of his hand.

"I have been thinking and would like to add a live Q and A in at the end of the interview. This is an opportunity to engage our viewers and make them feel involved."

"You think that is wise?"

"I think this interview will be massive for you. It's about your cousin and I respect that, however," Seth interrupted before he could continue.

"However…"

"However, for me, it's about business. This business is cutthroat and this will make the ratings hotter than ever. More calls equals more money and business is about money, it's what makes this and every other studio function. It's a win-win situation. You get your message across and we get more ratings, which comes with more money but it also allows you to hear and see things from the audience's perspective as well as maybe receive more intel."

"I understand your point of view. Can I have a moment to think about it? Erm, is that all?"

"Not exactly, I have also reviewed the questions you and Cassie prepared earlier and would like to add a couple myself."

"What would you like to add, Ted?"

"One, do you feel the police should do or should have done more? Two, why don't you discuss with us the leads you say you have? And three is about your idea of justice; you say that's what you want, what is justice to you? Good old-fashioned revenge?"

"Well, let's see, shall we. One, the police had evidence presented to them and they did what they could with what they had. I'm not mad with them but I will admit that I hope they will be open to what I have to say. In my mind, they have done their jobs and I am happy to investigate Eleandra's case myself, she is my family after all. And two, I can't share any information about my leads as I fear the evidence may fall into the hands of the wrong people and that is the last thing that I want. Oh and I nearly forgot three. Let me be very clear on this one, I want Justice, not revenge, Justice. There is a clear difference between the two and I want the person who murdered my cousin to spend the rest of their days locked away, where they can't harm anybody ever again."

Question three angered Seth and he couldn't stop himself from invading Ted's personal space. His response was spoken with a fierceness that not even Cassie had seen before. Taking a step back, Ted cleared his throat.

"Well, Seth if you answer those questions on-air then we can go ahead as planned."

"That is fine by me."

Making his way towards the door, Ted stopped abruptly and swung around to face all three of them.

"Actually, I want one more thing."

"Why not!" Seth answered through clenched teeth. He could feel himself raging inside and was almost past the boiling point. However, for the sake of Cassie, he managed to keep his temper under lock and key.

"I know this is going to be a major hit with the viewers and it will be what most people will be talking about, therefore, I want us to have exclusivity. If you speak, you speak only to us and only our station, we will have the latest and up-to-date knowledge of this investigation. I'll have a contract drawn up at once, that's if you accept."

Ted attempted to make himself seem unintimidated as Seth approached him. Grabbing firmly onto the man's hand, Seth proceeded to shake it most vigorously, whilst whispering quietly into his ear, ensuring Roy and Cassie were unable to hear the exchange. Ted rushed out of the room a few seconds later and was followed by a flustered Roy.

"What did you say to him, Seth?" asked Cassie.

"I said yes, the rest is between him and me."

"Hmm. We better get to makeup, follow me trouble."

"Makeup? I hadn't thought about that, is it a must?"

"Oh yes, it's a must! You are wearing makeup for the show like everyone does, now sit down."

Begrudgingly, Seth sat in the makeup chair as the artist fluffed about around him. He was so caught up in all the different makeup products displayed in front of him, that he hadn't noticed Cassie taking out her phone and recording his whole makeover process. Once the makeup was done and everyone was ready to go, Seth decided he should fill his aunty in on the discussion between him and Ted.

"How long till we go live, Cassie?"

"Six minutes."

"Quick phone call?"

Before she could protest, he ducked out the door and found a quiet space to keep his aunty up to date. He quickly summarised his encounter with Bruce and what had happened in the office with Ted and how angry he felt with the rude man. He finished his call on the agreement that he was meeting her in the morning to discuss thoroughly, in-depth about everything that had occurred today. Heading back towards makeup, Seth announced his presence to Cassie.

"I'm back. Told you I wouldn't be long."

"Good, they're ready for us, let's go."

"Cassie, I want you to know the only reason I'm doing this is because I trust you. If it was anyone else, I would have refused from the start."

"Over here please Seth," called a little plump lady at the back of the set.

Following her orders, Seth sat down on a chair directly opposite Cassie; it was centre of a small set. He waited patiently under the heat of the stage lights whilst the crew fitted clip-on microphones to their clothing and correctly positioned them as close to their mouths as they could be.

"Cassie, if anything happens to me, I want you to promise you will send all the information I have or I gather between now and then to the authorities."

"Seth, nothi…"

"Cassie, promise me."

"I promise you Seth if something happens, I will do as you ask."

"Thank you, for being the best friend that I could ever ask for and for being there for me when I needed you. You have been my rock through Eleandra's death."

Just before they went live, Seth noticed Roy's presence at the back near the makeup stand. He was busy talking to members of the crew who were attempting to fix his earpiece. Once this small task was completed, Seth watched as Roy turned to face him.

"Seth, can you hear me?"

"Yes Roy, I can."

"Good. Listen, I just wanted to apologise for Ted's demands. He is the boss but his rudeness is something I wish to say sorry for. His timing wasn't great and his interference can be disruptive." Seth was shocked. He wasn't expecting an apology, especially not from Roy. Cassie was right in asking him to give Roy a chance, he definitely surprised him.

"Roy, thank you for taking the time to say that, it's not needed, you personally did nothing wrong but I do appreciate it."

The conversation ended at that as a man Seth had never met, announced they were going live in thirty seconds.

"You ready?" Cassie whispered.

"Ready as I'll ever be."

The same man, who called out thirty seconds, was now silently counting down from five, four, three, two, one, with the use of his fingers. The cameras zoomed in on the two news anchors who perfectly introduced the show with their pre-rehearsed speech.

"Good evening and welcome to…"

"Seth this is exciting, we are about to do this for Eleandra," Cassie continued to whisper whilst leaning over and placing her hand on his.

Seth felt warm inside, there was no denying it now that he had it bad for Cassie. Her hand on his made him question why it had taken all of these years to realise his true feelings towards her. She leant back in her chair and the interview was about to begin.

"We now go live to our correspondent here in the studio, Cassie Bowl, Cassie are you there?"

"Good evening, Jeff, I am indeed here and today I am going to be speaking to Private investigator Seth Bronx. Many of you will remember that one year ago today, 21-year-old Eleandra Jacobson was reportedly murdered by Clarke Richards, a small-town family man who had no connection to her and no obvious reason to kill her. Seth is here to talk about his own investigation into Eleandra's murder and give you information as to why he cannot believe or accept that Clarke Richards was the one to have murdered her. But first, a video package."

A photo of Eleandra appeared on the screen with the year she was born and the year she had died. This was followed by a few clips of the warehouse she was found in and the voice of the lead officer involved in the case from a year ago sounded through the speakers.

"Such a tragedy to one so young."

Once the clip was finished, Seth took Cassie's lead and answered her questions. His replies were almost identical to that which he gave her earlier during their practice session, including the one's added last minute by Ted.

"I believe we have a caller on the line who would like to ask you a question."

"Yes, hello there, Seth, my name's Brenda. I'd just like to say that I lost my husband a few years ago and I really struggled. I ended up having some counselling and it really helped me with my grief, have you considered talking to someone to help with your own grief?"

"I haven't spoken to anyone professionally but today I managed to open up to a close friend and for the first time in a while, I felt a small weight had been lifted."

"Thank you for that Brenda. We have two more callers who have questions for you Seth. Next caller please."

"Hello, I'm actually calling to thank Seth. You pulled my little brother and me out of a fire,18 months ago at the Adam's ranch. The barn had caught fire and we were trapped inside but you saved us and because of that we are here to see another day. I know it was your job but we never got a chance to tell you how grateful we are. So now I can finally say thank you to you and all your colleagues for what you did for us."

"You are very welcome. Sorry what was your name?"

"Billy, Billy and Marshall Green."

"You are both welcome. Thank you for taking the time to call in."

"Last caller, are you there?"

"Yes, I'm here. Seth, I used to work with Clarke Richards and I know that he was a good man. I never thought he was guilty and I still don't. I know you are doing this for the truth about what happened to Eleandra but are you going to find out what happened to him too?"

"Although Eleandra is the main reason for my investigation, I am also determined to find out what happened to Clarke and why. I made a promise to his wife that I would get to the truth and for all of our sakes, I really hope I do."

"Thank you to all our callers for phoning in. Seth, any final words for the viewers?"

He repeated his same heartfelt speech from their discussion in the office earlier, only this time he added something more.

"I talk directly to the killer now, if you are watching then listen closely. You can't run and you can't hide. I am closing in on you, and I know for a fact you saw Eleandra the day before she died. I will be seeing you soon and karma will serve you the correct justice for what you have done to my cousin. I pray one day you see what you have done and repent for your sins. I just hope it's not too late to save your soul."

Seth was staring right into the camera, finally averting his gaze when a crew member and Roy approached them as Cassie finished up and handed back to Jeff.

"You two were sensational, the chemistry was phenomenal and everything just flowed so naturally. This is going to be massive, the numbers are already off the charts, potentially a new highest record of viewers. It's insane!"

"Wow that's amazing, this is definitely going to blow up over the next few days then," said Cassie.

"Do you think this will help me?" Seth inquired.

"Of course, I reckon the phones will be going off the hook very soon."

"Thank you for helping make this happen, Cassie, hopefully, Roy is right and the calls roll in."

"It's my pleasure, Seth, I'd do anything to help you with this. And that bluff about knowing the killer was with Eleandra the day before her death was insane, it's sure to have them on their toes."

Seth had a scarlet colour to his cheeks and a big smile on his face.

"Oh look, he's blushing, well three is a crowd so I will take my leave, hopefully, we speak soon." After Roy had left, Seth turned to face Cassie.

"For the record, I am not blushing."

"I never said that you were."

"Cassie before I head out, would you like to have dinner with me later?"

"Sounds grand, what time?"

"Eight o'clock? It gives me about ninety minutes to get my next visit all tied up."

"Eight o'clock it is, Sherbert's bar sounds good?"

"Perfect, I'll meet you there."

With a small kiss to her cheek and a tight hug, Seth bid his goodbyes to Cassie and headed out, still rosy-cheeked. He had a date with Cassie or wait, was it a date? Seth just realised he never clarified. What if she thinks it's just dinner between two friends and he has read it all wrong then goes in for a kiss? Does she even want him to kiss her? Seth now had a big dilemma on his hands, however, that was for later as he had a different engagement to focus on right now. He was off to visit the richest man in Kentsville, Quinton Forsythe IV.

Chapter Four

The journey to Quinton's unnecessarily large mansion took Seth approximately twelve minutes. Gazing up at this modern looking but actually very old built beauty, Seth remembered hearing how Quinton had inherited the property and all the surrounding land from his late parents. They had passed away a few years before Eleandra. Seth's eagerness to talk to Quinton stemmed from the knowledge that Eleandra was supposed to be giving Quinton a piano lesson the day before her death, however, Quinton himself had cancelled and Seth wanted to find out why. He pulled up to the majestically tall, golden gate, which was situated at the bottom of a long driveway. Seth thought about climbing the gate if he wasn't allowed in, however, he knew he had to approach this situation professionally, and considering the long day he already had, he didn't really fancy a climb. With this in mind, he pulled his car as close to the intercom as possible and pushed the button, waiting patiently as an older voice replied from the other end.

"Good evening."

"Evening, this is private investigator Seth Bronx, I was wondering if I could please speak to Mr Forsythe?"

"Mr Forsythe is not expecting any visitors tonight. What is the nature of this call?"

"Eleandra Jacobson, Mr Forsythe's old piano teacher, she was my cousin. It's a personal call."

"One moment please."

If the gentleman was as old as he sounded, Seth knew he would be taking a little while, however, he was back in mere moments.

"The gate will now open, please come in."

Seth drove his car up to the front door which was waiting open for him. A tall, thin, balding man was waiting for his arrival and greeted Seth with a curt nod as he approached him.

"Nice to put a face to the voice," said Seth.

"Follow me please, Mr Bronx."

Seth followed who he assumed was the butler through the house, thinking to himself that calling this place gigantic was an understatement. Although he was down to earth and didn't care for mansions and money, Seth had to admit this place was impressive. Following what seemed to be a never-ending corridor past countless rooms, they finally stopped in front of some large double, wooden doors. Upon entering this room, Seth instantly noticed a man sitting in a grand chair in front of a beautifully proud fireplace, which seemed to be the main source of light, bar a few dully lit candles.

"Sir, this is the gentleman I was talking about; Private investigator, Seth Bronx."

The man stood from his position in the chair and made his way towards the large grand piano on the other side of the room. His whole demeanour screamed smug and Seth couldn't help but feel the urge to knock him down a peg or two. It was already hard for Seth not to raise a brow at the man's awful looking dressing gown and greasy man bun that sat upon his mop of dark hair but now he had to restrain himself from returning the same attitude as the clearly hostile man.

"Anything else you need from me, sir?" Quinton shook his head and the old man took that as his cue to leave, shutting the door behind him. Seth hadn't moved; he had just stood in the same place, eyes fixed on Quinton.

"I am Quinton Forsythe IV, which you obviously already knew. What business does a man such as yourself have with me?"

Seth smiled widely, ensuring Quinton saw the condescending act.

"I'm Eleandra's cousin but I'm sure you know that already, which is why I know that you know why I am here. So let's skip this small chit chat session and get to it. Shall we?"

Quinton appeared to realise he wouldn't be able to outwit Seth so easily and stared intently at Seth for a small amount of time, another smug smile making its way onto his prudish face, before turning around and playing a soft tune on his piano.

"How much were you paying Eleandra for lessons?"

Quinton feigned ignorance and pretended that he didn't hear him, however, Seth knew otherwise, he knew he was trying to get under his skin and although it wasn't working, he toiled with the idea of pretending it did. Seth decided it was time for the tables to turn and that he would play Mr Forsythe at his own game, getting under his skin.

"She taught you very well, how many lessons did you have with her?"

Again nothing. Seth decided to start antagonising, just a little at first, unfortunately, his mouth didn't get the memo and he went full antagoniser straight away.

"Considering she did such a good job as your teacher, why did you murder her?"

"I would never murder her; I would never harm her at all. How dare you come into my home and cast such aspersions!!!"

Seth had hit a nerve. Quinton was shaking with rage and the fury was practically pouring out of his skin. He stood there at the piano, fists clenched, pure anger in his eyes, staring right through Seth with an almost empty look. After a minute or two of silence between them, he managed to compose himself and sat back down at the piano, continuing with the previous piece. "Why did your scheduled lesson get cancelled the day before her murder?"

Quinton was now back to playing ignorant to the questions again, so Seth returned to his previous tactic.

"Why did you cut open the body and rip out her organs? That's pretty messed up, wouldn't you agree?"

Unlike before, Quinton remained seated at the piano, however, his tone was harsh as he breathed out, "I told you I didn't do it, I couldn't do that to her, she was my only friend, my only true friend."

"Then what are you hiding? Why are you acting superior like you know something I don't?" Quinton looked smug again like he had just woken up to something that had happened.

"You knew I wouldn't be forthcoming with you Seth, so you decided to trigger an emotional outburst. I didn't give you enough credit; you are much brighter than I ever anticipated."

"I don't know much about you but as soon as I heard you play, I could hear in the music that she meant something to you. I felt triggering you, was the only way to get you to talk, to get me information that I need to get her justice."

"I will help you but you need to leave me out of it, out of the police reports, the media and the public eye, Deal?"

"I can agree to that Quinton."

"Tea?"

"No, thank you."

"Reginald, Reginald." The butler returned promptly.

"Another cup of pomegranate tea please."

The butler bowed and left again without speaking. Seth wondered if he had been waiting outside the door this whole time, he was rather quick to appear again.

"Common knowledge but one of the few things I do know, is your money comes from family wealth, correct?"

"Correct."

"And I believe you are the last of the Forsythe line?"

"Two for two so far Seth."

"If you don't mind me asking, how much is your net worth?"

"Money and the family home combined in a good market, between six hundred and seventy-five to seven hundred and fifty million."

"Wow, and about fifteen months ago you made a new will, didn't you?"

"Yes, I did, how did you know that?"

"It's my job to know who I'm questioning. Who did you leave your family estate and money too?"

"I'm going to have an educated guess and say you know the answer to that already Seth?"

"Do you not think that is seven hundred and fifty million potential reasons to kill Eleandra right there?"

Reginald reappeared with the tea and some biscuits. He placed the tray down near the fire on an antique coffee table and left again, bowing on the way out once more.

"Quinton, can you confirm who you left the money to in the new will you made 15 months ago?"

"It was split between several charities that my family had been involved with for years, with the bulk of it going to Eleandra. The house was to be left in Eleandra's guardianship to open as an orphanage."

"An orphanage?" said Seth.

"Yes, I have always wanted children but I understand that probably isn't going to happen now. I figured, this way children that don't have a home can make one from this. Eleandra would have been the perfect person to oversee this for me as she was so kind and selfless and was always willing to help everyone. I couldn't think of anyone who would have been better at spearheading the orphanage or at least getting it set up. Eleandra's values were something this world needs more of."

"I agree wholeheartedly with that, Quinton. How long had Reginald worked for the family?"

"In a few months, it will have been thirty-one years."

"Thirty-one years you say, does he have an alibi for the time of her death?"

"R-r-r-eginald, Reginald, he's a suspect?" Quinton stuttered.

"If you dedicated thirty-one years of your life to one family and then found out that if you outlived them, all that money would go to someone else, someone who is not even blood related and has only known you for a year, wouldn't you be a little bit pissed off?"

Quinton appeared to pause with his own thoughts for a few seconds.

"Valid reasoning. What do you suggest Seth?"

"For now, just keep an eye on him. If you think of anything else, please let me know. Oh! Why did you cancel the lesson the day before she was killed?"

"I didn't cancel the lesson, Eleandra did. She told me two days prior that she was in love and she wanted you and her mum to meet the person who had completed her soul, those were her words exactly. The next day she rang up to tell me that she had to cancel her lesson as something had come up regarding what she had mentioned the day before. I didn't press her on the matter, it wasn't my business, so we rescheduled for the day after her untimely passing."

"Hmm. I spoke to a lad named Bruce who mentioned Chelsea and her boyfriend; maybe it wasn't what they were arguing over but who they were arguing over. Maybe she fell in love with Chelsea's boyfriend and if he loved her in return but that wouldn't make sense as she saved Bruce from him," Seth mumbled out loud to himself.

"She never said who, only that she was in love for the first time."

"Keep an eye on Reginald for me and we may be seeing each other again soon Quinton."

"Seth, I know why you are doing this, and I want to tell you it's admirable that you are taking action. Most people would complain about the injustice and do nothing about it, so bravo to you."

"You aren't as pompous as you appear after all, are you Mr Forsythe?"

Seth shook Quinton's hand and left, he had a date, well, what he thought was a date, with Cassie. It would be rude to keep the lady waiting. Driving to the Sherbert bar, Seth could feel his heart trying to burst out of his chest, he was so excited and yet nervous at the same time. He mainly stuck to the speed limit, occasionally getting lost in his excitement and slightly tiptoeing over it. As he arrived outside, he pulled up next to Cassie who had just finished reversing in. He quickly walked over to her car and opened her door for her.

"What a gentleman."

"I can only try. How was work after I left?"

"It was crazy; the phone line we set up was going crazy, it was still ringing when I left. Unfortunately, it seems like people will phone in with anything, even things that are completely unrelated. One lady mentioned that her cat meowed at the screen every time they showed the photo of Clarke, which means in fact he is guilty and you should stop wasting your time. You know detective cat and all." She smiled whilst rolling her eyes.

"Wow, thank God for that, I can rest now I know for sure; Detective Puss Puss has solved the case."

They both shared a chuckle as Seth put his arm out for Cassie to hold onto, she happily accepted the gesture and they walked towards the steps to the Sherbert bar. They found a booth inside just to the left of the bar, which allowed Seth to put his wallet on the table and take his jacket off, laying it next to him. Cassie took off her coat and did the same, her handbag placed on top of it.

"What looks good to you?" Seth resisted the urge to say it was Cassie that looked good to him, even in his head he knew that sounded far too cheesy.

"I think I'm gonna have one of their famous Sherbert Cocktails and get a taxi home. I have four days off but I think I am going to go in for a couple of hours tomorrow, just to see if we have had any callers with real information."

"Nothing will top the cat. Why bother? However, four days off you say. Well, in that case, I guess we could have a sherbet cocktail or two."

"I think I'm going to have the Rainbow sherbert, its tropical flavours are a must-have. And you?" Cassie asked.

Seth studied the menu for a few more seconds and decided to have a rainbow one too.

"First round is on me, you know, to celebrate the success of the interview. I'm hoping it will really boost your chances of getting relevant information."

"The cocktail?"

"No you fool, the interview."

"Of course, now don't be daft, I'm paying."

"You can buy the next round, the first one's on me, no arguing."

"I will reluctantly accept as I'm buying dinner but you better not hold out on me, I want you to get anything you want, OK Cassie?"

"That I can do but only because you are looking extremely smart and handsome today, Seth." Cassie walked to the bar and Seth found himself checking her out, he enjoyed what he saw, she was beautiful to him and did she just say handsome and smart? Was he imagining it or was Cassie flirting with him? They always had banter and comradery but this felt different, it felt like something more and it was something he really wanted. Seth decided this was a date and for the rest of the night, he would treat it like one. He quickly checked his phone as Cassie was being served at the bar, his aunt had sent him a message. The message read, *'I'm really glad you are doing this, I feel really positive we will find the truth, I love you very much and I'm proud of you, have a great time with Cassie tonight xx.'*

He messaged her back that he loved her and he would speak to her tomorrow. Putting his phone away, he watched as Cassie made her way back to their table and placed his drink in front of him.

"For you."

"Thank you."

"Here's to Eleandra," she announced as she raised her glass, clinking it with Seth's

Seth sipped on his drink, which was filled with all different colours, a rainbow just like the name suggested. It wasn't the tropical taste he was expecting, instead it was very, very, sour.

"Wow, that's stronger than I expected," said Seth.

"I'd say it has a kick to it alright."

"I think I'll just have one of these and then maybe try something else."

"I think I can agree on that."

"Any idea what you want to eat yet, Cassie?"

"To be honest, I was going to ask if you wanted to share a pizza or some wings as I'm not overly hungry."

"That sounds great to me, BBQ Chicken and some hot wings?" Seth knew her favourite topping of pizza was BBQ chicken, hence the suggestion.

"Perfect."

"Now that's decided, what are your plans for tomorrow, Cassie, besides checking the phone lines?"

"Nothing much, just relax a bit in the garden if it's nice. You?"

Seth leaned in closer to her, ensuring that no one around could hear them.

"I am going to see someone called Chelsea Chive. Does she sound familiar to you?"

"I am sure that I have met her a couple of times but I couldn't really tell you much about her, well, except that she also teaches piano lessons like Eleandra did and she was the head cheerleader at school."

With Cassie this close to him, one word kept repeating itself in his head: kiss, kiss, kiss. He considered it and nearly went in for one too but he ignored his instincts and bottled up his desire, for now.

"Well, Quinton told me that Eleandra had found love and that she wanted to introduce whoever it was to me and her mum the day she died. Before that, Bruce told me the day before that he saw her arguing with Chelsea, so maybe she was seeing Chelsea's boyfriend and she found out. It's a bit of a stretch as they could have been arguing about anything and Eleandra wasn't normally the type of person to take someone's boyfriend but it's all I have right now. I decided that I need to confront her and see what she says. So, that's my main mission for tomorrow, see what she has to say."

"She was in love? I am so glad for her. I know it didn't last long because of what happened but I'm glad she got to experience that feeling." Cassie looked like she was going to cry.

"Are you OK, Cassie?"

"Yes, I am fine. I'll tell you something that will make me smile again. I had a dream last night about the time I had a sleep over at your house and we were up the whole night rapping. Do you remember? We were convinced that we were going to be the greatest rap duo of all time but we woke your aunty up twice and she shouted through the bedroom at us to go to sleep."

"Oh wow, I haven't thought about that in a long time. 'If you two don't go to bed right now, Cassie will sleep on the sofa and you will be grounded for a month," he said, imitating his aunt's voice, "she never meant what she said but it was always funny when she was trying to be stern."

They both started laughing at the memory. The laughter encouraged Seth to make a bold move, so he placed his hand on hers and asked her for a second date.

"Cassie, I'm going to be honest and tell you that I'm not sure if this is a date or not but I told myself that I would be disappointed if it wasn't. I want you to know that I think you look beautiful, you always look beautiful to me and if this is a date, then I would be honoured if you would accompany me to the Fire and Rescue Service's Charity Gala being held in the grand hall a week on Saturday, as my date. However, before you respond if it's not a date, I'd still like you to attend with me but as my friend. I don't want anything to change for us but at the same time, I want it to change completely."

His heart was pounding and he felt like it would rip right through his chest any minute.

"I'd be honoured to go with you, Seth."

"Perfect." He breathed a nervous laugh.

The nervous laughter faded but the smiles from both that took its place made them feel even elated.

"I'll go and order the food; I'll be right back."

He had walked a few steps towards the bar when Cassie called him.

"And Seth…"

Seth stopped and turned to look at her once more.

"Of course, this is a date."

He smiled once more at her and turned towards the bar for a second time. Seth was waiting to order the food when he felt a soft tap on his shoulder.

"Hey stranger, you come here often?" He turned to see that it was Cassie who was putting on an accent. If he hadn't looked, he would never have known it was her.

"First time, you?"

"Same, are you alone?"

"Actually, I am having a drink with a stunning young lady, however, you would be an above-average replacement if it didn't work out."

"Really! I went from stunning young lady to above-average replacement in a few seconds."

She laughed.

"I never was good at role-play or improv."

"I'm just popping to the Ladies room and if I don't return, it's because I jumped out the window. I'm sure you'd be able to find an above-average woman to take my place." She smiled and walked around the bar out of Seth's view.

After he had ordered, Seth returned to the booth and waited on Cassie to get back. He took some time to soak in his surroundings. There was a pool table, jukebox and a stage where a live act was advertised to perform this weekend just to the side, overall it seemed like a good night out could be had here. Although this was his first time, Seth really enjoyed the place. For the second time that night, he quietly watched Cassie make her way back to the booth.

"Didn't replace me then."

"I tried a few times but it turned out to be impossible to replace you. Plus no one else would have me."

"You are too sweet, I think."

"The barman said the food would be about twenty minutes. I was going to suggest we stalk Chelsea's social media and see what we could learn if you are up for it?"

"Yes, let's do…where did the lights go?"

Suddenly, the whole bar was invaded by darkness, no music, no vision, nothing.

"Don't panic, it's probably just a fuse tripped or something. I'll just go check the box out the back, remain calm, it'll be two seconds."

Someone shouted through the Sherbert bar. Seth thought he recognised the voice to be that of the barman as he had just been chatting with him.

"It really is quite dark in here, with the lights off I can barely see you, Seth."

SMACK!!!

Seth had felt something hard against the side of his face and it was clear that someone had just punched him on his jawline. They pushed Seth further into the booth and tried to take something from his pocket, however, were stopped by the force of Seth's defensive shove. He heard whoever it was hit the floor and quickly scurry away.

"Seth, are you OK?" Cassie said, sounding rather panicky.

Just then the lights came back on, causing Seth to look around for someone who may have looked out of place, however, he was at a loss as he had no idea who he was looking for. It was too dark to see anything at the time, so Seth couldn't put a face to the culprit.

"Are you OK?" she asked again.

"I'm just dandy thanks, Cassie, keep this quiet, please. It could have just been an opportune mugging because it was dark but something is telling me it more than likely had something to do with the case, after all my wallet is right there next to me on the table."

Cassie nodded in agreement.

"Sorry folks not sure what happened there but lights are back and the music will be on again in a second. Sorry about that and please enjoy the rest of your night."

This time Seth could see that it was in fact the barman shouting across the room.

"I tried to get a photo of the person but it's all black. I should have put the flash on, I just didn't think."

"The thought was there though, quick thinking. Anyway, no harm done. I'm more concerned about what the potential killer thought I had in my pocket?"

Chapter Five

The next morning Seth awoke feeling alive. The previous night went much better than he could have hoped for, even though he made no attempt to give Cassie an end of night kiss and for that, he was internally kicking himself. Not even the small hiccup of him being punched could put a damper on his mood today. After the said attack, Seth and Cassie looked deeper into the life of Chelsea and discovered that she worked part-time at her father's law firm as an assistant. As well as this, she taught piano privately, which they already knew and she played badminton at a local members-only club twice a week. They laughed, they talked about old times, they flirted all night and Seth couldn't believe Cassie appeared to have the same feelings towards him as he did her. Rising out of bed, Seth made his way towards the kitchen where he stuck two crumpets in the toaster and boiled the kettle. He turned his head towards the small table where his phone was currently vibrating, letting him know his aunty Dorothy was ready for a morning catch up.

"So did you kiss her?"

"Who, Cassie?"

"Of course, Cassie, who else?"

"No, I didn't kiss her, we are friends."

He didn't want to let on about his feelings at this moment.

"Seth, if you haven't realised that the two of you are more than friends by now, then you need to open your eyes."

"We are just friends."

"Oh please, everyone knows, everyone can see the spark between you."

"Everyone? Who's everyone?"

"Anyone who has ever seen the two of you together."

"Yeah, I'm going to stick with just friends."

"Just friends it is then, Seth."

"Let's talk about today, shall we?"

"Of course, what do you want to discuss?"

"I'm going to visit Chelsea Chive and see what she has to say about a heated argument taking place between her and Eleandra the day before she was murdered."

"All I will say as always Seth, be careful."

"I know and don't worry I will."

"Speak to you later, love you darling."

"Love you too, Aunty Dorothy."

Seth buttered his crumpets and poured himself a cup of hot chocolate before sitting at the small two-person table. He enjoyed his breakfast whilst listening to the radio, which seemed to make everything unusually sweeter that morning. Seth preferred the radio in the mornings, getting the day started with different music gave him enthusiasm going forward. Seth scrolled through Chelsea's social media accounts once more and had discovered that she had posted twice this morning already. He knew that she would be face painting at a fundraiser in town to raise money and awareness about homeless children in Kentsville and the neighbouring town Stoneymaids. This was a perfect opportunity for Seth to meet with her face to face and hopefully get some answers. Her first post gave Seth a little bit of an insight into her life. She was adopted at seven months old and had a good life with her adopted parents, hence why she felt the need to give something back to the community. Her second post gave away what her location would be and stated that she would be there from 10 AM till 1 PM. Seth decided he would relax for a little while and message Cassie, then head into town for 10.

Arriving at the fundraiser, Seth observed the crowds of people and took in the sight of numerous different stalls, ranging from cupcakes, pies, lemonade, coconut shy and many more. It had a real old town feel to it. There was also face painting, the dunk tank, tombola and the likes. He made his way towards the face painting stall where he managed to spot Chelsea right away. He watched as the girl lifted her head and locked her eyes with his as she stared at him in disbelief.

"You're him. I saw you last night on the news, you're really doing it?"

"If you mean investigating Eleandra's death, then yes I am."

"I don't normally watch the news but I heard about the interview and it piqued my interest."

"What piqued your interest?"

"Your investigation, of course. The police seem to think it was home and hosed."

"Do you think the findings were correct?"

"How would I know? It has nothing to do with me and I hardly knew her, we attended school and college together, that's it."

"When was the last time you saw Eleandra?"

"Just over a year ago."

"I'm gonna need a little more than that."

"I don't remember, I've slept since then, should have asked me last year."

"I get it, tough, sassy, a little spitfire, aren't you? I also get that you're lying, you know when you last saw her. So, care to share?"

"OK handsome, you really want to know, I saw her the day before she got killed."

"Well then, why not just say that? Not hiding something, are you?"

"Hm, nope. Saw her in passing and said hi, that's about it."

"Nothing else, just hi?"

"Yup, that's about it as far as I can remember." Seth stepped closer to Chelsea and looked her dead in the eye.

"Are you sure? Because that's a real good impression of you that someone must be doing."

"What are you talking about? What impression?"

"On the voice recording I have of you and Eleandra talking that day, it's a little bit muffled but my friend is working on clearing it up."

He gave her a smug look, similar to the one Quinton gave him and noticed that her face went very pale.

"You're lying."

"Can you be sure? Is that a risk you're really willing to take?"

Seth knew she could just call his bluff but he also knew that she was hiding something and he was hoping this might force her hand, he felt it worth a shot.

"Sorry I'm very busy, either have your face painted or leave."

Chelsea turned away from Seth but he wasn't going to leave it alone.

"I'd love to have my face painted, you any good?" She wasn't amused, she had gone from pale to bright red in the blink of an eye.

"Obviously, otherwise I wouldn't be painting children's faces, would I?"

"Well, let me sit down and then you can paint away."

He sat and the smug look was back, Chelsea was getting agitated and he knew it. She didn't know what to do as there were now children and parents within earshot, she had no choice but to paint Seth's face.

"Fine, I'll face your paint, I mean paint your face, what do you want? And no more questions."

She was getting flustered and he knew he had her on the ropes with all these people around.

"I'll go with Batman if that's not too much."

Seth decided to use the same tactic on Chelsea that he used on Quinton.

"So…"

"No more questions, please, I need to concentrate."

"Oh, I wasn't going to ask a question, I was going to say that soon to be Batman is wondering if you killed Eleandra."

Seth along with a few parents and children jumped a little when there was a loud crash on the floor. It seemed as though Chelsea had knocked her face painting box and the contents all over the floor and it had scattered everywhere. Seth turned to look at her and was surprised she was now crying floods of tears. He watched her drop the paintbrush from her hand onto the face painting table and proceed to rush off in the opposite direction of him. He quickly stood from his chair and jogged towards her, increasing his pace in order to keep up with her.

"Does this mean I'm not going to be Batman?"

"Leave me alone!"

"Chelsea, are you OK?"

"Leave me alone!"

"I was under the impression that you two argued the day before she was murdered because she was sleeping with your boyfriend. Am I wrong?"

"Yes, you are completely wrong."

"Then please explain why you are crying?"

She stopped abruptly, to which an out of breath Seth was grateful for, tears still running down her cheeks and her mascara everywhere.

"I miss her," she said.

That was not what Seth expected to hear.

"Chelsea, we should talk in private."

"Yes, I think that's for the best, where did you park the Jaguar?"

"Follow me, it's down here."

They walked in silence around the corner, Seth regularly checking back to make sure no one was following behind them. Once in the car, he handed her some tissues to wipe away her tears and to remove her smeared makeup.

"Can you drive, please?"

"First you need to tell me what's going on?"

"Drive and I will."

"OK, drive to where Chelsea?"

"Anywhere, just go and don't stop."

"Chelsea, start talking, I need to know what's going on."

"I don't know where to start."

"Just talk, it doesn't have to be poetry, just tell me what you know and why you are crying."

"What if I'm next?"

"What?"

"What if the killer comes back and I'm next?"

"Why would you be next?" Seth questioned.

This wasn't making any sense to him at all.

"What if he killed her and now, he wants to kill me because he knows my secret."

"Tell me, Chelsea, what is your secret?"

"You heard that Eleandra had a lover?"

"Yes. I don't know his name but I thought it was your ex-boyfriend."

She let out a laugh.

"You couldn't be more wrong if you tried."

"Really?"

"Yes, Seth, the real truth is…"

There was a pause and a deep breath before she shared her secret.

"I was her lover."

It took everything in him to not slam on his breaks right there. He managed to pull the car over at the side of the road safely, his mouth still gaping open in shock, he was gobsmacked. Chelsea dabbed at her eyes once more, she had stopped crying but she was still wiping away a few last tears.

"It's funny really Seth, I don't even know you and you are the only person in the world who knows about us, and maybe the killer."

"Lovers," Seth repeated this, a couple of times before he spoke again.

"Well, if you don't think Clarke killed Eleandra, then do you have ideas on who did?" he asked.

"Loads, each one as unsubstantiated as the next."

"Was there anything out of the ordinary, before or after she died? Any changes in her behaviour that you spotted?"

"Not anything that I noticed, well, she was nervous, as we were going to tell you and her mum about us and then we were going to tell my parents. I got cold feet that day before her death and we had that argument you know about. That was the last time I spoke to her; she said she felt like I was ashamed of her, ashamed of us. That wasn't true, Seth, I swear to you, I was only worried my parents wouldn't accept me. They took me in as a baby, they homed me, clothed me, loved me and adopted me. I couldn't handle being rejected by them if they didn't approve of me being gay. I regret the way things were left between us and now I can never change them."

"I'm sorry to hear that, is there anything else?"

"She was worried Ludlow would find out before I dumped him. I kept putting it off because we had the same group of friends and thought someone would put two and two together. I dumped him the day after Eleandra died, too little too late."

"I'm sorry, his name is Ludlow? Haha, Ludlow." Chelsea sniggered too.

"You're right, Ludlow, haha."

"Poor lad, I feel bad for him now."

"Ludlow Fenston, I should have run a mile when I heard the name."

"Fenston, I know the name Fenston. What does his dad do?"

"He works for NASA. He is very rarely around, always travelling. He sees him around twenty to thirty days of the year at most."

"Chelsea, do you think Ludlow is dangerous?"

"Ludlow and dangerous are two words you would never hear together. He isn't dangerous or clever for what it's worth."

"Maybe he knew about you? Maybe he stumbled upon an email or a message or possibly heard an exchange between the two of you."

"No, he didn't know."

"So why are you so fearful?"

"When I saw you on TV last night, I started thinking what if he comes back? What if he wants me next?"

"Do you have any photos on your phone of the two of you Chelsea, maybe he…"

Suddenly, it hit Seth, Eleandra's phone; they never got into it because they didn't know the password.

"Do you by any chance know the password for Eleandra's phone?"

"Unless she changed it after our fight, then yes, it's the same as mine."

"No one knew the password so we were never able to get into it but she had it on her when she died. What if there is a photo of the killer on there? Long shot but you never know."

"I won't give you the password."

"I'm sorry, I didn't hear what you said. It sounded like you said you wouldn't give me the password."

"I won't give you the password but I will open it for you."

"Chelsea, I don't want people getting involved more than need be, it could be dangerous."

"That is my condition, I loved her so much, I want to help, so either I unlock it or no one does."

Seth knew she had him over a barrel, so he agreed.

"Fine but I check the phone and then you can see it."

"Yes. I knew you'd cave."

"You are far too confident for your own good. We go do this now and then I take you back to the fair."

"I'm not going back there now, I can't face it, let's do this and then you can drop me home if you don't mind?"

Seth nodded and drove towards his office.

"We are like partners now," Chelsea said as they arrived.

"No. Same as I told Eleandra's mum, I do this alone so no one else's lives are at risk."

"Except your own."

"It's my life to risk Chelsea."

"When you see how I understood her like no one else did, you'll realise that you need my help."

"In advance, no, thank you but I appreciate you wanting to help."

"I don't want appreciation; I want to catch the son of a bitch who took her from me."

Seth entered into his office, there was silence as they entered, almost an anticipation of what clues the phone might hold. Seth hit the lights and walked over to his bag.

"I'm glad she found you, Chelsea, I'm glad she found love."

Seth brought the phone over to his desk and plugged it into the socket not too far behind. They both waited patiently for the phone to power up, it had been turned off for a long time but still had some battery once it came on. Seth handed it to Chelsea.

"No peeking now."

"Just enter the password please."

"Fine, it's three, five, two, two."

"Thank you, let's fire this thing up."

Seth first checked the gallery section and discovered that there were no photos taken on the day she was killed.

"No photos of the killer, I'm afraid, none on the day she died at all. I'll have a look through the rest to see if there's anything that jumps out, I won't keep anything from you as you are here."

"Thank you. You know she used to talk about you a lot."

"She did?"

"She was so proud of you, hero firefighter, great singing voice, looked after her and her mum, even though her mum was meant to look after you. Eleandra couldn't praise you enough. Singing voice aside, as I've never heard it, I can see you too were very alike and very fond of each other."

"To me, she was my little sister. I would have done anything for her. My aunt always said we were so alike, we never agreed with her but looking back I can see she was right."

"You were her hero, her idol. I can't believe you are doing this for Eleandra, she would be so proud of you."

"I am doing this for all of us, everyone who loved her, anyone whose lives she touched, we all deserve to know what happened to her."

Chelsea noticed a hat Seth had gotten out of his bag.

"She loved that hat, she said she had it for years and it always made her feel safe when she wore it."

"It was mine, she wanted one when she was ten so we went to the shop but they didn't have any more, so I gave her mine and bought a new one. She told me my hat wasn't as cool as hers, that mine was lame. I told her that hat would always keep her safe even when I wasn't around."

"She believed that, she told me so."

"Really? She told me I was stupid and it was just a hat."

"Well, she clearly thought otherwise." Seth smiled and continued looking through the phone, he found nothing noteworthy.

"Here's her phone, I can't find anything of relevance, if you find anything let me know, maybe you will see something I don't."

"Do you mind while I have the phone if I send the photos of us that are on here onto mine?"

"No, of course not, take whatever photos you want."

Seth understood her need for this as both he and his aunty would have done the same had they previously had access to the photos on the device.

"I don't know if it will be helpful but this isn't the email account she normally used, she had another one she used more frequently."

"Do you know what it is?"

"I do but not off the top of my head, I've got it written down somewhere indoors, the password is Piano3522."

"We need to go to your house; we need to read those emails."

"Sure, let's go. Does this mean I can help you?"

"With this, yes, with the rest of the investigation, it's still a big N and a little o."

They walked outside into the cold wet rain which was now falling from above, thoroughly drenching them as they swiftly took shelter in the car. Seth thought he noticed a man in the distance, and the odd feeling of being watched engulfed his body. Was he being followed? He stared intently at the spot whilst blinking rapidly in a failed attempt to clear his vision which was being blurred by the downpour of water hitting his back window. He turned on the engine and waited patiently as Chelsea directed him to her house. Approaching her home, Seth instantly noticed the police car parked by her driveway. He knew that this wasn't a coincidence, they didn't exist these days, at least not for him.

"Wait here," Chelsea said as she bolted into the house, with a disobedient Seth following behind. Inside the house, stood two police officers who seemed to be in deep conversation with a woman that Seth assumed was Chelsea's mum. Having never met her family before, he couldn't say for certain that it was but it seemed an obvious fit.

"Mum, what's going on here?"

"Sorry, are you Chelsea Chive?"

One of the officers asked.

"What gave it away? The whole Mum thing? What's going on?" she repeated.

Seth was unable to control the small smirk that made its way onto his face. Her boldness and sarcastic attitude that merely an hour ago annoyed and even frustrated him was now the reason behind his amusement. It was funny to him now that he was not the one on the receiving end of it. She really was a character and he understood what Eleandra saw in her, they would have been a great match for one another.

"There is no need to be so rude, Miss Chive. We have discussed with your mother what we needed to, and therefore, she will be able to bring you up to speed. Now if you will excuse us, we have some other business to attend."

As the two police officers made their exit, Seth decided to follow behind. His years spent working for the fire department enabled him to come across different people who worked in other branches of the emergency services. Therefore, Seth knew one of the officers who were previously speaking with Chelsea's mum and decided he would investigate the real purpose of their visit.

"Someone broke in when no one was home and vandalised Chelsea's room, put holes in the walls, turned her bed over, emptied the contents of her drawers onto the floor, you can go see it for yourself. Her mother called us out once she noticed the damage but there is nothing that points us to anyone, no one saw anything suspicious. Oh, how is the investigation going?"

"I'm making good progress but I'm sure there is someone following me around."

"Do they appear dangerous?"

"I can't say for sure; I've caught sight of them in the distance but they haven't approached me."

"If anything happens or if you need any help, then give me a call. Don't call the station, call me directly, I'm there if you need anything," said the shorter of the two officers.

"Thank you, Steve. I hope you guys have an uneventful night."

He watched the police car drive halfway up the street before re-entering the house. Chelsea and her mum were discussing the events that had taken place and Seth watched on silently for a cue to speak.

"Apologies, I don't actually know your name Mrs Chive."

"Her name's Vera, most people address her as Vee."

"Nice to meet you, Vee, did they take anything?" asked Seth.

"No, nothing looks missing but Chelsea will know for sure. Police think that it could have been some kids as they put a brick through the back window."

"Let me get this straight. They use a brick to smash the window, head upstairs for Chelsea's bedroom, completely trash it and leave?"

"Yes, exactly that."

"Odd."

Seth wasn't convinced that it was 'just some kids.' He was sure it was more likely the killer but he wasn't about to let Vee know this. Instead of voicing his concerns, Seth asked if he could see the bedroom, he hoped that he may find something that links to the case. He followed behind Chelsea as she led the way to her room, and even though pre-warned, Seth still managed to be slightly surprised by the wreckage. The pair stepped into the room and instantly began to rummage around in the mess, Seth eager to find any evidence, hair, saliva, blood or fingerprints. Anything that was able to help him identify who had broken into the room or possibly help him identify who the killer was. Surely, they were the same person? Or if not, then maybe they were connected somehow, right? Was this the same person as the one who was following him? "Chelsea, is anything missing?"

"No. It appears everything is here like my mum said, just all mixed together giving me the sheer pleasure of tidying it all up."

Seth helped Chelsea clean up the mess and gradually sort through all of the stuff that had been scattered onto the floor. After a while, the place had started to look a little normal again and was completely different from the mess they had first walked into. Pushing one of the bedside units back, Seth felt something crunching under his feet. Looking down, Seth noticed it was a picture of Eleandra and Chelsea smiling whilst looking at each other, and picked it up, smoothing out the creases.

"Chelsea, where was this photo when you left the house today?"

"Hidden in the bottom of my top drawer under my bras."

"If it was the killer who broke into your house today and he didn't know about you and Eleandra before, then he does now. This wasn't teenagers looking for kicks; this was him looking for something, the same as he was the other night. He thought I had evidence on me, he thought you might have evidence on you, he's scared that we have found something. You need to be really careful. I don't think he would come back here again but he might try and get you when you are alone."

"You keep saying he, do you know the killer is male or just assuming?"

"I think he's male, I think I may know who he is, I just can't prove anything."

"Who do you think it is?"

"I can't get into that with you. You are already in danger so the less you know, the better. Let's find this email and check if Eleandra has anything hidden that will help. I'm sorry this photo is screwed up and creased, it almost looks like two photos put together now."

He handed it back to Chelsea. They only had to rummage for a few minutes before they managed to find the piece of paper with the email address written down. Chelsea booted up her laptop and managed to get into the email account in no time, she sure had more tech knowledge than Seth. They looked through them together, and begrudgingly Seth had to admit that Chelsea was useful. She was able to get into the phone, she knew about the extra email account and she deserved to be here, especially given it's her house. Nothing in the inbox or the sent items jumped out at them, however, archived emails were the opposite. There were two conversations, one was between Eleandra and Chelsea and was mostly love letters, Seth didn't want to intrude into their relationship so decided it best to leave those unread, especially as he could see from the corner of his eye that Chelsea was starting to tear up.

"Let's check the other one."

Chelsea clicked on the other email that had no subject. Once opened, they could see it was an ongoing conversation going back and forth for about two weeks leading up to her murder. There was no name signed but from the text, it was clear that Eleandra knew who she was messaging. Someone was threatening her. Seth read one line over and over again.

"Drop this or I will drop you."

Eleandra had responded nonchalantly as though she did not perceive whoever this was to be a threat.

"Seth what if this is the killer?"

"I was thinking that myself, she knew him but felt he was all talk and no real threat. That is until one day he decided no more words, he decided to act and he killed her."

Seth left the Chive household shortly after with newfound confidence that the killer was watching their every move. He was more than sure now that the killer was the one who attempted to mug him and who trashed Chelsea's room. Whipping out his phone, he rang Cassie and his aunt, neither of which answered.

He wanted peace of mind that they were safe, so texted them both in hopes that they would respond shortly. Within minutes, his aunt replied to him, giving him the peace of mind that he needed. Cassie, however, was not so quick to reply but he told himself she was probably working and rang the news station, who confirmed she was there and put him through to her. He smiled at the sound of her voice and brought her up to date with the day's events.

"No quiet days for you, Seth. Actually, I'm glad you called, we seemed to have a call come through today that you may want to look into if you have the time."

"I have some time now before I head over to see my aunt."

"The call came in about half an hour ago. A lady claims that on the day of the murder she saw Eleandra talking to a young man near the warehouse where her body was found. She wasn't able to identify who he was or what it was they were talking about but if correct, he could potentially have been the last person to talk to her before her death. It's not a lot of detailed information but it's the best that has come through the phone lines so far."

"That would mean that Eleandra was murdered at the warehouse or close by it. I always figured she was killed elsewhere and then moved there. Cassie, thanks for this, if you hear anything else, please let me know."

"I will, speak later Seth and thank you again for last night, I had a great time."

"Me too, I can't wait to do it again soon."

"Me too. Bye Seth."

Seth made a U-turn in the middle of the road and headed to the warehouse where the body was found. He didn't know what he was looking for, he just had a hunch he should be there. Seth drove down the road to which the warehouse was situated; it was a semi-busy road with a few shops on either side. He parked outside an alley and walked through it towards the back entrance of the building. Although locked up, you could get in via the fire escape on the second floor, also known as the back entrance, everybody knew this. Once inside, it was clear to Seth that someone had been here, and maybe like the old paper mill, it could be teenagers or a homeless person so it didn't mean anything right now but someone was in here recently. Seth got to the point where Eleandra's body was found and paused, he needed a minute, not just to compose himself but to process. There was no getting away from what happened here as it was all over the media, however, Seth had never stepped foot in here before. He came to the solution that there was no need to; he wouldn't find any fresh evidence here, at least not after a year. Why should he visit this place? The place where it all happened, the place where she was found and in the manner in which she was. It felt surreal to him and after all this time, he just couldn't comprehend what had happened here. He welled up inside but did not shed any tears, he wouldn't let his emotions get the best of him and stop him from discovering what was to be found. Venturing further into the warehouse, he found a corner office with a desk, a lamp and a whiteboard. The whiteboard was full of photos, Seth, Chelsea, Cassie, Aunt Dorothy and Eleandra. In a moment of clear thinking, Seth decided that it would be worth setting up a small spy cam within the room to catch the real killer and uncover his true intentions. He headed back outside towards a second-hand gadget shop which was a minute's walk around the corner. It was worth a look to see if they had what he was looking for. The shop was closed when he got there, so he peered through the window but couldn't see anything of use. He headed back towards the warehouse, talking to himself as he went.

"I'll take photos of everything in the room and check if there's any hair or fingerprints and then report this to the police. As much as I don't want them to be involved, they might help keep him on his toes and force him into a mistake through all the pressure. This could be useful as mistakes are always noticed," Seth thought out loud.

Seth was welcomed by the familiar smell of smoke once he approached the warehouse once more. He could almost feel the burning from the other side of the wall, and looking into a window, saw that inside the fire was blazing high. He phoned his friends at the forty-eighth division, whilst attempting to work out if the culprit or the killer was nearby.

"There are no signs of anyone inside but I can only see one of the bigger areas, there's a lot of space in there," he told them.

People had started to notice smoke coming from the building and soon enough, a large crowd of men and women were approaching to get a better look at what was going on. The team from the fire department arrived within four minutes and quickly set to the task at hand, relentlessly working hard to set the blaze at bay. About an hour later, the flames were out, and even though the men were brave and worked tirelessly, the crime scene was all but gone. What once stood a gigantic structure was nothing more than dust and rubble. A few rooms remained, a balcony or two but the majority of it was gone, nothing but piles of ash. Seth sat down on the floor with his hands on his bent knees. Every time he moved towards the killer he was after or even remotely got close to him, he seemed to move further away, leaving nothing but frustration and questions behind. Seth knew this battle for justice wasn't going to be a picnic, he just needed the smallest slip-up and he would pounce, he would get the son of a bitch and Eleandra's soul could finally be at peace.

Chapter Six

"Seth Bronx?"

"Yes, who's asking?"

"I am the new Police Chief in charge in Kentsville. We have a few things we need to discuss about what has happened here. Would you please accompany me to the station so we could make a full report?"

"And why can't you ask your questions here and put them into a report later like you would normally do?" said Seth.

"As you are an eyewitness, I feel it would be best to do this down at the station."

He glanced at the multiple officers that surrounded him and instantly became uneasy.

"Why do I feel that you aren't asking me but rather telling me?"

"You misunderstand. I am not telling you to do anything, there is no arrest here, I am simply asking you to come to the station and receive our full protection while we ask you about what has occurred here. We need to know your version of events."

"My version of events! There is only one version of events and it's called the truth. I was in the building; I left and made my way towards the shops and when I came back it was on fire."

"Seems odd but I'm sure we can get to the bottom of this down at the station, your cooperation is greatly appreciated."

Seth decided it best not to cause a scene, the large crowd seemed to grow larger still now people were taking photos and videos. He got into one of the squad cars, thanking one of the officers who had opened the door for him. Although he was annoyed, he still remained polite and calm, after all the officers were just following orders and doing their jobs. The drive to the station was quiet with no one daring to speak. Seth was sat in the back of the car with one of the officers, whilst the new chief was sat in the front passenger side with a third officer behind the wheel. Seth wasn't familiar with any of these officers and internally kicked himself for not being up to date with the latest additions on the force. It was a rather odd feeling not knowing who any of them were as Seth was used to being friendly with all the previous officers, due to his old position in his fire and rescue team. At the station, Seth was taken in via the back door which he was told was due to avoiding any lurking press who may be situated out front. His interview on live TV the previous night had gained Seth some popularity, therefore the officers thought it best to deal with this matter discreetly. Once inside, Seth was guided towards a holding cell where he was made to sit and wait. This was apparently routine according to one of the officers but Seth thought otherwise and was beginning to feel like he was being treated as a criminal. He didn't know for sure if this was standard protocol as he had never been in this situation before but he was sure that they were trying to intimidate him.

"Seth Bronx, could you follow me please?"

"Of course."

His tone was sharp and it was clear that he was becoming frustrated. He was led to an interrogation room, one where he sat down on a single chair at a small, bleak table and watched as the officer left the room, shutting the door behind him. He didn't hear the door being locked and assumed the officer was standing guard on the other side. The door opened and in walked the new chief, alone.

"Seth, I have a few questions for you."

"I feel like all I've done since yesterday morning is ask and answer questions."

"Well, then you'll enjoy a few more to complete the set."

The chief's tone was now very hostile, a stark contrast to that of earlier when he had first approached Seth, which was a more fitted match to his overall presence. He was roughly six foot two and rather large around the middle, his hair not doing much to cover his large forehead and his receding hairline showing off his very obvious bald patch on the top of his head. He was clean-shaven and Seth could see a scar on the left of his face by his jaw about two inches long, it looked nasty. Seth took the brief pause as a cue for himself to start asking questions but before he could, the chief continued speaking.

"Why were you at the warehouse in the first place, Mr Detective?"

"Just Detective is fine and I had information that suggested to me someone may be in there."

"Who? The killer perhaps?"

The new chief still hadn't given Seth his name, and with a killer on the loose, Seth wasn't prepared to take any chances on this whole coincidence business.

"Sorry, I never did catch your name back at what's left of the warehouse."

"You're right. I never gave you my name, did I? I am Police Chief Abraham, Glenn Abraham to be exact. I was moved here to lead this department forward as Police Chief of Kentsville. As of this morning, I am attempting to sort out the shambled mess in which they call a police force here in this town. Now I understand that you are leading your own investigation into the murder of your cousin Eleandra, and although I respect you for that and agree with you on many aspects regarding her death, I don't like the fact you are running around with the media in tow. You are not a policeman Seth, if you have any new evidence to suggest any wrongdoing with Mr Richards being found guilty of Eleandra's murder, which is needed to re-open the case, then tell me what it is."

"Well, Mr Abraham, apologies if you think I'm stepping on your toes, that's not my intention but I feel you need to know a few things. Firstly, I will never stop until the real killer is found and brought to justice, never. Secondly, I don't care who you are or what you are doing, don't get in my way, this is personal, this is family and I thank you for putting me on notice and please carry on doing a great job for this town, my town. Remember, that I was born and raised here, you just showed up. Now, did you want me for anything else, Chief?"

"Don't forget your place, Seth, you are a member of the public only, I always get results, always. If you get in the way of this police department, I have no problem with locking you up until we are finished."

"I'm glad we have both made ourselves very clear Chief, now may I go? I have an investigation to get on with."

"You may go, I will show you out but remember I will be watching you, Seth."

"You won't be alone; I'm already being watched. If you really want to do your job, then watch the man watching me. Maybe you could even try catching the man who's watching me."

Seth turned and walked away from him and the station, he didn't look back. It was only a short walk back to the warehouse and his car; he didn't ask but he assumed he wouldn't be getting a lift. The excitement from today was more than enough for him and he decided that tonight he would do some more investigating from indoors. He wanted to be the one who brought Eleandra's killer in, now he had this guy to compete with. He knew justice was all that mattered but it would have meant the world to him if he could do it. He caught his reflection in a window on the way to his car and looked himself straight in the eye.

"I guess it doesn't matter who finds him, as long as he's found."

Maybe I should accept some help, he thought. He deliberated this on the way back to his office, he did have three women who wanted to help him after all. He decided to go to his aunt's house instead of the office and so made a sharp turn in her direction. Pulling up outside, Seth parked his car and whipped out his phone quickly creating a group chat with Cassie, Chelsea and his aunt, asking them all if they were free in an hour's time.

"Hi, Seth," his aunt said, opening the car door.

"Oh dear God, you made me jump, Aunty Dorothy."

"Sorry, darling, nice surprise, what's this message I just got?"

"Let's go inside, I'll make us a cuppa and I'll tell you all about it."

"Alright then, deary."

Dorothy's house was warm and cosy with a nice, homely feel, completely different to that of Seth's house. They went into the kitchen and Dorothy sat at the dining table while Seth put his jacket on the back of the chair opposite and proceeded to make the drinks. He went to get the biscuit tin out for her too, however, she stopped him before he could proceed.

"No Seth not the biscuit tin, I fancy a slice of cake."

"Sounds good to me, top left cupboard?"

"I knew you'd remember where the cake was kept. You never remember where the dustpan and brush are or where the washing up liquid lives but the cake's location you always seem to know."

They shared a chuckle and Seth got both the cakes out. He couldn't decide between the chocolate or salted caramel but he knew his aunt would let him have a slice of both.

"If you don't mind the company, could Cassie and Chelsea come over tonight? I want to talk to the three of you together."

"I am curious as to what it is but, of course they can, my darling."

"Thank you, I'll update the group."

They had both replied and fortunately were both available.

"Great news, I'd like to have a conversation tonight about Eleandra and my investigation. Could you meet me at my aunt Dorothy's house, please? Chelsea, do you know where that is?"

"Yes, I know, I shall meet you there."

It took Cassie longer to respond but soon enough, she was able to confirm her attendance.

"Seems there will be four of us tonight and I haven't prepared dinner. I'll order takeaway when everyone is here."

"You don't need to do that; we can eat later."

"No, guests of mine will be here at teatime and not eat, put the cake back and we shall have the apple crumble I made for dessert after dinner." Seth reluctantly put the cake back into the cupboard; the salted caramel sponge looked so tasty that it made his mouth water just looking down at it.

Seth filled his aunt in about the warehouse and the police station, she wasn't happy about the new man in charge and how he was attempting to interfere.

"You should make a complaint, that's ridiculous threatening to throw you in jail, what law are you breaking? You are a private investigator. I will be having words with the commissioner of the county; I will write a letter and post it first thing in the morning."

"I don't think that is necessary, it's his way of letting me know he's the 'top dog' in town. I don't care what he does, it won't stop me, you know that."

"I know that. Oh Seth, I just miss her so much." Seth put his arm around her and she rested her head on his shoulder, he saw the wet teardrops appear on his shirt and held her tighter. This was always a sensitive subject for her and he hated seeing how withdrawn it made her sometimes.

"I miss her too. It feels like yesterday we got the news; I was in shock and completely numb, my heart has never hurt that bad."

"Oh Seth, what I wouldn't give to see her smiling back at me one more time. I'd move the Earth for it."

"Me too, me too."

"Right, no more tears, we must be positive, not negative, let's power through. What do you fancy to eat? Chinese sound good?"

"Yes, that gets my vote and Cassie's too probably, she loves a nice Chinese."

"Oh yes, Cassie, I knew there was a subject we had to discuss."

"There is nothing to discuss like I told you before, just friends."

"Seth, life is precious, it's limited, time flies by so fast and one day what you have becomes what you had. Let Eleandra stand as an example, if you love Cassie, don't play around with it, do something about it, there is never enough time in this life to waste precious moments of it."

"I do love her, it's taken me so long to realise what was right in front of my face but I have no idea what to do, what if we ruin our friendship? She is the best person in my life, no offence."

"None taken darling. Just tell her how you feel, it's that simple, tell her your innermost feelings and do it sooner rather than later."

"Yes, it all sounds very simple."

"Exactly, now they will be here shortly, so let me refill the kettle. Could you go and grab my glasses? I'm getting a bit of a headache."

"Of course, where are they?" he asked.

"Next to the TV remote, darling." He grabbed them for her as she took some painkillers.

"I'm going to grab some paper out of the draw if you don't mind, I want to make some notes prior to them arriving."

Seth picked something out of the drawer and started staring at it, it was something he hadn't seen for years.

"What is it, Seth?" Dorothy asked.

"It's the poem I wrote for my parents' funeral. I haven't seen this in years. Where did you find it?"

"I was moving some stuff around in the loft yesterday looking for my sewing kit and I came across it mixed in with some old photos. They were of you and your parents, all of your beautiful family before their accident."

"Wow, I don't think I've read this since the funeral."

"Will you read it to me, Seth? I mean, I read it yesterday but you wrote it and it would be better if I heard you read it out loud."

"Sure."

Seth took a deep breath reading over the first line in his head over and over again.

"You alright?"

"Yes, I'm fine. I just can't believe how long they've actually been gone."

"I know, as much as I and Eleandra loved having you live with us, it was so unfair that you didn't get to be with them growing up."

"I know, but I still had a good upbringing, thanks to you. Anyway, here goes nothing.

'*My mum and dad were the best any kid could ever ask for, He was fast, strong and funny, while she was really clever and her demeanour was always sunny.*

They both loved to laugh and they both loved me, Dad took me to football and Mum taught me how to ski.

In my opinion, they were out of this world, He was a great pool player for his team and she made the best chocolate cake with cream.

When I found out they were gone, I completely lost my breath. Gone but never forgotten, love you always your son Seth'."

"That was beautiful, Seth," said Dorothy.

"I remember Cassie helped me write it as I couldn't rhyme anything, the truth is, without her my poem would have looked like a bag of scrabble tiles."

"I'm sure you would have done just fine but I'm glad she helped you, you two have always been there for each other even as children."

"Yeah, we really have."

Grabbing some paper and a pen from the drawer, Seth started making notes about the case so far. He wanted to make sure he hadn't missed anything, he wanted them all singing from the same hymn book. At that moment, the doorbell rang.

"Come in Chelsea." Seth led her to the kitchen and prompted her to sit down at the table.

"I've told Cassie to come in about five minutes, I wanted us to talk first. Aunt Dorothy, this is Chelsea, she was Eleandra's girlfriend, they were in love."

Neither of them was sure how she would react, so were a little surprised when she walked around to her chair and wrapped her up in a warm embrace.

"I'm so glad Eleandra knew love and I'm so happy you are here. Anyone who loved my daughter is welcome in this house and this family."

Chelsea broke down into tears, which seemed to become a common thing with people who were around Seth. He still never knew what to do or say in these types of situations, thankfully, his aunt did.

"Chelsea, it's good to cry, get a few tears out, our girl was one of a kind. I'm sure that gets said on a day-to-day basis about others but with her, it was true. No one came close."

"She was the gift you gave me without even knowing who I was. I couldn't describe to you how Eleandra made me feel, made me act, and when I was with her, I felt untouchable like nothing could bring me down. My life was so much better with her in it, in my eyes she was perfection."

Her words brought tears to Seth's eyes too, he welled up inside also longing for her to be back in their lives.

"No more sadness, only happiness, for Eleandra," said Chelsea.

"Agreed. Chelsea, have you told your parents about your sexual preferences yet?"

"No, I wanted to tell them and I wanted them to meet Eleandra but I didn't believe that my dad would accept me, so I've kept it hidden, you are the only ones who know."

"When you are ready to tell them, no matter what the outcome, I will be here for you if you need me, it's what Eleandra would have wanted," said Dorothy.

"Thank you so much. She was right, you know, she was always saying how she had the best family ever, I couldn't be more jealous of her."

"Be jealous no more, Chelsea, we are your family now too."

"That must be Cassie, I'll go and let her in," he said excitedly.

The doorbell had rung once again and Seth couldn't be happier. He was eager to fill Cassie in and get started on asking for their collective help.

"Hi Cassie, it's been too long, how are you?" Dorothy beamed from ear to ear.

"I'm doing really well, thank you, you?"

"Same old, same old. I potter along doing what I can, little bits here and there."

"You are far too modest, Dotty, I heard about the charity work you're doing and the relief packages that you send abroad. Not many are as involved as you."

"I just want to make her proud, as we all do. I do no more than I think she would."

Dorothy had a big smile on her face.

"Sorry, where are my manners, drinks?"

"Yes please, a cup of tea would be nice," said Cassie.

"Chelsea?"

"I'll also have a cup of tea, please."

"Seth, out on a limb here but I'm guessing hot chocolate?"

"Yes please, Aunt Dorothy, that would be nice."

"While Dorothy makes the drinks, can I just say Hi to Chelsea. We met once or twice a few years back, glad to see you are well. Seth, I got word that there was a call earlier from Mrs Richards, she would like to speak to you but didn't get your number when you spoke the other day. Oh, and out of curiosity, why have you gathered us all here?"

"Yes, I am wondering the same thing, Seth," Chelsea piped up with interest.

"Let's sit and wait for my aunty, and then I shall make it all clear."

Dorothy brought the drinks over on a tray and placed them centre of the table with some biscuits.

"OK then Seth, do you want to explain?"

At that moment, Seth's phone started to ring; it was a mobile number that again was unknown to him. *How is everybody is getting my phone number?* He thought.

"Hello."

"Hello Seth, it's Chief Abraham here, I have been thinking about what you said earlier, why don't we go catch the person supposedly following you?"

"You actually want to do something to help me, Chief Abraham?"

"I want to check out your story, see if someone is actually following you."

Seth shook his head, he wasn't surprised, he didn't believe him but at the same time, he kind of was. *It's one thing to dislike, even hate me but to accuse me of making things up is different,* Seth thought. He decided to agree with the Chief's idea and catch the man following him that proved he was telling the truth and would hopefully, shut him up for a while at least.

"What did you have in mind Chief?"

"Very simple Seth, we get you to go somewhere obscure with lots of open space so there is nowhere for him to hide and we wait and see who turns up or if anyone turns up," said Chief Abraham.

"How about we do this now? said Seth."

"I can't do it now, I need to set the operation up first, I will make arrangements and be in touch soon though."

"Soon, sure, well I guess, I will speak to you then," said Seth.

Seth hung up the phone without another word, he couldn't be bothered with Chief Abraham anymore, he was just taking time away from the real investigation.

"That was Chief Abraham but frankly what he said isn't worth mentioning."

Seth stood up and grabbed the paperwork he had written up while waiting for Cassie and Chelsea to arrive. He handed one to each of the women and sat back down at the table with his notepad and pen in front of him.

"Over the last two days, you have all shown an interest in helping me with the case. I in turn have told you all it's too dangerous, which I still stand by. Regardless of that fact, I have decided that if you would like to help contribute to this investigation, I would like to gratefully accept your offers. If they still stand?"

"Brilliant, I'm in." Cassie beamed.

"I echo those words, Seth." Dorothy smiled, expressing her pleasure at the statement.

"I want to help you, Seth, for Eleandra, I also want to ask for your help in return."

"What is it you want Chelsea?"

"I want to tell my parents that I'm gay. Will you be there when I do? I know you offered to be there Dorothy and I know it's a strange request as we only just met but Eleandra just had such a high opinion of you and I feel my dad will be the one who has the most trouble with it out of the two of them. I'd really like a man there for support if you would?"

"Of course, I'll be there for that if you're sure that's what you want?"

"I'm in this for the long haul. I'll tell them my truth once this is solved, once justice has been served, I'll come out to my parents."

"Eleandra would have been proud of you Chelsea and I know my daughter will be with you when you do tell them. She will be your strength and it will make you so brave."

"Then if everyone is in agreement let me inform you all of everything I know so far, feel free to ask any questions to get you up to speed."

"What is the paper for?"

"Each other's contact details and a few notes I made."

Each of them briefly skimmed over the paper as Seth filled them all in on recent events.

"To recap, Reginald the butler doesn't have an alibi that I know of yet and someone was seen talking to Eleandra the morning she was killed in close proximity to the warehouse. Someone, presumably the killer, has been working from said warehouse and there is a new police Chief who may want to reopen the case and doesn't want me anywhere near it. Oh, and the Killer may have been following me. Also, Clarke Richards left late for work that day and would have had a very small time frame to kill her. In fact, it would be damn near impossible for him to have done it. So that rules him out, well almost. Do we have any questions?"

Cassie spoke first, only to ask to use the toilet.

"Of course dear, you know where it is. Also, I am ordering Chinese, would anyone like anything specific? Or shall I buy a mix of bits to share?"

"That's very kind of you, I won't turn down a Chinese. Can I have some sweet and sour chicken balls please?" asked Chelsea.

"Of course, anyone else?"

"I'm not fussy so order whatever you'd like but really I need the little girls room. I'll be right back," said Cassie.

"Can you get some chicken fried rice, please aunty?"

"No worries, I'll order the food now and then we can continue when Cassie returns."

Dorothy pulled out her phone and proceeded to place the order with the man on the other end. Cassie returned just as she had put the phone down and soon, they were all back to discussing business at hand.

"The way I see it ladies is that four heads are better than one. Plus, if I'm being watched by both the police and someone, I am unsure of, I could be a great distraction to them whilst you all help me uncover more evidence."

"So simple and yet so clever."

"You sound surprised Cassie?"

"Not surprised, I'd say more like impressed."

"Well, thank you. If we divide and conquer, we could cover more ground and move things along faster. I do have one condition to this proposal for all of you though."

The three women all looked at each other, Chelsea took the lead.

"Go on then Seth, what's your condition?"

"I want you to swear to me that if there is any trouble or danger you walk away and call me and the police. Acceptable?"

"I am an investigative reporter; I will promise not to get into danger on purpose if that helps?"

"That's kind of OK, Cassie."

"I promise not to get into trouble either Seth, I am older though and the memory does play up from time to time but I agree in principle," Dorothy said with a smile.

"Chelsea?"

"I agree to behave, I am headstrong and very inquisitive, so apologies in advance."

"You three are overwhelming me with confidence." Seth's tone dripped with sarcasm.

"Seth, we will be fine, honest. We will call you if we feel in danger."

Cassie's words were followed by murmurs and smiles to suggest all was in agreement.

"Well, on that note, I have your first assignments."

Chapter Seven

"Fire away darling," said Dorothy.

"I am going to visit the mortuary, try and gather additional information on the deaths from the woman who did the post-mortem. Cassie, if you could please speak to Chelsea's ex-boyfriend Ludlow, ask him where he was when he heard about Eleandra's death. Ask him if he knew her and remind him that they went to the same school. Don't ask him for an alibi and don't ask him directly if he has anything to do with her death, just see what he knows generally, make up some excuse about it being for the news."

"Sounds pretty routine for me," said Cassie.

"Chelsea doesn't think he would be involved but no harm in figuring out what he's all about."

"Chelsea, you are going to be Quinton Forsythe IV's new piano teacher, I'll let him know that I've set this up. He has already agreed to keep an eye on Reginald, so you can be a go-between without arousing his suspicions."

"You reckon he will pay me; we've got to make it look convincing, right?"

"You will have to ask him but I doubt it. Plus, it's not like you need the money with your family wealth, is it?"

"True. But taking money from an even richer man is fun and in the off chance that he does, I'll just donate it to charity or something, happy?"

"Happy enough, Chelsea, no harm in asking him. Aunty Dorothy, I will send you some photos later of Reginald, Clarke and Ludlow, show them around the warehouse area and see if anyone can identify them in association to last year. I want to know if any of them were near the warehouse around the time of her death, slight long shot but may turn something up."

"Will do. I'll make sure to catch up with the ladies at the cafe; they're always good for gossip, see if they know any real news."

"Good. Be yourselves, don't lie and pretend to be someone else, there's no point. With the interview the other night and a small town like Kentsville, most people know about this by now anyway."

The doorbell rang again.

"Must be the food, Seth could you get that for me deary while I put the plates out?"

"Of course."

Plates laid and stacked with food, everyone began to tuck in.

"This salt and pepper chicken is delicious aunty, thank you for ordering this."

"You don't need to thank me, we all need to eat and, in my house, no one goes hungry."

"It's only 8:30 and the night is young, why don't we all go out? They do karaoke at the Sherbert bar tonight if you all fancy it?"

"Cassie, I am beginning to think I may have to stage an intervention, you are addicted to the Sherbert Bar," he said.

"You aren't wrong, I love it there."

"She has good taste, Seth, it's really fun," added Chelsea.

"Well, I'll go but only if you girls can persuade my dear aunty Dorothy to go, then and only then I guess I'll be in too."

"No need to try and persuade me of anything. I love karaoke, I'm in."

"You are?" Seth said very surprised, this was becoming a habit.

"Then I guess if Aunt Dorothy is in, we are all going for a sing-song," he declared sullenly.

"This is going to be great fun. Seth has a great voice but he never does karaoke, he's too shy."

"Well, tonight, Dorothy, we will make him sing us a song," said Chelsea.

They carried on eating with the three girls really looking forward to the exciting times ahead later in the night. Seth couldn't wait to go out, he was just a bit apprehensive about singing in public. Most people sing in the shower but Seth didn't even do that anymore, he just lost his appetite for singing and wasn't really sure why.

Once they were all fed and watered, Dorothy cleared up and they headed out to the Sherbert bar. "Girls, could you go ahead and grab us a table? I need a word with Seth," said Dorothy.

Once the other two were out of earshot, Seth asked his aunt if she was alright.

"Seth, I know I've mentioned it before but you and Cassie, you should say something. I notice the way she looks at you, she is in as deep as you are. Don't waste your chance, go for it."

"I am working on it; I just don't know what to say at all."

"Come on, let's go and have a sing, I know you'll figure it out once you're ready."

Cassie was at the bar whilst Chelsea was in the toilet. Seth and Dorothy approached her and helped carry the drinks she had ordered to a free booth; the first round was clearly on her. Chelsea made her way towards them, stopping at a small table in the corner to grab some karaoke slips and a pen.

"I'm going to put my name down, I'm feeling *firework*." Chelsea declared.

"Ooh I love that song, what are you thinking Dorothy? Seth?"

"I'll probably dazzle you all with a classic from yester-year Cassie, like me."

"Seth?"

"Not a scooby, Cassie, I'll have a look and think about it."

"Next up, a big cheer for Andrew singing *Eiffel Sixty-Five, Blue*."

There was a smattering of applause. The place was pretty busy and they had only missed one or two performances, so plenty of music to come.

"I got mine, I'm singing *from here to the moon and back*, by the fabulous, Miss Dolly Parton," said Dorothy.

"That leaves just you and I Seth, decisions, decisions."

"Great, what are you thinking Cassie?"

"I don't know. I'm waiting to be inspired, and this guy is just not going to do it."

There were smiles mirrored all around the booth with a chorus of chuckles as well. This guy wasn't doing the best job singing the song but it wasn't the worst cover they had heard.

"A solid six I'd say, he couldn't get those da be da ba de's in tune," said Chelsea.

"He had the guts to get up there at least, the majority of the people in here wouldn't and most of them are half my age."

Seth didn't know what was coming over him but he knew what he had to do to declare his feelings for Cassie. He would sing her favourite song. He nestled the pen in his hand and wrote the slip out discreetly, allowing only his aunty to see, before handing it in to the DJ. Dorothy smiled at Seth, and although she didn't know that the song was Cassie's favourite, she knew it was going to be a big romantic gesture, especially since it would take a lot of courage for Seth to sing in front of all these people.

"Just you now then Cassie. Me, Chelsea and Seth are in and have chosen our songs. What are you going to sing?"

"I will go for a bit of Rihanna, probably *Umbrella*."

"Ooh nice, I like Rihanna. She's not as good and legendary as Dolly but she's my favourite of the modern singers."

"Give Andrew a big hand, well-done dude. Next up is Chelsea, where you hiding?"

Chelsea approached the stage with swagger and conviction, she was a born entertainer but Seth couldn't help but wonder if her singing voice was as great as the way she held herself. He wouldn't have to wonder for long.

Do you ever feel like a plastic bag, drifting through the wind ready to start again?

"She's good, really good."

"I agree, Dorothy, she has a good voice and star potential."

You just gotta ignite.

"GO ON GIRL," shouted Cassie.

Baby you're a firework.

"She's a natural at this, we should make this a weekly thing Dorothy."

"That is a great idea, Cassie, but I don't think Seth would be up for that."

The idea of singing every week was daunting, well if Seth's now pale face was anything to go by.

"It's OK Seth, your aunty and I will grab Chelsea and have a weekly girls' night, you are off the hook, I mean after tonight that is."

"Well at least that's something," said Seth.

Make them go oh oh oh as I shoot across the sky sky sky, make them go ah ah ah, you're gonna leave them in awe awe awe.

The place was full of cheers and wolf whistles. A tall guy made mostly of muscles took his shirt off and threw it on the stage. Chelsea picked it up and pretended to wipe her sweat with it and threw it back in his direction.

"Thanks, gorgeous."

"That was amazing, me and Cassie were in awe, you are a born entertainer young lady." Dorothy beamed at Chelsea as she made her way back to them.

"Thanks, Dorothy, I love it, it gives me a rush being up on stage and the guys seemed to enjoy it too."

"Yes, my dear, but they only want one thing and it's not to hear your dulcet tones."

"Sorry lads, I'm into girls."

"Well, that was sensational, apologies for my bias but good luck following that. Next up we have Gavin. Gavin come to the stage dude."

The shirtless guy still dressing himself was walking to the stage. Blowing kisses to the women as he went, including Chelsea and Cassie.

Gavin was awful from the start, he was gyrating to all the words and thrusting so badly. Seth reckoned if he looked in any dictionary right now this would be the meaning of repulsive.

"I think in his mind, everyone wants him. What's your opinion ladies?" asked Seth.

Cassie shook her head.

"Not for me."

"He's too young for me, plus he is vulgar so I'm out." Dorothy faked gagged.

Chelsea just laughed and that answered that.

"Mic Drop."

Gavin did just what he said; an unpleasant noise filled the room for a second.

"Chelsea was always going to be a hard act to follow Gavin and unfortunately, the alcohol or the pressure or the *COUGH STEROIDS COUGH* got to you there, unlucky dude," the DJ mocked.

The crowd chuckled and Gavin stormed out followed by his friends, who were laughing and gyrating in mimicry.

"Next up and this lucky lady has a free pass after that disaster, it's Dorothy."

"Go on Dorothy," roared Cassie.

I could hold out my arms, Say I love you this much. I could tell you how long I would long for your touch.

"Aww she's so cute up there rocking out to Dolly Parton, Seth you must be so proud of her, her strength is unwavering."

"Eleandra got her strength from her mum and now her memory powers my aunt on, it went full circle."

From here to the moon and back, who else in the world will love you like that?

"My grandad used to sing that song to her and my mum, I haven't actually heard this since I was a baby, my mum used to sing it to me and Aunt Dorothy used to sing it to Eleandra too."

Seth's eyes were glazed with tears, he turned to the bar and wiped them clear. Cassie was quick to notice and put her hand on his. Chelsea saw this but didn't say anything, she instead turned her attention back to the stage.

"Wooooooo, go Dorothy."

And I'll spend forever just proving that fact, from here to the mooooooon and back.

"Dorothy, Dorothy, Dorothy, Dorothy." Chelsea had become a one-woman cheerleading section, she was a head cheerleader, so she was putting her experience to good use.

"Dorothy I am in awe, I see where Eleandra got her enthusiasm for the stage from."

"Thank you, Chelsea, I loved it, it was so nerve-racking though."

"I guess you'll be next Seth."

"Oh goody," was his retort.

"Well done, Dorothy, even Dolly would have loved that performance. We are taking a quick ten-minute break and then back with our next singer, Cassie."

"I guess they got them mixed up, not me next after all."

"We haven't got any drinks left; I'll pop to the bar as I'm on next, might be an idea to go to the toilet to empty my bladder too. What would we all like?"

"I'll come with you Cassie, I have two empty hands and it's my round, you got the first one."

"My hero, what a gentleman."

"Could you grab me a tomato juice please if they have it, if not I'll have a bottle of water instead."

"Tomato juice for Dorothy, Chelsea?"

"I'll have a vodka, lemonade and lime if you're offering Cassie?"

"I can do that."

Seth ordered so Cassie could go to the toilet as there were two people already waiting to be served. Seth was still waiting to be served when she returned.

"While we have a minute, there was something I wanted to tell you."

"Yes, what is it, Seth?"

"The song, I'm singing, well you kind of inspired it, I'm singing it to you."

"Singing it to me! I am intrigued, it's not something daft like Vindaloo, is it?"

"Haha no. Guess I missed the boat on that one, could have been legendary."

"Well, that's a relief, so what is it?"

"I won't tell you the song just yet, you can wait and see, the main reason I chose that is because I realised something the other day Cassie, something I guess I have known for ages but…"

"What's your order guys and girls?"

He was interrupted at precisely the wrong moment, he was going to do it, he was going to bare his soul and then the barman turned up and ruined it.

"Ruined," he muttered.

"Sorry, did you say Rum and coke?"

"No sorry, no rum but can we have a Tomato juice, a Vodka lemonade and lime, Cassie what did you want?"

"I'll have a sherbet Mocktail please, surprise me with which one just as long as it's a mocktail version."

"And I'll have a bottle of hooch please," said Seth.

"Tomato juice, a bottle of hooch and a mocktail in the same order, that's never happened before." The barman went off chuckling to himself.

"Not sure why that's funny but sorry Seth, what were you saying before he interrupted?"

Seth took a deep breath and got ready to tell Cassie how he felt, it was going to happen now.

"I was trying to say that…"

"There's your hooch and the tomato juice, I'll just get the Vodka and then I'll bring the mocktail over to you in a jiffy, that's fourteen pounds fifty please."

Seth paid and once the change was given, they made their way back to the booth without him finishing his confession.

"Third time lucky Seth," said Cassie, Seth was fully aware that Chelsea and his aunty Dorothy were listening as well, not exactly a romantic moment to announce his feelings, he went for it anyway, he wanted to tell her officially, even though his aunt insists she already knows and that Cassie feels the same way.

"Oh why not, I was saying that…"

"We are back and as promised next up a big round of applause for Cassie singing Umbrella-ella-ella. Big cheer for Cassie please."

The crowd where now all very lively, a few drinks in most of them and they were listening intently. There was a big cheer as Cassie walked up to the stage. There was an eerie silence, the song didn't start, Cassie waited and waited but still nothing.

"Sorry guys and girls, minor technical issue, delay over, let's hear it once more for Cassie."

A smaller round of applause at the second attempt but at least the music played this time. Cassie wasn't the worst singer in the world, better than Andrew from earlier but not as good as Chelsea or Dorothy, this didn't seem to faze her though as she was smiling from ear to ear and was a hit with the crowd, even with the slightly shaky voice.

When the sun shines, we shine together told you I'll be here forever, said I'll always be your friend, took an oath that Imma stick it out 'til the end.

"She's so captivating stood up there."

"She's alright Seth, not really my cup of tea," Chelsea explained.

It's raining, raining, ooh baby it's raining, raining, baby, come into me.

"I think she is having so much fun up there, that's the point so many young people forget these days," Dorothy said.

"It's true aunty, I'm the same, everyone just gets caught up in the day-to-day slog, fun gets forgotten sometimes."

"And the crowd goes wild," Seth proclaimed to Cassie as she returned to the table.

"I was fine, not like you two though, you were both much better."

"I am a born entertainer no doubt about it, Cassie, but you were really in your groove up there, give yourself some props for that girl."

"Thanks, Chelsea, thanks everyone."

"Next up, slowing us down a bit more is Seth. Big cheers for my main man, Seth."

The music started and Cassie knew the song, it was her favourite and she knew he knew that. He locked her eyes with his and sang with all his heart, he had so much passion in his voice, and the way he sang was like it was only her in the whole bar. His declaration of love shone right through and he felt amazing, the nerves and apprehension were gone, all that was left was Cassie.

I can't believe you're here with me and now it feels my world's complete and I never want this moment to end. I close my eyes and still, I see my dreams become reality.

There were wolf whistles from the ladies in the audience and his chiselled good looks and suit had them all in frenzy. Seth blocked them all out; there was only one woman in the room with him and only one woman for him.

I finally found what I've been looking for and now you know I'm gonna love you more hold me tight cause it's always been you. To think that you were always there, to be my friend and wipe away my tears now it's clear that it's always been you.

"Cassie one thing is clear, ole Sethy boy can't take his eyes off of you." Chelsea chuckled.

"I can't believe he is singing this for me, to me even, I didn't know if he felt the same way but Dorothy I...I...I love him."

Dorothy grabbed her hand and smiled at her. Cassie wasn't sure whether to smile or cry, she did neither. She just stared at Seth and he stared back.

Now it's clear that it's always been you.

The music died and the crowd went mad, the women went mad, there were whistles, cheers, applause, they loved it.

"What a fantastic performance, top of the sherbert's tonight, give it up for the suave and oh so slick, Seth."

Seth didn't get a chance to sit down in his chair as Cassie marched up to him a few feet from the table and laid a smacker on him.

"Ewwww gross," Chelsea joked.

"Not in front of me, please dearest nephew."

Seth's love had turned to lust, this was a much more common feeling for him. Their tongues massaged each other's for just a second or two as more rapturous cheers sounded from the whole room. Seth took her by the hand and they walked the last few steps together.

"Well, it only took you about twenty-five years."

"So, you would approve Dorothy?"

"My dear, if you agree to lower your standards to my Seth, I'd march you up the aisle myself before you had the sense to change your mind."

"Thank you, your blessing means a lot, not that I really know what this is, we should probably talk."

She turned to Seth. "We should probably talk."

"Talking sounds like a plan Cassie."

"Yes, probably should have done that a long time ago too."

"Shall we take a walk?" Cassie nodded and Seth took her by the hand, a smile from ear to ear on both their faces.

"Aunty, Chelsea, we are going to head off, catch up with you on the other side."

"Night Seth, night Cassie."

"Have fun, lovers in the night," Chelsea said with a smirk now on her face.

Seth and Cassie agreed to meet at his, Cassie drove off first and he followed closely behind. Seth knew in his heart that finally, he had the girl of his dreams. His night would end with Cassie in his arms. What seemed like forever to Seth, in reality took just a few minutes, they were back at his before he knew what was happening, they were kissing again, this time with more vigour and passion than before.

"No Seth, I'm taking off your shirt, don't touch it."

"You'd better take it off quicker than that Cassie; I want to feel your hands on my chest."

"Mmmmm so manly, I knew I wanted you, I just never knew how badly. I don't think I can ever put you down."

"Who said you have to? And white panties, you don't seem very innocent to me right now."

"I like white, just because I'm not innocent doesn't mean I'm not pure. Come and taste how pure I really am."

Seth pushed Cassie onto his dining table; she really was a sight to behold, one of pure golden beauty. Looking at her in all her beautiful glory as she stared up at him, Seth knew she really was the love of his life. He kissed her with a hot burning passion and she grabbed at the buckle of his trousers, rapidly attempting to undo it.

"It's not fair really, I'm just in my underwear and you still have these on."

"You want them off? Then take them off."

She nodded as she undid the button and slipped his trousers down enough to get her hands in his boxers. He cupped her right breast and squeezed softly before running his hands down her body to her knickers. He rubbed at her delicate bud through her white panties and kissed her body slowly and softly, her back arched slightly off the table and Seth knew she wanted him the way he wanted her, maybe even more. He slipped his hand inside her knickers and teased around her clit, feeling how wet she was for him only made his want for her intensify. Cassie then shimmied his trousers down his legs allowing room for him to step out of them. This action excited Seth more, which caused him to jump up on the table onto his knees towering above her.

THWACK!!!

Seth toppled off the table taking Cassie along with him, she landed on the floor at his side. Thankfully, he was damage free, Cassie, however, wasn't so fortunate. Seth looked to his right to see her holding her head and blood running down the side of her face from under her hand. He leapt to her aid checking her cut. It was a nasty one but thankfully, wasn't too deep. He scurried off in just his socks and boxers and returned to administer some first aid to her wound.

"Well, that's one for the record books, never made a girl bleed before."

"You are clearly doing something wrong then."

Cassie had a cheeky smile on her face and Seth smiled back at her, glad to see she hadn't lost her sense of humour. He patched her up and cleaned any remaining mess, ensuring to properly dispose of anything with blood on it.

"This is gonna be some story you know. My aunty will ask about how tonight went and I'm sure she will find a way to wiggle it out of me."

"I'm sure she will find the funny side of it. Let's maybe not add too many details; we were kissing on the table and BOOM."

"I'm good with that, it covers the basics."

With that settled and her head patched up, Seth kissed her softly once more. Cassie grabbed his hand and led him down the hallway to his bedroom. Even though the situation moments ago would have put a damper on anyone's mood, Cassie was eager to continue what they had started.

"Cassie, we shouldn't, you might have a concussion."

"That's OK Seth, instead of me playing nurse like we used to, you can play doctor instead. Oh doctor, I think my lady parts need attention too, would you come and inspect them for me."

Seth didn't say a word, he just nodded and smiled and followed Cassie into his bedroom for a night neither would ever forget.

Chapter Eight

The next morning, Seth was awoken by the loud ringing of his phone. He hadn't set an alarm for that morning as he was eager to spend more time with Cassie tangled in his arms, so someone must have been calling, that someone being his aunt Dorothy. The time on his phone read 6:47 AM. *She wouldn't be ringing at this time of the morning unless there was an emergency*, he thought.

"It's my aunt, I have to take this. No more bad news, please." Seth mumbled that last part under his breath.

"Seth."

"It's 6:47 in the morning, so I'm assuming something serious has happened. What is the matter?"

"I couldn't wait to speak to you about this."

"What is it, do I need to come over?"

"Yes, get dressed straight away, is Cassie with you or did she go home?"

"Yes, she's here, do you want her to come too?"

"Yes, come to mine ASAP, the both of you."

"Can't you tell me now?"

"I need to do this face-to-face Seth."

"We are on our way."

Seth ended the call and proceeded to get completely out of the bed.

"My aunty needs us both, can you follow me to her house?"

"Of course," Cassie let out with a yawn.

"Sorry, I didn't mean to yawn in your face."

"The perks of a relationship, I mean…I err…if that's what this is?"

"If that's you asking me out Seth, then I guess I accept your kind offer, if of course, that's indeed what that was?"

"Cassie let me go one better, would you like to move in with me? I know that seems sudden but…"

She put a finger over his lips, and then kissed him.

"I'd love to move in with you," she said.

Wrapped up in his love for her, Seth forgot about having to promptly be at his aunt's house, well until Cassie reminded him that is. With the bubble burst, they got moving.

"Oh crap, we need to go."

"My clothes are on the floor out there; I'll just go and get them. Do you have a spare toothbrush?"

"Yes, I do, get dressed and I'll meet you in the bathroom."

Maybe it was the fact they were woken up by the lovely Aunt Dorothy with some secret news but Seth felt no awkwardness at all this morning. Asking Cassie to move in was sincere and unexpected to him but it was natural and he felt great, impending bad news apart. They both got into their separate cars and headed for Dorothy's house. Seth looked at the clock on his car radio taking note of the time, three minutes past seven in the morning to be precise, very impressive considering they were both in bed wrapped in each other's arms just sixteen minutes ago. Seth didn't ring the bell as usual instead he used his spare key to let them both in. He didn't want to delay the potential bad news that his aunty had waiting for him.

"Seth, Cassie, so good to see you both this morning. Please come through to the kitchen, I have prepared breakfast."

"Sorry Dotty, you prepared breakfast?"

"Yes, that's correct. The kettle's boiling now if you don't mind making the drinks Seth. Plus there is fresh juice on the table too."

"Wow, aunty this is a full spread! What time did you get up?"

"I woke up around 5:30 today, no alarm, I was just awake and decided to do breakfast for the three of us."

"So what is it that you needed to tell us?" Seth questioned, hoping it wasn't serious.

"Oh, I don't need to tell you anything. You need to tell me something."

"Sorry, I'm confused aunty."

"Last night. Details, details."

"Oh Dorothy, you called us here for that?"

"Well, yes deary, I have been waiting for many years for the two of you to wake up and smell the flowers. You've both been in love with each other for a long time and have kept it hidden from each other. Even kept it hidden from yourselves but I've always known. Please leave out the gory details and give me the general gossip."

"It was going well until we got too carried away." Cassie smiled, lifting her hair back and revealing the covered-up wound.

"Oh dear, what happened?"

"We had an argument, she tried to put the toilet roll over, when everyone knows it goes under," Seth said.

"Such a Joker," added Cassie.

"Oh Seth, it looks nasty Cassie, what actually happened?"

"Well, we were kissing on the table, getting caught up in the heat of the moment and well, he fell off. I grabbed him to try and stop him but I went down with him and well, here we are."

"Oh wow, that's quite the story, how does it feel this morning?"

"I'm actually OK. No pain this morning, thankfully."

"And, are you two, well, are you a two?"

Seth took Cassie's hand and placed a gentle, yet loving kiss upon it.

"You could have just said yes, Seth, no need to put me off the breakfast I've just cooked for us all."

Cassie smiled in response to Dorothy's statement, whilst Seth merely chuckled walking towards the kettle to make the tea and coffee. They enjoyed a lovely sit-down breakfast together; crumpets, full English and croissants with jam. It was both appetising and filling.

"Eleandra and I once had a bet about the two of you. I always told her that the pair of you would one day figure out what was right in front of you and finally be together. She always believed that you were both too dumb and stubborn to admit your love for one another and that she'd be sixty by the time you both figured it out and admitted it. I guess that's one-nil to me."

"I can't believe you two had a bet on us, that's terrible Dotty," Cassie said.

"I know, I'm wicked really." She chuckled.

"So what was the stake on the bet," Seth asked curiously.

"If I was right, then she had to give up chocolate for a year. If she was right, well we would have had to have crossed that bridge if I was still around."

DING DONG.

"Are we expecting anyone else, Aunty?"

"No Seth, not that I'm aware of."

The doorbell ringing at breakfast was a surprise, it was still early and Dorothy said she had no idea who was outside.

"I'll go and get it."

Seth walked towards the kitchen door then stopped, spun one hundred and eighty degrees and kissed Cassie. It was passionate, firm and completely off the cuff.

"That was amazing, what was it for," said Cassie.

"Just to remind you that no matter what happens, I will always be here and I will always love you."

Seth's answer put a huge smile on Cassie's beautiful face; he had to admit that as beautiful as she was her smile made her face even more spectacular to look at and his eyes would never get tired of adoring her.

DING DONG.

"Well, whoever it is, they're rather impatient," he said.

This time Seth actually left for the front door. Once it was opened, his eyes took a few seconds to recognise who exactly it was. He was looking at a short woman his age, she was very attractive with her slim figure made even more impressive by her tight jeans and snug off the shoulder top. Her name was Eshima, she and Seth had a brief sexual encounter about seven years ago and he hadn't seen or heard from her since as she moved away. Before she spoke, Seth started to question in his mind what on Earth she was doing here at his aunt's house after all these years.

"Hi there, how long has it been, seven years?" he asked.

"Yes, it has been a while, a long while, in fact."

"What are you doing here at my aunt Dorothy's house? I assume you were looking for me?"

"Yes, I am here to talk to you, Seth."

Seth was hoping for more of an explanation if he was honest but he guessed he would have to ask more to find out what she wanted.

"So, what is it you are after me for after all these years?"

"Well, you might wanna sit down before I tell you."

Seth asked her in and they went and sat in the kitchen with Dorothy and Cassie, upon seeing the two of them in the kitchen, she spoke again.

"I was kind of hoping we could do this in private."

"Here is fine, we are family, I will just tell them whatever you say to me when you leave anyway. Do you want a drink?" Seth asked.

"No, thank you, I am fine," she said.

"OK, well, this is my aunty Dorothy and this is Cassie Bowl. Ladies, this is Eshima, a lady I met about seven years ago."

"It's nice to meet you both, sorry it had to be under these circumstances."

"Please take a seat and explain exactly what these circumstances are," said Seth.

She sat down, took a deep breath, looked Seth straight in the eye and began.

"Well, there is no easy way to say this but I have a brain tumour and I need to have an operation, it will be happening in Stoneymaids in seven days."

"I'm terribly sorry to hear that and I don't want to seem insensitive but we haven't seen each other in seven years, I believe you moved up north somewhere, so why did you come all this way to tell me your news?"

"Well, you see, Seth, I don't have anybody else, except my babysitter, so I'd rather set things up now in case the operation I'm having goes awry."

"I'm sorry, Eshima, I'm not following you. The operation obviously has its risks, I get that but what is it exactly you're asking me to do if something bad does happen to you?"

"There's no easy way to say this but after we hooked up seven years ago, I did indeed move away, when I was settled in my new house, I started getting sick, I went to see the doctor…"

"Please continue," said Seth.

"And I…I found out I was pregnant. I wanted to tell you but I had moved and we weren't even dating, it was just a fun night, so I decided to raise the baby alone."

Seth sat open-mouthed for a few moments; he couldn't believe the bombshell he had just heard. He had a child, six years old that he had never known about. After a few seconds to get his head around it, he took a big sip from his drink and then responded.

"I'm sorry, you're telling me that for six years now I have had a child that I had no prior knowledge of because you wanted to go it alone."

"I'm really sorry, Seth, I thought it would be for the best, obviously, it wasn't right of me but the longer it went, the harder it was to contact you."

"So what, now you might die and you thought it was a great idea to just turn up and be like surprise, it's Fathers' Day very soon and you can have a present this year."

"Seth let's calm down," said Cassie.

"Sorry, Cassie, but I won't calm down, this is outrageous. How could you keep this from me, I know we were never dating or even friends but even still it's just wrong."

"I know that and I wish I had made different choices back then but now he needs you; I might not come back from this operation and he will need his father."

"He?" said Seth.

"Yes, he, his name is Lucas Noah Bronx. I never told you about him but I wanted to give him your name still. I understand you're upset and probably angry, I deserve that but Lucas doesn't."

"So what exactly do you want from me?"

"I want you to have him and get to know him when I go in for my op. It will give you time to bond in case the worst should happen to me. I know it's a lot to ask but please Seth, you're his dad," she said.

Seth took a deep breath and held his own thoughts for a few seconds.

"Of course, I will have Lucas, he is my son, I've already missed out on six years, I don't want to miss out on another day."

"Thank you. I know it will be difficult at first but he is a great kid and you two will have so much fun together I just know it."

"I have to ask what your plan is after your operation when you have finished your recovery. What happens then?" asked Seth.

"What do you mean?"

"I assume he will return to you and you will move back away again, correct?"

"Yes, Seth, that is the plan."

"So after no contact with my son for six years, because you neglected to tell me of his existence, you then want me to look after him while you're in the hospital and then once you are healed up enough, he just goes away again?"

"Seth, I don't have all the answers for the future but for now I need you to take him and if everything is OK after the operation, then we can discuss long term, together."

"So when do I get to meet him?" Seth asked.

"Well, he doesn't know about you yet so I am going to tell him in the next few days and answer any questions he has and then I will bring him around to meet you if that's OK? It will give you some time to get your head around the news as well."

"OK then, well if there's nothing else, I'll let you get back to Lucas."

"No that's it, I will ring you in a few days' time and we can make the necessary arrangements."

Seth gave Eshima his phone number and then stood up.

"I will see you out then," he said.

Seth led the way to the front door, his head still spinning. At the door before leaving, Eshima hesitated to walk away, Seth stood behind her as she was in the doorway not sure why she had just stopped.

"Seth," she said with her back to him still, "I am really sorry about all of this, I hope one day you can forgive me."

"Maybe but that day is not today, I will speak to you soon."

With that response, Eshima left Dorothy's house and Seth returned to the kitchen and sat down at the dining table once more.

"Well, Aunty Dorothy, what do you say to that?"

"I am not really sure what to say Seth, I mean it's shocking."

"Cassie?"

"I agree with Dotty, it's out of the blue. What are you going to do?"

"Well, for now I am going to try and concentrate on the investigation, it won't be easy not to think about it but at least for the next few days I will put it to the back of my mind and crack on. First, though, I want to see what she looks like, so I'm gonna search her social media accounts and see if I can see her photos of Lucas, my son. Wow, my son, it feels good to say that."

"I am really happy for you Seth and I know it was unexpected and with everything going on not ideal timing, however, I think you will make a brilliant dad," said Cassie.

"I just want you to know, in my mind, this changes nothing between us, I know it's a surprise but what I feel for you isn't going away and I don't want this too either."

"Seth, nothing has changed between us since last night, Lucas won't come in and change that, yes some things might have to but I love you and I promise I will always be here for you and for your son."

Seth gave her another kiss and then Cassie threw her arms around him.

"Eleandra would have been so happy to see you two like this, I know because I myself am over the moon. Seth, Cassie is right, it might have come as a shock after not seeing this woman for seven years but children are a gift and you will excel at being a father, I have no doubts," said Dorothy.

"Thank you both, I might not have a big family but I certainly have the best."

"Well, on that note, breakfast has been lovely Dotty but I really need to go home and get some fresh clothes on," said Cassie.

That fresh smile hasn't left her face since she woke up, she was practically glowing, thought Seth.

"I need to go too; we all have our tasks for today and I am eager to get started on mine. Did you and Chelsea enjoy the rest of your night?"

"Yes, we did, and I'm so glad someone else knew Eleandra for the amazing person she was. She touched so many people's lives but for us select few, she was magic."

"Yes, she really did. Over the last few days, I have seen how many people she had an impact on, it's amazing how she managed to just be there for everyone she met."

Dorothy showed them out, waving them goodbye as they all parted ways. Seth headed back to his car, Cassie back to hers and Dorothy, well she just waved then turned around and closed the door.

Seth decided to make his way to the mortuary considering he was already dressed and well-fed. It was on the opposite side of Kentsville, stationed on the border of Stoneymaids. Both towns had access to it considering there was only a small mortuary at the hospital. This meant that eighty percent of corpses were transferred there for post-mortems. Seth made his way inside the building where he spotted a short lady with wavy black hair.

"Hello, I'm wondering if you have a moment in which I may be able to talk to you?"

"That depends, are you Seth Bronx?"

"Answering a question with another question. Well in that case, yes I am Seth Bronx, which makes me think that you know why I'm here."

"I think I may have an idea as to why. Please come on in."

Seth walked through the dimly lit building that practically screamed death. Fitting for the type of place in which it was. Seth followed the woman down a long hallway towards a set of large double white doors.

"How are you with dead bodies?"

"Personally, I prefer the living but I won't freak out if I see one if that's what you are wondering."

"Great, because I have one on the other side of this door that I need to examine and considering I'm short for time and you wish to speak with me, we will have to have this conversation in here not far from it."

As they walked past the corpse, Seth stopped dead in his tracks, his face went as white as a ghost.

"I can't believe he's dead!" he said.

"You knew him?"

"Yes, he was good friends with my parents and always very friendly to me. I spoke with him just two mornings ago, he seemed his normal self. How did he die?"

"He was brought in at four this morning. His neighbour said his dogs were barking for over an hour and they usually never bark, so they went and checked on him through the living room window to find him lying on the floor. They kicked the front door down to help him but it was to no avail. Paramedics informed me he had lost his life before they arrived and they suspect that it may be due to heart failure. I will find out soon enough."

"A sad day. Another great person taken from the world."

She nodded her head in agreement and led him into the office at the back of the room, leaving Jerry alone on the table in the middle of the room once more.

"I wonder what will happen to his shop. He has no family and his poor dogs."

"I'm sure the local authorities will work something out. They won't let what he worked so hard for go to waste." Seth assured her.

"Now I'm assuming you are here to ask about Eleandra's post-mortem?"

"I am indeed. I know you examined her, did you do it alone?"

"Yes. I was the only person in the room whilst the post-mortem was being completed."

"I know she had rope marks around her neck and on her wrists, which suggests she was tied up tightly. Was there any indication she was unconscious due to substances before she died?"

"There was no sign of drugs in her system if that's what you mean. However, she did have some blunt force trauma to her temple, not enough to kill her but enough to make her lose consciousness."

"Her cause of death was a puncture wound to the heart. Is that correct?" Seth asked.

"Yes. It seemed that she was stabbed with something, just once, a long blade of some kind, however, it was never recovered."

Seth didn't want to hear anymore; he had heard enough already and it was becoming too painful to bear. He considered Eleandra a sister and even though he knew this information, to hear out loud that she was knocked out, tied up and stabbed in the heart made him want to vomit. He had to continue; he wanted more answers. He needed now more than ever to find who killed her. "Could you tell what organ was removed first?"

"Unfortunately not. The way in which her body was cut open was far too severe to know what was removed first but it is evident that this person was no expert when it comes to removing body parts. It was an amateurish mess."

"Her heart. Other than the puncture wounds, was there any other damage to it?"

"No. The heart minus the singular puncture wound was probably the most intact organ of them all. The rest of her organs had some knicks and gashes."

"The heart was placed at the centre of her body by her feet, I wondered if there was any meaning to that?" asked Seth.

"I'd say judging by the fact she was stabbed and her heart was placed in the middle and in the best condition compared to the rest, then yes. I have done a bit of psychological profiling before and everything in these kinds of cases is normally done for a reason."

"Well, thank you for that information, I really appreciate it. I know I'm not related to Mr Clarke Richards but can I ask you some questions about his death?"

"You can but I'm afraid I don't know very much about that."

"Oh. Was his autopsy performed by someone else?"

"No. No autopsy was done on his body."

"I'm sorry, you said no autopsy was performed, may I ask why not?"

"The police told me to prioritise Eleandra as they wanted as much information as I could give them so that they were able to inform your aunty. After I had completed my work on Eleandra, I wanted one performed on him and I again pushed for it but they said it wasn't needed due to him committing suicide. They were pushing for my report on your cousin."

"That doesn't sound odd to you?"

"Very odd, Seth, and completely wrong."

"If you did an autopsy on a year-old corpse, could you tell anything?"

"I could still tell you a lot about the body even now but my results wouldn't be as informed as to when the corpse was still fresh. Your chances of getting them to agree to dig the corpse are pretty slim. You would need written consent from his next of kin and there is loads of red tape to get through, lots of toes you would be stepping on. If you want to do this, you'd need to speak to the new police chief in town."

"Oh, we've met already, he's delightful," Seth replied sarcastically.

"Interesting, that was my opinion too."

"Well, thank you for your help today. Your cooperation is greatly appreciated and I feel that I am maybe getting somewhere with this case. With that in mind, I wish you a very lovely day."

Seth wasn't sure that was the appropriate thing to say to her as she was going to be cutting up a body or two but it was the first thing that came into his head. Seth thought his time spent at the mortuary was productive, even if he didn't have much more information than what he started with. It looked as though it was a crime of passion judging by the information about the heart, which would lean more back towards Ludlow than Reginald. He checked his messages as he sat in his car to see if anyone else had an update for him. Nothing had come through yet but the screen showed that Cassie was typing, so he thought that he may as well wait a few seconds for her to hit send.

"Seth, Ludlow didn't want to talk to me at first but I managed to get a few words out of him. He was very tight-lipped about everything, only disclosing what we already knew, that they went to the same school together. He claimed that he never really spoke to her that much, and that was about it."

"Would you say he was very hostile or in a rush to get away from the conversation?" Seth asked.

"I feel that he is hiding something. Do you reckon you could do some social media stalking on him, see what you come up with?"

He didn't wait for a response from her as he knew it would be positive, so he put his phone away and drove off. Seth headed towards the police station, eager to see if the new police chief had been informed of the lack of autopsy performed on Clarke Richards' dead body. He could have easily asked him over the phone, that's if he answered the call but he wanted to look at him face to face so he could see his reaction. He was made to sit in the waiting area at the station as Chief Abraham was supposedly tied up. He waited for over an hour, wondering if he was actually busy or just making him stew. During the hour, Seth checked the football news, his messages, of which he had two and browsed Facebook. Cassie had responded and said yes, he expected nothing less of her. The other message was from Chelsea.

"Quinton wasn't happy about the new arrangement, you forgot to pre-warn him. He has agreed to go along with it for now with a lesson scheduled for tomorrow and then one every other day after that. He isn't going to pay me but it was worth a try."

Seth shook his head.

"She has certainly got character." He chuckled to himself.

He was just about to play a game on his phone to kill more time when Chief Abraham appeared. "Seth, would you like to follow me to my office?"

"Your Office this time, all the interrogation rooms busy, are they?"

"No, my office will be fine."

Seth sat down opposite the Chief; he had a big smirk on his face. He couldn't wait to put him on the back foot, maybe it would get him off his case and hopefully, leave his investigation alone.

Chapter Nine

Neither man spoke at first, Seth wanted to see if he had anything to say before he asked about Clarke.

"So Seth, what have you come in for today?"

"Are you aware of all that went on in Eleandra's case?"

"I am indeed. I have gone over all the case files and spoke to a few officers who dealt with it. I believe I am fully informed."

"Brilliant, so maybe you can tell me why Clarke Richards body never had an autopsy performed on it?"

There was silence, and judging by his face, Seth could tell he didn't have the answer. His plan was working, he was unaware of this fact and it gave Seth the upper hand, at least he thought.

"I want to know why not? I feel that an autopsy could tell you a lot; it's a massive oversight and has compromised the case findings. Mr Richards could have been drugged or had something in his system that showed he was a victim too. Now, we will never know."

"I was unaware that one was not performed. I was reading Eleandra's notes yesterday after we spoke but I didn't think to check for Clarke's autopsy."

"Could we dig the body back up? I reckon his wife would agree to it if I explained to her why."

"Digging up his body and examining it now wouldn't be of much use. It may prove what we both already believe, that he was killed and it wasn't suicide but you wouldn't get much more evidence from a pile of bones. It would be a waste of time and resources."

"Is there anything we can do about why there wasn't an autopsy completed?"

"Not publicly, it would be too damaging to the station's reputation. I won't let the mistakes of one or two individuals reflect badly on the department, I will handle this privately."

"Well, there's nothing more I want, so I guess I'll take my leave."

"Seth, before you go, I want to apologise."

"You want to apologise, to me? Yesterday you wanted to lock me up."

"I misjudged you. I have spoken to some of the officers and residents within the town and I realised I was wrong. If you need our help, we are here to assist you in any way we can."

"Then I accept your apology, thank you."

A solid handshake between the two and Seth was on his way. He still hadn't heard from his aunt, so he decided to give her a call. He rang her four times but no answer. He decided to go to her house and check in on her to ensure everything was OK. His phone started vibrating against the dashboard of his car, so he immediately answered it, putting it on loudspeaker so he could continue to drive.

"I assume you have a good reason for ignoring four calls from your favourite nephew?"

"My only nephew you mean. I didn't realise you had rung, sorry darling. I am down in the cafe at the moment having a nice mocha and a doughnut."

"Everything alright?"

"Yes, everything is going well. I have been showing the photos that you have given me around but no one seems to have seen them around here recently or on that day that they can remember. I'll keep persevering though."

"I am done so I will come join you if you'd like some quality, only nephew time?"

"That would be lovely. Come and meet me in the cafe first for a lovely warm drink and then we can head out together."

"Great idea. See you soon."

"Yes, see you shortly, love you, Seth."

"Love you too, Aunt Dorothy."

Today had been going smoothly for Seth. The mortuary and visit to the police station seemed to have Seth leaving with a feeling of accomplishment. Even Cassie and Chelsea had been rather plain sailing with their tasks, although no real results as of yet. It had been a stop-start the last few days so it made a refreshing change for everything to go to plan with no nasty surprises so far. Seth could use a mocha now that his aunt Dorothy had mentioned the drink and he would be sure to get one as soon as he got to the cafe.

"A brownie to accompany it, of course," he said to himself.

He parked up swiftly once outside the cafe and was soon giving his aunt a hug, sitting down across from her with his drink in front of him and his brownie in his mouth.

"I love the brownies here. So full of flavour and the texture is perfect," Seth muffled through a mouthful of the delicious brown delight.

"The aroma is something like a fairy-tale and it smells fantastic."

"No talking with your mouth full dear. Now, I'm personally not a fan of brownies but you can give me a doughnut any day."

"Sorry," Seth said with a clearing of his throat.

"So, where have you been so far aunty?"

"I walked up and down the main road and up Cook Street, then just off the road down the end there." She pointed to behind Seth.

"No one who was in the area that day can recall seeing any of the three men I have shown to them, and others who are often in the area can't recall ever seeing them around before."

"We will find someone. Hold that thought, it's Cassie."

Seth answered his phone, smiling to himself at the sound of her sweet voice.

"Seth, I found something. Not sure if it relates to the case but I was going back through his Facebook page and not long after he and Chelsea had broken up, his relationship status changed again, he was no longer single. However, the change in status doesn't say who it was with, just that he was in a relationship. I don't know if it helps us in any way but I could have another crack at him, maybe get some in-depth intel?"

"I'd like to be with you when you do. I want him to feel intimidated, maybe he will crack under pressure. Where are you at? I'll come meet you."

"I'll meet you at the rowing club and don't worry I'll wait outside till you get here."

Seth hung up the phone and turned towards Dorothy.

"Sorry aunty, rain check?"

"Sure, love is calling after all, see you later, darling."

Seth went to meet Cassie out the front of the rowing club as she mentioned, to go and see Ludlow together this time. The morning visit wasn't productive but Seth felt optimistic about this one with the new information to play with. Cassie was currently sitting in a little park just opposite the rowing club entrance and Seth saw her as he arrived and he parked up and they walked over together.

"Ludlow," Cassie shouted once she had spotted him.

Ludlow turned to face them both with a look that had them believing he was sucking on something sour.

"You again. Oh and look, you brought the detective with you too. That's just great."

"I just had a few more questions for you, if you have a few minutes."

"I am just leaving, so can I say no?"

"You see, that's the good thing about being a private eye. It's my job to persist with people until I am satisfied, I get the information I want. So what I'm trying to say is that I have nothing better to do but investigate, so I can meet you wherever you are going and talk there if you'd prefer?" Seth had a big smirk on his face which clearly made Ludlow angry.

"Listen to me Mr Detective. I don't care what you do with your time, as long as it doesn't involve me." He started to walk away, at quite a pace, almost jog even.

"Why the rush to leave, are you hiding something, boy?"

Seth was really pushing him to see what he would do; he nearly fell over himself as he came to a speedy halt. He had swung himself around and marched back to Seth with a purpose.

"BOY! I have a name and it's certainly not BOY."

"If I were you, Ludlow, I'd step back rather quickly," Seth warned.

Ludlow and Seth were eye to eye, nose to nose, with their chests rising and falling at a remarkable pace. Ludlow's nose was slightly crooked as if it had been broken previously and his eyes were dark brown as opposed to Seth's blue.

"Can you both calm down please, I don't need to be showered in testosterone. If you have nothing to hide, then what harm can it do to speak to us."

"Ask your damn questions," he huffed out.

He was very aggressive and Seth wasn't impressed that he was being so hostile to Cassie as well.

"Watch your tone with her, lad."

"You come into my rowing club and start telling me what to do and how to behave. I make the rules around here, not you. Now ask your damn questions or leave."

Seth went to speak again but Cassie not wanting to go around and around in circles, cut him off at the pass.

"What are you hiding about Eleandra?"

"Nothing about killing her, if that's what you are implying, Cassie."

"So you admit you are hiding something about her?"

"That not what I said."

"That's how it was worded," said Seth.

"I have nothing to hide, so are we done?" He turned his back to them and started to leave. Seth put his hand on his shoulder and pulled him back around towards him.

"If I find out that you had something to do with it, I will find you and I will deal with you personally."

"Sounds like a threat. Remember that you are an ex-fireman and an investigator, not Rambo. I think I'll be OK." He laughed out smugly.

"That's what Chuck thought in the third grade and then Seth hit him with a stapler and gave him a black eye," Cassie said, raising her eyebrow at him.

"That was an accident Cassie, what I'd do to Ludlow here if I find out he killed Eleandra or had anything to do with her death whatsoever, would be completely purposeful."

This time it was Ludlow that Cassie cut off before he could retort to Seth's last comments.

"Ludlow, after you and Chelsea broke up, you moved on pretty quickly. You were rumoured to be in a relationship just two weeks later. My question is with who?"

"Like you said Cassie, rumoured, don't believe everything you hear."

"Sorry, let me reword that. This screenshot I have is of you posting that you are in a relationship. So, who with?"

Ludlow went from angry to sheepish in about point two seconds.

"Sorry, Ludlow, did you say something? All I could hear was your silence," said Seth, very cocky indeed.

"It was one of those joke things with my mates. You would know what I'm on about if you had any mates."

"Thank God I was used to putting out fires for a living Ludlow, it means I am adequately trained to deal with that burn."

"Was that a joke, Seth?"

"No Ludlow. The real joke here is you, thinking you can hide the truth from me."

"Who was the new relationship with?" she repeated the question again.

Seth noticed she wasn't going to give up until she got an answer to it.

"What was Chelsea's reaction to your new relationship status?"

"That psycho, I don't know and I don't bloody well care. I was just glad it was over."

"Really, so you dumped her?"

"Yes, actually, I did. She was psychotic and possessive, I couldn't have fun with her around. I was a horrible person when I was with her."

"Strange, as she isn't here now and yet you're still a dick," said Seth.

"Go fuck yourself, Seth."

"Alright, we are done here, for now. Seth let's go," Cassie urged.

They walked one way whilst Ludlow went another.

"Oh Ludlow, what was her name again?" Cassie shouted.

"Goodbye!" he shouted back.

"That's an unusual name."

Once they were outside, Seth looked around to make sure they were alone.

"That was fun, we are great at this. Dream team, am I right?"

"Wait, you weren't actually angry? I thought you were going to pummel him. You looked as if your blood was boiling over."

"I meant what I said to him but my blood was cold as ice. I just wanted to get a reaction from him and it worked, it works with everyone. So what did you think?" Seth questioned, pondering on what had just taken place moments ago.

"I think the only honest thing he said was when he was talking about Chelsea."

"Really? You think what he said about her was true?" Seth asked, sounding surprised at Cassie's answer.

"Not necessarily what he said but the way he had said it. He was clearly glad to be out of the relationship but I can't understand why. Maybe he knew about her and Eleandra, maybe the new relationship status he put up was a fake to try and make her jealous. I don't know, all I can tell you is that he is definitely hiding something."

"That, Cassie, we agree on, but the question is what exactly?"

The car journey back home was full of theories and scenarios, both had lots to say as they loudspeakered a phone conversation all the way. Nothing they came up with seemed to make sense. Cassie said she couldn't shake the idea that what Ludlow was hiding was important to the case. Seth on the other hand wasn't so sure. Yes, he was hiding something but it could be related to anything, not just the case. Seth had to be sure, he couldn't afford to make any mistakes.

"So are we thinking more towards Reginald than Ludlow?" she said.

"I don't know, is there may be a third option?" Seth offered.

"Like who? Are you having a gut moment?"

"A gut moment, what's a gut moment?" He wasn't sure what Cassie was asking.

"You know, the great Leeroy Jethro Gibbs gut, a gut moment?"

"Oh you mean like a gut feeling; I get you now. I do love a bit of NCIS. Well, I think maybe I've been looking at this all wrong. What if it's definitely the murderer who has been following me? They could be one step ahead, leading me where they want me to go and following to make sure I am not on the right path. Or do you think that's a bit far-fetched?"

"If you are sure someone was following you the other day, then I guess it's possible, Seth."

He considered who else could be the killer. Obviously, his aunt and Cassie were ruled out as suspects, plus Chelsea, Quinton and Bruce. He racked his brain, who else was there?

"I have a theory for you, Seth, thinking outside the box, of course. What if Mrs Richards thought Eleandra was having an affair with her husband, could she have done it? That would be a strong motive."

"What? No way. That one's definitely out there, Cassie. I can't see her dissecting a frog in a science class let alone overpowering and cutting up a human being," Seth said.

"I did say it was outside the box. Here's another one for you. What if Eleandra rejected Quinton's advances after he was set to leave her all that money, and in a moment of rage, he enlisted the help of Reginald, with the promise of a small fortune, to help him murder her. What do you think about that?"

"Still no but it's more plausible than Mrs Richards."

"I put money on it being Reginald. I haven't spoken to him but he had reason to do it, what bigger motive is there than seven hundred and fifty million pounds?"

"I can't argue with that Cassie. I think he is an important person of interest; I'm just not ruling Ludlow out."

"So who else do you think could be a suspect?" she said.

"I'm not sure really, for now, we will see if Chelsea and Quinton come up with anything on the butler."

"Seth, do you think if I could get Roy to agree to another interview tonight at six, would your aunty Dorothy appear?"

Seth went silent. He wasn't sure if she would agree to do it, and he wasn't sure if he wanted her exposed on TV like that. However, it wasn't his decision, it was her's.

"You should ask her Cassie, we can head to her house now if you want, actually I should ring her she might still be down by the warehouse showing photos."

"We had such a positive reaction to you being on the show that I feel if Dorothy made an appearance, even more people would be willing to pick up and call. It's a mother losing her daughter and that resonates with all mums. It could be the push we need, maybe even get us some key evidence that we have been lacking so far."

"I'll ring her from my phone, I'll pop you on hold then I don't have to ring you back after." Seth still had her on loudspeaker when he searched for her.

"Here we are, there's no place like home."

"That's what she's saved as?"

"You like it? I thought it was funny."

"There's no place like home, Wizard of Oz reference, it's cute."

"Well, her name is Dorothy, and it was Eleandra's favourite film, so it made sense. Anyway, I'll ring her now, speak to you soon."

The phone rang a few times before it was picked up.

"Hello."

"Hey Aunty, I have Cassie on hold, this is just a quick one, we were wondering if you were still at the same place where I left you earlier on?"

"I am indeed. I was just about to leave but I can wait here for you both if you'd like me to?"

"We are a few minutes away from you, just coming past Wallerion's woods."

"I shall get us a booth in the cafe, I'm feeling a bit peckish. See you soon."

"Bye."

Now she had mentioned it, Seth felt he could do with some food too.

"Cassie, we are meeting her at the cafe for some lunch, you can ask her then."

"Oh, thank god, my stomach has been rumbling this whole conversation."

"I can tell Cassie, it's so loud it sounded like you'd popped a tyre, repeatedly. We can grab food and then speak to her about possibly doing an interview. Sound good?"

"Well, my stomach says yes, and Seth on a different note, I'm so happy right now."

Seth felt his heart could sing to the rafters when he heard those words, and even though he wasn't with Cassie at this exact moment in person, he knew that Cassie was feeling the same. Upon entering the street in which the cafe and the warehouse were situated on, Cassie exclaimed her disbelief.

"Wow, it's completely destroyed. It's almost just rubble and dust."

"Barely anything of the building is left. I always thought if the building was gone that I would feel happy but it's strange, I felt nothing as I watched it burn. The building's timely demise makes me realise that it being gone doesn't actually change what happened and it doesn't bring her back," said Seth.

"I get what you mean, and you're right but I promise everything will soon fall into place. Whoever is guilty of this, will pay. Should we go find Dorothy?"

"Yes, let's go find her and get some grub."

Neither could see her as they entered the cafe. They looked in all the booths and Cassie checked the ladies but there was no sign of her. Seth went to ring her but realised that he must have left his phone in the car, and Cassie didn't have her number, so they sat down and were soon approached by a waitress.

"Hello, my name is Jade and I'll be your waitress today, what can I get you?"

She was carrying a glass pot presumably filled with coffee. Seth was unsure though as the strong smell of her perfume was overriding the scent of what was in the pot. Jade was about five foot tall, roughly a size eight and looked around 18 or 19 years of age.

"Oh. I know you. You're Cassie Bowl! And you, you're Seth Bronx! I've seen you both on the news."

"Yes, that's right. Please, may I have a glass of water?" Cassie asked nicely.

"Of course. You know, I want to be a reporter so bad. You are like my idol."

"I'm honoured you look up to me that way, Jade, and I'm sure one day with hard work you will be a fine reporter." Cassie smiled.

"I hope so, I want to be just like you."

Seth thought it funny that Cassie was turning a little red due to her very obvious fan girl.

"May I also have a glass of water, please; I'm feeling very thirsty."

"I'm so sorry, of course. I forget myself sometimes and get so carried away."

"I understand. I forget myself too sometimes in the presence of Cassie." Seth smirked, making Cassie turn even more red in the face.

"Not just Cassie, you too, Mr Bronx. I have been following your investigation and I'm eager to find out what the result will be. You are somewhat of a local celebrity."

"A celebrity?" Seth questioned.

"Yes! I was just wondering when you were going to be doing an interview again. Here I was thinking of you and the case and all of a sudden you walked in, must be fate."

"Not fate, famished. Please can I have that water?"

"Oh God, what am I like I forgot about the coffee, it's all cold now. I'll be right back with some more."

Before Seth could repeat his wish for water once more, she was out of earshot and getting fresh coffee.

"I'm sure she will bring out that water for us when she returns with the coffee."

"No Cassie, I don't think she will, she is away in la la land. I'd hazard a guess she's related to your receptionist." Cassie giggled and then the waitress returned, with coffee.

"Coffee?" she questioned.

"No, just some water, please," Seth said.

"A water for you Seth and for you Cassie?"

"I'll have water also. Oh, and could I also have a Fanta, please?"

"Of course. Would you like it in a glass?"

"Yes please, Jade."

"Excuse me. I'll be right back."

"Oh, must she return, we've only just got here and I'm already exhausted."

"Oh Seth, you are a man of no patience or understanding."

Seth ignored that comment and went to check his phone remembering he had left it in the car. Cursing his stupidity, he hoped his aunt would appear shortly and put his mind at ease.

"Still nothing? That's strange, she knew we were meeting her. She should be here by now," said Cassie worryingly.

"Cassie, if you wouldn't mind waiting here, I'm going to go find her car; it should be parked around here somewhere."

"Of course, I'll get you that glass of water from the sink myself if Jade forgets again," Cassie joked.

Seth shook his head and kissed Cassie on the forehead, leaving the cafe in search of her car.

"Excuse me, that's my auntie's car. Does anyone know what happened? Why is the window smashed?" Seth asked a group of people close by.

"I canna tell ya, pal. I saw it was like this when I was standing over there," said a tall, brunette Scottish man.

There were no obvious signs of a struggle as the doors were intact, however, there was broken glass all over the front seats and down by the pedals. Seth was starting to worry that something bad had happened to her and a million thoughts were running through his mind. What if he was the cause? What if something really did happen to her because of him and this investigation? Could it be the person who was following him? Does the killer have her?

Chapter Ten

Seth feared the worst when he felt his phone ringing in his pocket, taking it out he discovered it was Chelsea.

"Chelsea, I'll have to call you back, I'm dealing with something important at the moment."

"Seth, this can't wait. Reginald handed his notice in this morning. He told Quinton he is leaving at the end of next week and didn't give a reason."

"Tell Quinton not to let him leave the house. Make up some excuse. I don't care what it is; I want eyes on him until I can get there. I have to go; I have an incoming call."

Seth didn't wait for her response. Hanging up the phone, he quickly accepted Cassie's call. "Please tell me she's with you?" said Seth in an almost desperate voice.

"Yes, she's here. She has just walked in."

Seth's heart started to slow down; it had been beating quite rapidly for the last few minutes. He proceeded to tell Cassie about his findings and encouraged them to make their way towards him. He needed to see for himself that his aunty was safe. Once they had arrived, Seth embraced Dorothy in a loving hug, his anxiety calming down some more.

"Seth, that isn't my car," Dorothy exclaimed.

"Yes, it is."

"It's the same make and model as mine, however, I'm parked over the other side, three cars down."

Seth turned and saw the same car where she had said it was. He felt like an idiot but he also felt relieved.

"Thank goodness. I was worried that you had been in an accident or something bad had happened to you."

"Oh darling, I'm fine. I was having a serious conversation with someone who wishes to remain anonymous. They have important intel on the day of the murder. How about we go and sit in my car? I want to go somewhere that we can be guaranteed privacy, and I don't believe the cafe is a good place for that; too many listening ears."

"And leave Jade, oh no, we couldn't possibly do that, let's go."

"Seth, you are ruthless," said Cassie and she laughed.

"Wait, who is Jade?" Dorothy asked, making them both laugh.

Seth sat in the front passenger seat with Cassie in the middle seat in the back, leaning forward to look at Dorothy.

"I was canvassing like you asked. At first, I was getting a lot of no's and sorry's, when all of a sudden, this man approached me, must have been about thirty-five to forty years of age, and asked me what I was looking for. I wasn't sure if he was a creep, a weirdo or if he was a gentleman who saw me as a damsel in distress and wanted to help. Well anyways, I decided to show him the photos you had given me, figuring that if he was just some creep who wanted to waste my time, I could walk away safely due to all the people around. I showed him the photos and he said that he hadn't seen Reginald around, however, he had seen Ludlow. I asked him if he was sure that it was Ludlow and he said yes, he was wearing a rowing hoodie."

"So when was Ludlow supposedly here?" Seth quizzed.

"He said that he saw Ludlow here three days in a row, including the day Eleandra was killed. He also claimed he saw Eleandra talking to him around 6:30 AM on the morning of her death."

"We need to talk to him again but first I need to go visit Quinton. Aunt Dorothy, Cassie, could you both go to your house," he said looking at his aunt.

"Actually, Dorothy, first I'd like to ask you something. I spoke to Seth about possibly interviewing you on the news tonight like I did with him. He is unsure, but he understands that you are an adult and therefore told me to speak to you directly. Would you be up for being on the news tonight?" Cassie asked.

"If you think it will make an impact on the people watching, then absolutely, I'd love to."

"Then how about we make our way to the news station instead?"

"Perfect. Seth, out you pop and let Cassie get into the front seat. We are off to do some butt-kicking. I'll see you soon, my darling," said Dorothy.

"Actually, we came separately, I'll meet you at the station, Dotty."

"And I'll meet you both there later on then."

Seth waved them off and walked back to his Jag. He couldn't make up his mind about who was more guilty, Reginald or Ludlow. On one hand, the evidence leaned more towards Ludlow but why was Reginald now all of a sudden deciding to quit? And why leave so quickly? Seth felt he was closing in on the killer, he could just feel it in his bones. He once again took the photo of Eleandra from his pocket and spoke to her.

"You would be so proud of your mum; she is so tough and gritty. You probably already know that she has cancer, I found a letter from the hospital in her kitchen draw. I don't think she is planning on telling me though, you know what she's like. Unfortunately, you are going to have to wait to be reunited with her again because I'm gonna help her fight this all the way, I'm just not ready to lose her too. I'm more than sure that I am close to finding your killer, I can feel it. And I know that trying to find him is giving your mum the strength and inspiration to beat her illness, so I promise we won't give up, for the both of you. I'd like to think you are looking down on us now, so you must also already know that Cassie and I are together and that I asked her to move in with me. Apparently, you said it wouldn't happen till you were sixty but you know what I'm like, always proving you wrong. I hope you are happy for me and I want you to know that I will always love you like the sister I always wanted. I love you Eleandra, send me your love, strength and some luck too would be nice."

Seth pulled into the street where Quinton lived, driving slowly down the road so that he would have a few moments to think. He wanted to question Reginald himself, however, thought it best to speak with Quinton first to see if he had noticed anything out of the ordinary or if he thought Reginald was suspicious of his request for Quinton to keep an eye on him. Pulling up to the familiar gates, Seth was met with the same intercom system and conversation with Reginald, 'did he have an appointment' blah blah blah. Once Reginald was given the go-ahead by Quinton to let Seth in, he proceeded to drive up the long driveway towards the door.

"Please come in, Mr Bronx, he is sitting in the same room as the last time you visited. Do you require me to take you or are you capable of finding your own way?" Reginald asked politely.

"No, it's OK. I can manage if you are needed elsewhere."

"Very well. I'll take my leave."

He bowed before turning and making his way up the stairs and out of Seth's sight. Seth waited until he was completely gone before he made his way into the room where Quinton was. He wasn't at all surprised to find him sitting at the grand piano.

"I asked Reginald to let you in and then change my bedding for me, that should buy us a few minutes without interruption," Quinton said, his eyes never leaving the piano.

Seth ignored his lack of greeting. His tone wasn't hostile and therefore, Seth knew this was just normal behaviour for him.

"That was quick thinking. Chelsea tells me that he has resigned and is leaving very soon. What did he say to you?"

"He didn't really say anything. Just that it was with regret that he had to leave and that he has loved his near thirty-one years with the family. He handed me this piece of paper and walked out. I was with Chelsea at the time completing a 'lesson', so I didn't really get the chance to speak with him. Can I ask why she is here?"

"I needed a cover, someone to keep an eye on Reginald. This way you are able to relay any important information to her that she can pass on to me, without you being suspected of anything like if I was ringing you or messaging you all the time."

"I see. And you trust her? Who is she exactly?"

"Chelsea is the person of whom Eleandra spoke, she wasn't seeing her ex-boyfriend, she was with her."

"Excuse me. Surely, you are mistaken. Eleandra wasn't gay. I once had a delivery guy here when Reginald was at the store, so she took it in for me as I don't like to open the door to people."

"Your point, Quinton?"

"She was all hot and flustered. They were flirting with each other for ten minutes. I remember because it wrote into my lesson time."

"So you think Chelsea is lying?" Seth questioned.

"Eleandra liked men, I'm not saying she didn't like women as well but I know for a fact she liked men. And anyways, I'm more than sure she would have been honest with me if she did."

"Chelsea knew the password to her phone. She knew the password to her email and about the secret second email account that Eleandra had that no one else knew about, explain to me how she would possibly know about that if they weren't dating?"

"That I can't offer an opinion or knowledge on."

"Right. So let's put a pin in that and go back to Reginald."

"I want you to ask him why he's leaving and why now?"

"I will do that but if I'm being honest, I don't think he is a suspect."

"Any reasoning behind that?"

"I have known him for thirty-one years since I was a teenager. He didn't do it, I would know. I would notice a change in his work levels or a change in his demeanour. He may seem like a robot but he's actually a really emotional guy and I would know if something was wrong, you just need to know how to look. I don't believe this is his crime. You should probably focus your efforts elsewhere."

"Thank you for that but I have to follow all the theories and can't leave anything out. I would like to see why he is leaving all of a sudden."

"Very well, Reginald. Reginald, could you come in here please."

They sat in silence, Seth taking in what Quinton had just said. He didn't know Quinton that well but he certainly seemed to have passion for Eleandra when they last spoke. He seemed eager to catch her killer, he still does but Seth couldn't eliminate the possibility that he could be protecting Reginald. After all, he had classed him as part of his family for a lot longer than what he had done to Eleandra. Could he live an adult life without a butler? He had been waited on hand and foot by Reginald for most of his life, surely that would give him a motive to try and protect him.

"You called sir? How can I be of service?"

"Please Reginald, take a seat."

"Why, of course, sir."

"As you know this is Seth Bronx, a private investigator working on the Eleandra Jacobson murder case. I'm sorry to do this Reginald, and in front of Seth too but he wanted to be here for this."

"Here for what sir?" asked Reginald, genuinely confused.

"He wanted to be here when I asked you why you are leaving this household. You have served so magnificently for the majority of my life."

"Sir, I served this household, I served the family name and I served your parents. If I'm honest, I never liked you as a child or even as a young adult, you were too arrogant and too entitled, nothing like your parents. I saw a change in you once they had both passed away. You were secluded and lonely, so I stayed, continuing to serve you and your family home."

"Indeed, you have been a great servant of our household for so long, are you retiring?"

"No sir, I will not retire. I will seek alternative employment after a well-earned vacation."

"Then why do you leave your post here?"

Seth had sat quietly throughout the conversation, wanting to jump in but felt it wasn't his place, so he sat, listened and observed.

"I am leaving sir because of your dishonesty and lack of trust towards me with this man."

"Dishonesty, lack of trust?"

"Yes sir. Do you deny that you have been keeping an eye on me?"

"No Reginald, I do not deny it. I'm sorry, I do not deny helping Seth. He is trying to catch Eleandra's killer and he asked me if I would pay attention to your actions and your whereabouts."

"All you had to do was ask me, sir, look into my eyes and ask me."

Seth finally got involved; he has caused this friction and wanted to help fix this if he could.

"Quinton was only doing what I had asked. I put the notion in his head that it was a possibility that you were a suspect because he had changed his will and left the majority of his money and wealth to Eleandra."

"I see. I was unaware of this change to his will, not that it matters to me, I am not interested in receiving his wealth. Nonetheless, I feel, although he acted on your behalf, he still acted. And after nearly thirty-one years of loyal service, I feel it was a kick in the teeth."

"Reginald, I can only offer you my deepest and most sincere apology. I meant no offence and I didn't take how you would feel into consideration. I appreciate everything you have done for this family and I am so sorry that I have disrespected you and your loyalty to us in this way. I may own this house but it is your home too and if you still want to resign, then I understand. I will, of course, miss your tireless hard work and your companionship but please if you would like, stay in the house until you find a new job. You need not pay a penny for accommodation elsewhere when you can be here for as long as you like. I would like you to reconsider your position here as well but I will accept and agree to your leaving if that is what you wish."

"Reginald, I feel that I should tell you, in Quinton's defence, he was praising your character before you came in. He did act badly, yes, but I put him up to it to find the killer. I would in fact still like to ask you a few questions if you wouldn't object though?"

"I have nothing to hide detective, please go ahead."

"Do you have an alibi for the morning that Eleandra died?"

"I do, and she will corroborate it for me."

"Who were you with?"

"Miss Delilah Hills."

"The town dentist?" asked Seth.

"Yes, that is her profession. We have a book club once a week with one other as well. That week, it was on the night before Eleandra's death, and we decided afterwards to go for a few drinks. Delilah started to feel sick, and since we had both been drinking, she had let me use her spare room instead of driving home as the pub was around the corner from her house."

"Again, I want to reiterate how sorry I am for doubting you Reginald," said Quinton.

"Your apologies are accepted, sir. I am unsure if I can continue to serve you knowing you don't trust me, I thought all my years of loyalty proved that and although I don't entirely care about your money, it is a bit disappointing that someone you have known for a year, triumphs over me."

"I believed that if anything happened to me, Eleandra would do good things with the money, like develop and plan an orphanage, it's not an insult to you in any way, I just wanted the money to do good in my absence."

"I get that sir. What I don't get is why your life has to end for your money to be well spent. You don't really live a lavish life apart from this house, your money sits there collecting dust. You could do all the things you wanted Eleandra to do with the money by yourself. Get out of the house and be involved with the community."

"I have been away from people for too long and forget about children, I don't know how to speak to them."

"Well, if there is nothing else sir, I will take my leave and get back to changing the bed sheets."

"Before you go, may I make a suggestion to you both?" Seth piped up.

A lightbulb had gone off in his brain upon hearing the two men speak. It had nothing to do with the case and more to do with money.

"Quinton, Reginald, consider this. You start a charity together, The Forsythe Foundation for instance. You use your money to set it up, be the backer or founder if you will, and Reginald runs it for you. You could hire someone else as a butler to help around the household and also stay close to Reginald who will help you with building it up from the ground. That way he won't have to look for a new job and you can still have him in your life."

Quinton stood to his feet and used the momentary silence to pace back and forth. It wasn't inevident if he was in agreement with Seth's suggestion.

"Reginald, what do you think of this suggestion?" Quinton asked.

Seth couldn't tell his feelings on the matter either, he wasn't really all that great on reading facial expressions, that was Cassie's expertise.

"I'm not entirely in disagreement with the idea but I would like to hear a solid plan. What charity do you suggest?" Reginald asked, intrigued by the idea.

"Did you have a full plan in mind Seth?" Quinton questioned.

"Not really. It was just an idea I created in the moment. I hoped the two of you would be able to work that out but you could always go with an animal or a children's charity, they are always popular."

"I do like the idea of a children's charity, Reginald. I'm not an expert when it comes to children and I have little to no experience with them but you do. When I was a child, no matter how difficult I was, you always stood by me and guided me, I trust you to do the same now."

"Thank you for your kind words, sir. The idea of building a charity with you sounds amazing, and I would be honoured to help you but I am still feeling hurt by what has happened and although I would like to do this with you, I hope you understand that it will take a little while for me to trust you again. We will have to work on that."

"I understand Reginald. I will do everything I can to make you trust me again, I won't let you down," Quinton said, lowering his head in guilt.

They agreed that this was something they were both willing to pursue and arranged a time to sit down and discuss in more detail in order to come up with a solid, worthwhile plan. Looking at the two finally getting along, Seth felt a small amount of relief, he managed to fix a situation in which he accidentally broke in the first place.

"I shall finish the last of my household tasks and then will come back and we can get started on our plans."

"Brilliant, thank you, Reginald."

Reginald said a polite goodbye before exiting the room.

"Well, Seth, I think it is evident by now that Reginald is innocent."

"I must say that I think I agree. I'm sorry for causing a strain on your relationship Quinton and I hope the charity works itself out. If you think of anything else that could be of use to the investigation, non-Reginald related, then please give me a call."

"Of course, Seth. And I must thank you also, you helped me realise that although he has been my butler for all these years, he has also been my friend and my family. Eleandra was the only person I could talk to, at least I thought so. I was wrong, you and she are very much alike and I feel she would be really proud of you. I hope you find whoever the killer is."

"Me and you both. I have to go now, duty calls. Goodbye for now, Quinton."

Quinton gestured his goodbye with a nod of his head and actually took the time to show Seth out himself. Just as he was leaving, Seth's phone started ringing. He looked at the screen and it said unknown caller.

"Hello," he answered.

"Hello there pal, how's your day going?"

Seth recognised the voice but couldn't place a face to it. He decided to be honest and blunt and just admit he didn't know who was calling him.

"My day is going as it normally does these days, a mixed bag, I can't quite place your voice though, who is this calling?"

"It's Roy, from the news station. Don't tell me you have forgotten me already. I'm hurt."

"Oh hi, Roy. I assume Cassie gave you my number?"

"Yes, your new girlfriend hooked me up with it."

"So what can I do for you, Roy?"

"Well, Seth, Cassie's phone has died and is currently on charge, and the lovely Dorothy has left her phone in the cafe, women eh. So I am ringing to inform you that we won't be doing the interview live tonight, we will instead be pre-recording it in about thirty minutes or so to show it on the six o'clock news tonight."

"I will be right there, Roy, thank you for calling me. I have some time so I shall swing by the cafe and retrieve the left phone and then make my way to you all at the station."

"Perfect! I'll let the ladies know, see you soon buddy."

"Yeah, see you soon, Roy."

He was going to say pal but decided on Roy that seemed like a good enough response after all it was his name. Seth wasn't the making-friends type, well, at least not anymore, so a short reply would suffice. He swung by the cafe and asked if anyone had handed in a phone and to his luck, they had, however, handing it over wasn't a walk in the park. They questioned him about the kind of phone it was and what the background picture was. They had wanted to be sure it was really his and once satisfied, handed it over to him. It was put in the office and after a few minutes, was given to him after he was again questioned about the background picture for security to see if he knew what it was. As he was leaving, he bumped into Chelsea.

"Seth, I'm glad I ran into you, I wanted to chat to you when you have time."

"I have five minutes now for a quick chat or do you wanna speak later as I'm going to the news station soon."

"No, no. I won't hold you up. I'd like to chat in-depth about something, so go do what you need to and we can catch up tomorrow."

"Yes, that should be fine. I haven't decided what's happening tomorrow, I might even have the day off to clear my head and relax. It's been a very full few days since this all started."

"I understand. Taking a day off is a very good idea; the mind needs rest as well as the body."

"See you then."

"Bye Seth."

On the way to the news station, Seth had a few moments to think to himself. He thought about what had happened at Quinton's, if Reginald was out of the picture, then his only lead was Ludlow. He needed to turn the pressure upon him and knew he needed a plan of how to do that, so after they were done at the news station tonight, he would ask the two girls to come up with a way to squeeze more out of him, he didn't want to ask Chelsea given their history. Arriving outside the station, Seth wasn't too eager to put up with the receptionist once again, so decided it best to give Roy a call.

"Hello Seth, are you here yet?"

"Yes, I'm outside. Could you pop down to the car park and meet me please?"

"The car park? Why don't you come in and I'll meet you in the waiting area?"

"No Roy, I'll wait here. I'd like a word in private."

"Sure thing, good buddy, I'll make my way down now."

"Thank you."

Seth only had to wait a few minutes for Roy's arrival.

"There you are, how's things?"

"Roy, I won't beat around the bush. If at any time during this interview she doesn't feel like she can continue, it stops. I don't care about ratings, I don't care about the buzz, I care about my aunty Dorothy. Do I have your understanding?"

"Seth, I won't do anything that will cause harm or offence to your aunty and you know Cassie won't either."

"So I have your word?"

"Yes Seth, you do."

Roy offered his hand out and Seth obliged. After they shook hands, they headed into the building and up the lift. Stopping at the third floor, the news floor, both men got out of the lift and headed towards the two women who were being worked on by hair and makeup artists. Seth remembered this floor; it was the same floor in which he himself had been interviewed a few days back.

"Aunty Dorothy."

"Oh hi, darling, you made it just in time. We are starting shortly."

"I had to make a quick pit stop first, believe you were missing something." He smirked, handing her the phone.

"You went and got my phone for me? Oh, you are the best."

"I can only try but yeah I know."

"Hello beautiful."

Seth smiled towards Cassie, although Roy thought he was talking to him at first, causing a very estranged look on his face.

"Sorry Roy but I think he meant me." Cassie laughed, taking a photo and capturing the look on his face.

"Oh, I hope you don't plan to post that online. I can only imagine it's not flattering to look at."

"Oh Roy, I will only post it to our network website," said Cassie beaming from ear to ear.

"I'll go and stand behind the camera."

Roy moved himself into position whilst Seth, Cassie and Dorothy chatted about the interview.

"We are going to attempt to shoot it in one take, maybe have a break in the middle if we need to and then if anything goes wrong or there's anything you don't like, we can edit it out before the show goes on," Roy explained from his new position.

"Great, shall we get started?" Cassie asked.

"Aunty, don't bottle anything up. It really helped me on a personal level speaking to Cassie and I know there will be a lot of people seeing this but right here it's just the two of you and a few crew members, say what you have to say."

"Seth, don't worry about me, I know what I have to do and anyway, Cassie says they can edit stuff out so it will be fine. Sit down, relax and watch me become a star."

Chapter Eleven

Seth did as was asked, he still felt uneasy about it, he didn't want the world to see her break down. He did have to admit though that she was extremely tough and very resilient, he was probably worrying over nothing.

"Cassie, you ready?"

"I am indeed."

"Dorothy, are you ready?"

"Yes, I'm ready."

"Then five, four, three, two, one." Roy waved his hand to indicate that the cameras were now rolling.

"Good evening to all our viewers. I am Cassie Bowl and this evening I bring you another interview from the Eleandra Jacobson case. Today, I am very honoured to be speaking to an amazing woman but don't take my word for it, judge for yourself. Please let me introduce, Eleandra's mother, Dorothy Jacobson. Welcome."

"Thank you for having me here, Cassie."

"We didn't have a lot of time to sit down and speak before this, so I'm going to ask you a few basic questions and then go from your answers if that's OK with you?"

"Yes, Cassie that is fine."

"First, let me ask where you were when you heard the devastating news about your daughter Eleandra?"

"I was indoors, I was doing the ironing in my kitchen with the back door open enjoying the sunlight. I thought it was a magical day, the sun was out, the flowers in my garden which I watered briefly beforehand looked beautiful and I was in a really pleasant mood."

"Then you got a call that changed your world, how did you feel?"

"I dropped the iron on the floor, and I sunk to my knees and cried. There was no more sunshine, no more light breeze, all there was in that moment was darkness. It was like a vacuum, a black hole had sucked away all the good, all the life that I was just rejoicing about had all vanished in a heartbeat."

Her voice wobbled but Seth was so proud she got her next words out brilliantly as he knew she could.

"I felt a cold shiver down my spine like she was flying past me to say goodbye before she left us. I knew it was real, no mistake, no walking through the door any minute, I knew it was going to be the worst day that I would ever remember."

"Dorothy, what did they tell you on the phone?"

"A police officer rang and told me that they had discovered a body and it was believed to be my daughter Eleandra. They needed me to go down to the town morgue to look at the body and to identify that it was her. I don't even know if it had sunk into me like really sunk in. I told them that I'd be there soon and hung up. I picked my iron up and continued on like nothing was the matter. It wasn't till I went to walk out the door that it hit me again like really hit me."

"So they didn't come to see you in person or arrange to take you there?"

"No, they didn't do any of that. It was my nephew, Seth who came to my house, he had a friend in the police force who had heard what had happened, so he went to see Seth at work as he was just finishing his shift and was heading home. He believed someone would have been coming to see me but no one did."

"So no one came at all? That's unbelievable. When Seth was being interviewed on here, he didn't want to say anything negative about the police here in Kentsville, but I am ashamed by that behaviour."

"Looking at it now, I agree. If anyone else ever loses a loved one, I hope they get a much better handling and more sympathy and support than I received. However, at the time, I was devastated, I didn't really process the small things like that, I just wanted my daughter to be alive and in my arms."

"I knew Eleandra and I can speak from first-hand experience that she was the last person you would expect to be a victim in a crime like this. She never offended people, even when it was probably warranted. She didn't break laws; she was a kind-hearted soul. Do you have any reason why she would be treated the way she was after her death?"

"I don't know why this happened. I don't know why she died or why the killer did what he did after her death. All I know is that Seth will find whoever did this, and he will get my daughter the justice she deserves."

"Do you have any idea as to who could have been behind it?"

Dorothy nodded her head in an up and down motion to indicate that yes, she knew. This surprised both Cassie and Seth. Seth was hoping she wasn't just about to drop some important information about the investigation.

"Is that a yes, Dorothy?"

"Yes, Cassie, I do."

"Are you able to share your views with us?"

"I'm afraid I can't share them at this moment for fear of bungling my nephew's investigation. I will share something with the killer though if they are watching of course. You can run but you can't hide. You will pay for what you have done, not just to my family but what you did to this town. You put Kentsville on the map for all the wrong reasons and hopefully, your capture will help rectify some of the damage you have caused to me, my nephew and this town."

"Dorothy, I have to applaud you for your bravery and your passion."

"I have always been a passionate person but I was not brave before any of this. Now, I will never be scared ever again, my daughter is my strength. They took my baby from me, there is nothing more they can do to hurt me, I will stand in the face of the killer if I get the chance and tell them that to their face. I, Dorothy Jacobson, will never be fearful of them and neither will anyone else in this town again, not while I draw breath."

"Dorothy, you are an inspiration to me and I'm sure so many women and children all across the town and beyond. How do you feel about yourself today now that we have passed the one-year anniversary of her death?"

"I'm no different to the rest of the world; I cried, I cried and then I cried some more. I spent it thinking of the good times we had, I miss her, I miss her every day. It's one of the things that makes us human, it's what separates us from every other creature, that and our opposable thumbs." Dorothy gave a small smile.

"Before the murder, you worked full time but you gave that up. What do you do now?"

"Nowadays, I split my time between volunteering locally, arranging relief packages to go to a number of third world countries and of course, I love a nice Netflix and chill time."

Cassie chuckled.

"You're not alone. I think we all like them, Dorothy. So what do you think the future holds for you?"

"I will just keep plodding along, helping people out where I can. I plan to go on holiday next year but I didn't really feel up to it this year."

"That sounds nice, anything in mind?"

"Maybe a cruise, never been on one of those big, beautiful boats before."

"Well, that sounds lovely, I hope when you go you really enjoy it. Is there anything else you'd like to say before we go?"

"Yes, there is one thing." She turned to face the camera that was on her left, rather than the one in front of her.

"I like this camera better so I'll speak to this one. If anyone watching takes anything from what has happened to me, what happened to my daughter, then take this. Hug your children, kiss your children, tell them you love them. I'm not saying to smother them and wrap them in cotton wool, let them have their adventures, let them live their lives, just don't forget, you don't know what's around the corner for you or them. So let the people who are important to you know just how much they mean to you as often as you can."

"Dorothy, thank you so much for coming in and chatting today. Remember, the phone number is at the bottom of the screen, and we are pleased to say that we have had some really good information come through, so please keep it coming. Together this town and community can bring a killer to justice for Dorothy and her much beloved and missed daughter, Eleandra. Thank you and goodnight."

Cassie stood up and Dorothy mirrored her. Seth approached the women, wanting to tell his aunt she had done great but he didn't get the chance.

"ROY!" someone shouted across the room.

"Roy, please explain why I wasn't consulted on this?"

Ted boomed; face beet red from all his pent-up anger.

"Ted, I did ring you but you didn't answer so we went ahead."

"Without consulting me first, Roy?" the angry man growled, getting angrier.

"Indeed without consulting you. After all, you do pay me to run this news station, not assist you in running it."

Roy seemed to infuriate Ted further and he was getting very red and sweaty.

"Now listen to me, Roy, you are great at what you do but this is my news station, MINE! And I want to be consulted on these things before they happen or else."

"Or else what Ted? Are you threatening me?" Roy fired back, becoming angry himself.

"Only with your job."

"Now you listen to me, you stupid prick, I love this job but if you get in my face again you can stick it up that dark alleyway of yours, where the sun doesn't shine if you catch my drift."

"Oh, I get your drift, Roy, now get my drift you overpaid wanker, YOU ARE FIRED, GOT IT, FIRED," he bellowed.

Seth thought it was all completely unnecessary and out totally of order, Ted was overstepping the line, even if he did own the station.

"I will run this place myself until I find someone who will do as they are told. Roy, you can leave and take the rest of your circus with you. Cassie back to work."

"I'm on holiday, just in on my day off, twice this week actually, because of the case. So I'm going home."

"Of course. Why does no one seem to work hard enough around here," He shot out sarcastically.

"Excuse me Ted, but if you are going to treat myself and the other employees like this, then maybe I won't come back," said Cassie.

"Then don't, you can fuck off as well you little tramp."

Seth boiled over and saw scarlet; no way was anyone going to disrespect his girlfriend like that. Without thinking, he balled up his fist and swung it towards Ted's face, however, was unsuccessful. Before he could strike the guy, who was blaspheming his new love, Roy grabbed his arm.

"Roy, move," Seth said.

"Seth, I can't allow you to do that, if he presses charges against you what happens to the investigation?"

Seth didn't want to admit it but he was right.

"You're right, Roy, cooler heads should prevail."

"Oh, I never said that, I merely pointed out you shouldn't hit him as it harms the investigation. I, on the other hand, am not investigating anything."

Before anyone could even react, Roy spun around making direct contact, hitting Ted square in the nose, with the velocity of the strike making him fly backwards into the drinks table.

Seth felt as if he was watching it all unfold in slow motion. He was expecting something to happen, he was gonna hit Ted, he wasn't expecting Roy to do it instead. He was very happy with what just took place and he couldn't help but shake Roy's hand afterwards as a show of respect. Dorothy walked over to where Ted lay.

"Learn some manners and some respect, you stupid buffoon."

"Shall we show ourselves out, Cassie?"

"Great idea Seth, everyone ready?"

With a chorus of 'yes's', they were all marching out of the building with their heads held high. Roy felt like an action hero, Dorothy happy that he had stood up for Cassie and stopped Seth from getting in trouble. Cassie was glad she had made a stand against Ted the tyrant and Seth was a little disappointed he didn't get to hit him but enjoyed watching Roy make him fly.

They had all exited the building and were walking across the car park when they heard a ruckus behind them.

"Wait up please," came a small voice from behind them.

"What are all of you doing out here?" Cassie questioned the crowd of crew members trailing behind them.

"Everyone stood up and took your lead Cassie, we told Ted whilst he was cowering on the floor that we are all on strike. He doesn't hire you two back, then we won't work for him for a very long time."

Roy stepped forward and addressed the workforce.

"You are all amazing and I am glad to have had the pleasure of working with each and every one of you, however, there is no need for you all to lose your jobs as well, the show must go on."

Roy noticed his phone was vibrating in his pocket.

"Ted is ringing me."

He spoke to him for only a few seconds and then hung up.

"I guess he can't run a news station with no team. Cassie, you go and enjoy what's left of your mini holiday, the rest of you get back inside, we have a show to do and I'm pretty sure after today we are all getting a pay rise, I'll make sure of it."

There was a loud cheer as everyone followed Roy back in, Seth imagined that right now he felt like a King. After the noise had died down and the three of them were left alone, they got into their cars and tried to head to Dorothy's house. However, before Seth was able to reverse, he was blocked by a police car that had come speeding into the news station car park stopping everyone from exiting. They all got out their cars to see what had caused such a commotion with the Chief of police.

"Seth, you are not going to believe this but there has been another murder."

"The same as Eleandra?"

"Not exactly," said Chief Abraham.

"How do you know it's linked then or even the same person?"

"Although the body wasn't cut open with the organs removed this time, it's definitely related. This time someone carved Eleandra's name into the victim's chest and placed a coat hanger in his dead hand."

"Who is the victim?" asked Seth.

"I don't know if any of you actually knew him personally but you'd know him best as Mr Chive, Chelsea's dad."

Shock and unease were the emotions running through Seth's body right now. He didn't understand what was going on, why would someone kill Chelsea's dad? Why was Eleandra's name carved into his chest and a coat hanger left? None of it made any sense. He didn't understand the link between them, was there even a link? Nothing seemed to add up and Seth needed to bring himself out of his stunned state sharpish in order to see things through a clearer mind, he needed to focus. His first move was to find out as much information as he could from the police Chief, maybe he had a lead or a suspect in mind.

"Is there any evidence or any leads as to who did this?" Seth asked once he had got himself straight.

"Unfortunately not. The body was found in the back garden of their home. Mrs Chive was at the beauty salon and Chelsea said she was at Quinton Forsythe's house for a lesson before she bumped into you at Caitlin's Cafe."

"Yes, I saw her there just before I came here. I went to the cafe to pick up my aunt Dorothy's phone that she had left there earlier on in the day."

Seth watched as the Chief let out a long sigh and rubbed his hand across his face. He didn't notice it before but the Chief looked as if he hadn't slept in a few days.

"Seth, as of tomorrow morning the case will officially be reopened and properly investigated as it should have been from the start. I can't stop you from investigating it yourself, however, you won't have as much free reign as you have had up to this point. We will be doing the same as what you are doing now and unfortunately, I won't be able to share certain information with you."

"I understand that, Chief Abraham."

"If you do have a serious lead, then I encourage you to chase it up now. I know what this means to you, Seth, so I will give you as long as I can before I do a press release, to solve this yourself. Once the release has been done, everyone will know that we are officially leading our own investigation and due to security reasons, I will have to advise my officers not to disclose any information with you."

"I know you are doing what is right and you are acting according to protocol, so I won't get in your way, you have my word. However, you must know that I won't stop searching for the killer, I made a promise to myself and even more importantly, to Eleandra."

"I figured as much Seth and I respect that. Do you have any leads?"

"I have one, Ludlow. Chelsea Chive's ex-boyfriend."

"I know of him. May I ask why he is a suspect?"

"Chelsea broke up with him to be with Eleandra. My theory is that he became so enraged that he wanted revenge and what better way to hurt his former lover than by taking away her new one. When we questioned him, he seemed to still hold some of that pent up anger towards her. So maybe he still wants to hurt her, that would be a good motive for taking away her dad's life too, you'd have to agree?"

"I definitely agree that right there is a strong motive. Did you find out if he had an alibi or not?"

"He wouldn't give us an answer and kept beating around the bush. He became very agitated and aggressive when I and Cassie pushed his buttons. He is hiding something, I know it, I just can't prove what."

"Seth, would you consider a proposal?"

"What kind of proposal? I mean no offence but I already have a girlfriend."

"No Seth, I didn't mean that. I was thinking you should come and work on the case as a specialist with me for the police force. That way I can give you some access to information that we acquire and you would be able to assist in an arrest when needed."

"Seth, that's a really good idea," Cassie chimed in, having been silent this whole time.

"You think so?"

"Yes, I really do. It could help you solve the case much quicker as you will have more resources and support. What do you think, Dotty?"

"I'm with Cassie darling. I think you and the chief should do this together. I can still canvas the area around the warehouse showing photos but Cassie will be back at work soon and Chelsea has just lost her dad. Her head won't be in this, even if her heart is."

"So Seth, what do you say?" asked the Chief.

In his head, Seth agreed with Cassie and his aunt Dorothy, the extra manpower would help and he would be able to go anywhere and question anyone when he needed to without the police stopping him. Completing the rest of the investigation on his own may limit him in certain aspects and certain areas, especially if the police are now carrying out their own. If he managed to get any real proof, he would need their help for an official arrest, so joining the team in this role would be beneficial to both parties.

"I accept. In fact, why delay the press conference? Let me join it. Let's do it tomorrow morning together. I won't speak but I think us standing side by side would have a strong statement to the community and to the killer."

"Wow Seth, be careful there, you're starting to sound like a police officer yourself."

"Oh no, I'm afraid in my heart I'll always be a fireman."

With all in agreement, they left for Dorothy's house like they had originally planned. Seth couldn't help but go over it again and again in his head, why Chelsea's dad? He thought about it more and more and it still made no sense to him at all. What did the killer have to gain by doing this now? Why did they kill again? Did he know something that related to Eleandra's death? Maybe he had some information on the killer. Again, this was just him clutching at straws, he didn't really have a clue why he had been murdered, he never even met the man. Walking through the front door, Dorothy walked straight through the living room and into the kitchen to put the kettle on. The sound of the boiling kettle sliced through the dead silence in the room. They each had taken off their coats and sat around her small coffee table which was situated in the middle of the living room with the kitchen door open. The kettle whistled; it was ready.

"Poor Chelsea, first she lost our Eleandra and now her dad, she must be devastated," said Dorothy, letting out a large sigh.

"I can't imagine how the poor soul is feeling. She has only just been able to finally talk to us about losing the one she loved and now she has lost someone she loves again," Cassie stated, almost with tears in her eyes.

Cassie and Dorothy had both wanted to message Chelsea but decided against it. They all agreed that it should be Seth who would message her. Cassie had taken Seth's phone and started to type a message to Chelsea. She was writing on behalf of him as he just wasn't the type of delicate that Chelsea would need at this moment.

"Chelsea, I am really sorry. I have just heard about what has happened and wanted to convey my condolences on the loss of your father. If there is anything I can do for you, anything at all, then please let me know. I am here for you, Seth."

"She will know that's not me Cassie," said Seth.

"That doesn't matter, Seth. All that matters is that she knows that she has people there for her if she needs them."

"I guess so. Aunt Dorothy, cup of tea?"

"Yes please, Seth. Can you put two sugars in for me?"

"Two sugars? You're pushing the boat out, aren't you?"

"I'm just craving sugar this evening. It's probably the stress from today's news and events."

"Two sugars it is. So I'm going to be working with the police from tomorrow but for this evening, can we discuss where we currently are with the investigation and then we can have a nice evening watching something on Netflix if there are no objections?"

"That sounds lovely, Seth," said Dorothy as she smiled.

"Yes, I'd like that too, Mr Bronx."

"Mr Bronx, I could get used to that Cassie."

Seth made the two women their drinks, ensuring to add the sugar into his aunt's tea. He brought up the fact that Reginald wasn't a suspect for him anymore and added the charity idea that he had mentioned to him and Quinton earlier in the day. The girls both agreed that it was a really nice outcome to a difficult situation and it was sweet that Quinton realised he had a friend instead of just a butler. Dorothy knew Reginald and she was glad he wasn't a suspect anymore. She wouldn't say they were buddies but she bumped into him now and then when volunteering and he always seemed like a nice guy. It made her happy knowing that she could go back to thinking that. Cassie pointed out that Ludlow was now the only suspect they had and wondered if there was anyone else, they had missed or any other leads that they could look into. Seth thought back to the phone call with Chief Abraham from the other day, catching the idiot following him but without the police assistance.

"Cassie let's do it, let's catch the guy following me."

"You want to let the police catch him? What if it is the killer? Then they will bring him in themselves and you won't get the answers you want. I think you should wait until you join forces with them like you agreed."

"No Cassie, just me and you. You get in my car and drive to the paper mill, the person following me will think I'm meeting someone there. You go inside quickly before he gets a proper good look at you and wait. I'll see who's following you, tail them and then call you to come out once I've dealt with them."

"What if he gets violent, Seth?" asked Cassie.

"You don't need to worry, I'll deal with him, remember I will have the element of surprise, he will think I'm in the paper mill, he won't be looking back, only forwards."

"OK, I will help you catch him, Seth."

"Brilliant, let's get started."

Seth and Cassie went looking for clothes, they found an old knee-length coat and a flat cap in a box marked charity that Dorothy had collected and was planning to deliver in a few days. Seth went down to the car and attached Cassie's phone to the boot of his car, the camera pointing out of the rear window, then he face-timed his phone from hers and answered so he could see if anyone was following her. He went back inside and Cassie went to his car, Seth stayed in the house as Dorothy waved her off. Seth was sitting at the kitchen table when Dorothy returned to the house and joined him in watching the phone. About three minutes driving down the road, Seth noticed a car had been following her in the distance for a few roads, Cassie had noticed it too. "Cassie, you have a tail, I'm gonna come follow you now. Keep to the plan and slow down a bit to give me more time to catch up to him. I don't know about you but we can't quite make out the license plate from here, if he gets close enough to do so though, I will get aunty Dorothy to take a screenshot in case we lose him."

Seth added his aunt to the call.

"Could you be our third person, our eyes and ears, watch it from here take screenshots if and when you think it's needed and let us know if you spot anything we don't?" Seth asked.

"Of course and I know you'll promise to be careful so I won't bother to say it but you and Cassie watch out for each other, OK?"

"Got it aunty, see you soon." Seth headed out in Cassie's car and raced towards the paper mill with haste. Windows open on this blisteringly hot day, he was starting to regret wearing a suit but it looked so professional, he thought he should look smart.

"Cassie, I am nearly on the other car, I should only be about a minute and I'll be there, continue the plan, get inside and hide. I doubt he will actually follow you in but just to be safe make sure you aren't visible."

"Understood, I'll make sure I'm not easy to find even if he comes in, you just let me know when you've got him."

"Oh and don't take your phone with you, leave it in the car."

"I'm pulling up now, I'll speak to you soon, good luck." Seth heard nothing more from Cassie and as the car had stopped moving, he knew she had gone into the paper mill as instructed earlier. The only potential issue now was where would the guy following Seth or in this case Cassie, park. Seth drove past the entrance like he did when he met Bruce there, he circled around looking for any cars other than his. He saw just one; it was the one he was after, the one that thought they were following him, he would solve two mysteries right now, who was the person in the car? And why were they almost stalking him around town? The car in question was parked just past the entrance to the car park so Seth drove in and turned in the road to cover half of each side of the road, whoever it was wouldn't be able to drive past unless they rammed Seth's car or smashed into some trees, they were trapped. He got out and approached the car, he stopped three or four metres from the bonnet and he could see someone in the front seat who had clearly heard and seen him arrive and had slid down trying to hide himself from view when the person walked past. The problem for this guy was that Seth wasn't walking by, he had stopped and was standing there staring down the car in front of him.

"Let's finally find out who you are."

Chapter Twelve

"I can see the top of your baseball cap, I know you are in there, I have called the police, they are on their way, get out now and I won't press charges, try to run and you are going to jail for illegal surveillance of me."

The car door opened and someone stepped out with their head bowed, slowly but surely, they straightened up and their face became visible to Seth.

"Bruce!! You're the one who's been following me? Are you kidding me? You're not the killer."

"No, I never killed anyone, especially not Eleandra."

"What the hell are you doing watching me and following me around for then?"

Seth had walked towards Bruce and was right in his face, he was both angry and frustrated and Bruce knew it.

"I'm sorry, I just wanted to make sure you weren't on your own in case someone attacked you, I wanted to repay Eleandra for stopping my bullies by protecting you Seth in case someone came for you."

Seth's anger dissipated and he managed a smile.

"So in your mind, you're protecting me from the killer?" Seth asked.

"Well, yes."

"No offence Bruce but not only have you wasted my time but you're also the least most intimidating person I've ever met in my life. Your heart may be in the right place which is admirable, however, if the killer did attack me, you would offer no real protection and could potentially end up getting yourself and me hurt or worse, killed. Go home and stop following me, if you have any more information then feel free to let me know, otherwise stay out of harm's way and stay out of my investigation, please."

Seth sent Bruce on his way and went into the papermill to catch up with Cassie on what just happened.

"You are alone, did he get away or did you send him to swim with the fishes?"

"Wow Cassie, you make it sound so gangster like I'm the Kentsville mafia. No, I'm afraid I found out who was following me these past few days and it wasn't the killer. It was bloody Bruce."

"Bruce, why on Earth was he following you around Seth?"

"Hello, can you hear me?" Dorothy's voice came from Seth's pocket, he took the phone out and saw his aunt's face on the screen.

"I'm sorry I forgot we were on FaceTime; did you hear everything?"

"Yes, I heard. I'll let you go so you can update Cassie and I'll see you when you get back. Speak soon."

"Yes, bye for now."

"Bye, Cassie."

"Bye, Dotty."

With the facetime over, Seth and Cassie continued their chat about Bruce.

"Bruce was apparently following me for my protection."

Cassie let out a loud laugh.

"I don't mean to be mean but I'm ten times better protection than Bruce is, what was he thinking?"

"Like I told him, his heart was in the right place. I don't think he will be following me anymore. Now this distraction is out the way, I believe we have an investigation to get back to."

"And you have a meeting with your son to prepare for as well, Seth."

"Indeed."

"As it's just me and you here and you've had some time to digest the news now, can I ask how you are feeling about it?" Cassie asked.

"I am excited but a little bit nervous. I am proud to be a father but at the same time a father to a child I don't know and who doesn't know me, it's scary. I know with your support, I will be alright and no matter what happens to Eshima, the future will be bright for us all."

"Seth, you are going to be a great dad, I know it."

"Thank you, Cassie, you are the best."

"Oh I know, just glad you know it too."

A few kisses and a big hug later and they were heading back to their cars to make the short journey to Dorothy's.

"Bloody Bruce," said Seth.

He pulled up at Dorothy's house just behind Cassie and his phone started to ring.

"Hello," he said.

"Hi, Seth, it's Eshima."

"Oh, hi Eshima, I didn't save your phone number yet so I wasn't sure who was calling me. How are you? How's Lucas?"

"We are both really good, thank you, I was wondering if we could meet this Sunday?"

"I am not doing anything this Sunday, so that would be great. When is the operation again?"

"It's on Thursday, so if we could do a meeting on Sunday and then he could hang out with you maybe Monday and Tuesday too and then he will feel a bit more comfortable around you when I go into the hospital."

"That sounds like a good plan to me, I am happy to do that, I was wondering if your babysitter would be able to have Lucas so we could have lunch together tomorrow, just for an hour or so, I'd like to learn what things he likes and doesn't like, allergies, bedtimes etc so he has a smooth transition when staying with me."

"I'm sure I can manage that, one o'clock good?" Eshima asked.

"Perfect, so my place at one?"

"That would be great, just message me the address and I will see you there."

"Awesome, bye Eshima."

Seth entered the house once again. Cassie had gone in already as she saw he was on the phone, Dorothy let her in and they left the door on the latch in case he didn't have his spare key.

"Hey Darling, I forgot to ask you earlier, what was the mortician like? Did she seem honest, no hidden agenda?" Dorothy asked.

"The mortician, why would she be a suspect, Aunty?"

"She was the one who performed the autopsy. How can we be sure that she wasn't involved? Was she really ordered to not do an autopsy on Clarke? I mean, doesn't that seem a bit far-fetched?"

"No, she was very professional and sincere but then who am I to judge."

"Who is anyone?" Dorothy said.

"Cassie, I want to know your honest opinion, do you think Ludlow is the killer?"

"No Seth, I don't."

He turned to Dorothy and asked the same question, to which she afforded him the same answer as Cassie. Seth scratched his head, literally scratched his head, it wasn't itchy and it wasn't because he was bored, he was just stumped. He didn't have the answers he wanted, and he couldn't just come up with them. If the two people who he loved and trusted most didn't believe that Ludlow was the killer, then who was? Even if Ludlow wasn't the killer, he was still hiding something that related to Eleandra and to Seth, that was worth pursuing.

"We need to follow up on Ludlow, he may not be the killer but I believe he knows something that concerns our case."

"Seth, I do agree that he's hiding something but I don't believe that it has to do with this case or her death," said Cassie.

"Either way, we need to find out what exactly it is. We can go together tomorrow to see him if you'd like. I have to go to the station to speak with the chief, so we can go just before that."

"That would be nice, my last investigative adventure before I'm back at work again."

"Do you want me to do anything, Seth?" Dorothy inquired.

"Actually, I do. Could you go to the news station and work the phones alongside the news team? I think it would be good if some of the callers could talk to you themselves, it would help them connect more to us and the investigation."

"I like that idea, Seth, I love talking to people."

"Let me know instantly if anything important or serious comes up and I'll be right there."

Dorothy cleared the cups into the sink and wiped the table down.

"No offence to you both but I am going to take a nice bath, do some of my crossword book and then have an early night. Feel free to stay if you want."

"I think I am going to go for a run, then shower and then an early night sounds good to me too," said Seth.

They all said their goodbyes and Cassie and Seth headed to their respective homes. Seth drove back to his cottage and then changed into some shorts, although it was into the evening now and the sun was nowhere near as bright as earlier today, it was still very hot and so shorts and t-shirt were the right call for jogging, he felt. He headed out for a few miles and then lapped back around to his house, getting out on his own always cleared his head. It was something he hadn't done enough of recently and something he intended to do more of when this case was over. Seth jumped into the shower and let the sweat wash away before wrapping a towel around himself grabbing a bottle of water from the fridge in the kitchen and making himself comfortable on the sofa. Tomorrow, Eshima would come around for lunch and would tell him all about his son, he still couldn't believe it, his son.

Although he was excited, he was also a tad nervous and in turn, worried that he wouldn't sleep much that night. He finished his bottle of water, grabbed some boxers to wear and brushed his teeth. He fell onto the bed a few minutes later, and to his surprise, what seemed like only a few seconds later, he was waking up to birds chirping outside his bedroom window the next day. He couldn't believe it when he looked at the clock and it was just gone 11 AM.

"I don't even remember falling asleep." He got up and got his day underway. After he was up and dressed, he checked his phone, he had a message from Cassie wishing him a good morning and one from Eshima confirming she would see him later on. After replying to both he grabbed himself a drink, a nice hot chocolate and some shortbread biscuits, not the healthiest breakfast but he decided he'd had a nice lay in so he would pair that with a tasty drink and a snack. Before he knew it, he would have company as planned. He went over to the oven and started to prepare lunch. Just then, Seth heard someone knocking at his door, barely, it was very faint. He turned the heat down low and walked from the oven where he was preparing the eggs and bacon to the front door. He assumed it would be Eshima and it was.

"Hello."

"Hi, please come in. Can I take your jacket?"

"Yes, thank you, Seth."

She handed him her jacket and Seth hung it over the back of the sofa and headed back to the cooker and Eshima followed him over to the kitchen area.

"Eggs and Bacon, looks good."

"Do you want them in a sandwich or just on a plate?"

"Whatever you are having is fine with me too, Seth."

Seth dished up the food in silence and walked two plates over to the table. There was salt, pepper and ketchup on the table already.

"Please sit and enjoy, I'll just grab some orange juice if that's OK for you?" he asked.

"Yes, orange juice is fine, thank you."

They enjoyed a nice lunch and then Seth put the plates in to soak in the sink. They sat on the sofa and he started the conversation up about Lucas. "So what can you tell me about him? Did you bring any photos?"

"I didn't bring any photos no, I'm sorry. You can take lots of him and with him soon enough though. Lucas has brown hair and blue eyes just like you, although he looks a lot like me. He loves football, he is always asking me to go to the park and he makes me go in goal and then he sends the ball flying towards me. He is really into Lego; he builds for hours at a time."

"Is he smart?" asked Seth.

"If you mean is he intelligent, yes, he is, teachers say he's top of the class. At least once a week he gets sent home with certificates or stickers for his efforts at school."

"Eshima, I know I was mad the other day, I just couldn't believe you hadn't told me about him, it really hurt, not being a part of my son's life for six years. I promise that even though I don't have any experience at being a parent, I will make sure he wants for nothing and always knows I am here for him, always."

"I know you will Seth, I have no doubt about it."

"Is it just you and Lucas back home?" Seth asked.

"If you mean do I have a boyfriend, then the answer is no. I have dated a couple of people over the years but nothing long term and I've never introduced anyone to our son."

"How do you feel about him meeting Cassie and my aunt Dorothy?"

"I would like him to meet just you the first time but I have no problem with him meeting either of them on the next visit."

"Great, so what else do I need to know, Eshima?"

"Well, he normally goes to bed about 7, 7:30 at the latest and he's a great sleeper, goes right the way around to the next morning at 8."

"He really does like to sleep."

"Yes, I can't complain he never really has me up at night. He is currently learning to swim, he's not great but improving fast. He has no allergies I know of but he doesn't like tomatoes or peas."

"Tomatoes or peas, check. Anything else?"

"No Seth, that's it really, you are up to speed and you'll be fine."

"Eshima, I know it can't be easy for you to come to me after all this time knowing I would be angry. I have to respect you; you came and told me the whole truth regardless of what I might say because you felt it best for our son. You're a great mum."

"Oh, why did you have to go and be all nice like that, it would be easier if you were still mad."

"Would you rather I had continued being mean to you, Eshima?" Seth asked.

"No, obviously not, it's just I haven't exactly told you the whole truth as I didn't know how to say it."

"What else do you need to tell me?"

"I'm sorry to have to bring this up but you have a right to know everything. Lucas isn't your only child. I was pregnant with twins."

"So we have two children now?"

Seth paused and took a drink.

"What's gonna happen the next time we talk, we will suddenly have three?"

Seth was trying to keep his cool but this was not proving easy.

"No, we only have one child Seth."

Eshima started to cry.

"Eshima, what happened?"

Seth knew he was about to hear something he didn't want to hear but he also knew he had to know what she was about to say and pressed her to go on.

"Just tell me Eshima."

"I gave birth to Lucas and he was perfectly healthy, then when the second baby was born, they said she wasn't breathing. Lola lived in an incubator for seventeen hours before we lost her."

Her tears were now accompanied by loud sobs. Seth was raging inside, he couldn't understand how she could keep a child from him, let alone a second child that had died. He stood up and walked to the front door, he put his head against it and took some deep breaths, his anger suddenly melted away and all he felt was hollow. Lola, his little girl who he never got to meet, to see or to hold, was gone. His insides were twisted and knotting tighter and tighter by each second.

"Eshima, I think it's best if you go, I need to be alone."

She didn't speak, she just nodded and made her way to the door and towards Seth. Seth stopped her with a gentle hand on her shoulder and gave her a hug as she went to pass by him.

"I am sorry for my outburst; I can't imagine the pain you went through when that happened to you but I also am very hurt right now and I can't look at you without feeling angry. So it's bye for now Eshima."

Eshima didn't argue she just left with her head hung. Seth was thinking she must know how this feels as she has been through it before and maybe she was the one person he could talk to that could understand his pain but then he thought about his aunty Dorothy. Losing Eleandra was the toughest thing she ever had to deal with; he needed to talk to her. Other than Eshima, if anyone would know his pain, it would be her. Seth grabbed his keys and headed for her house; he just knew she would have the words he needed to hear. Seth sat in his car in silence, he mulled over the information he had just received about his daughter, Lola. He wasn't sure which emotion he felt more, sadness or anger. He was both upset and livid with Eshima and right now he knew he couldn't be around her no matter how much he wanted to meet Lucas. He thought it might be a good idea to delay meeting his son that way he could get some time to wrap his head around everything Eshima had told him the past few days but he knew there was a timeline. After taking a few minutes, he headed inside to speak to his aunt Dorothy.

"Hi, Seth, I thought you would be longer with Eshima, I didn't think I'd be seeing you just yet. Are you OK? You look a bit down."

Down was an understatement, he thought, he also thought it would be a good idea to tell her what Eshima told him and he didn't take too long in doing so.

"Oh, I am so sorry to hear that Seth, you were so happy about Lucas, you must be devastated to find that out about Lola. Give me a cuddle, darling."

Dorothy wrapped him up in a warm embrace that gave Seth some comfort if nothing else.

"I don't know how I am meant to react; I am supposed to be meeting Lucas but I am worried I will be angry with her and I don't want him to see that, I don't want him to be scared of me, I'm already no more than a stranger to him."

"Seth, it's your decision, take your time and do what you think is best for you and the boy. In the end, you will make the right choices for you both, you are a great man and I have every faith in you," said Dorothy.

"I think I'll just carry on with the case today and then ring Eshima tonight. I'll probably go ahead with it though but I'm not a hundred percent on that. Either way, it's not Lucas's fault and I've already missed the first six years of his life; I don't want to miss any more."

"If that's what you want then do it, I know Cassie will be there for you as will I."

"Thank you for always being there for me, aunty."

"I always will be Seth."

"Well, I guess we should crack on with today but first I'm going for a nice walk and I'll tell Cassie later when I see her."

Seth decided this would help to sort out his head; he would go for a walk along the river, alone. He wasn't sure if he was going to think about the investigation, distraction-free or to just not think at all. He had so much on his plate, more than he ever imagined he would at this point. He was with Cassie, something which made him immensely happy, he found out he had a son, then he found out he had a daughter that passed away, a daughter that he would never get to meet, a secret that had been kept from him for years. On top of that, the investigation into Eleandra's death had been up, down and all around, he just needed peace, quiet and some space. Seth parked up next to the part of the lake where crowds of parents would gather with their children to feed the ducks, he thought he could do this one day with Lucas. He walked past all the families feeding the ducks and what looked like the making of some great memories, similar memories that he had of his parents taking him there as a small boy. Oh, how he would love to hear their voices and see their faces right now. Next, he walked towards and past the crazy golf area which wasn't opened just now and he remembered when he was here with his dad. He was so bad, swinging the golf club like it was an axe attempting to cut down a tree, yet somehow at the end his dad said the scorecard showed Seth had won. At that age, he never questioned it but now looking back he knew his dad clearly let him win, he could barely hit the ball let alone putt it. Seth continued his walk up around the lake to the miniature railway, he loved trains when he was little but this hadn't been put in until after he had grown up. He thought this would be something else he could do with Lucas when he came to stay with him. Lucas, what would he say to him when they meet? He had no idea how to be a dad and even though he was so excited to meet him he was very nervous about messing up. With Cassie and his aunt Dorothy for support, he would be OK but that didn't stop him from worrying about when they weren't around. Seth continued pacing around the beautiful water view in front of him, when his phone started vibrating in his pocket.

"Oh, the peace ends," he said.

He looked at the screen; it was an unknown number, not much of a surprise these days. *Now what*, he thought to himself, he was hoping for good news as opposed to bad.

"Hello, Seth speaking."

"I know who it is, I am ringing you."

Seth's initial thoughts were to hang up, whoever the man was on the phone he was rude and interrupting his quiet time.

"Well, I don't know who you are, so inform me or I'll just go."

"You won't hang up though Seth, not unless you want to waste this opportunity to get intel on Clarke Richards."

"Clarke Richards is innocent; I don't need intel on him but thank you for your call."

"If he was so innocent then why does he have a bag full of cash in his locker that Mrs Richards hasn't opened yet?"

"You're lying," said Seth.

"Oh no, I am not, go ask her for the key and see for yourself."

"If this is true, how do you happen to know about it?"

There was silence from the other end.

"Hello, hello," Seth said.

"The other person has cleared," came an automated voice.

Seth put the phone back in his pocket. They didn't give their name; they didn't say how they knew about the information. They didn't really explain anything, just that there's money in Clarke's locker for some unknown reason and he hadn't told his wife. Or maybe he had and she was too scared to access it. Even though he was adamant Clarke was innocent, especially after learning what time he left for work on the morning Eleandra was murdered, he still had to go check this lead out. He started walking back to his car when he got another phone call, he looked to the sky.

"Really, is it too much to ask for some peace and quiet?"

He took his phone out again and this time, he saw it was Cassie, he smiled and the annoying state he was in for a fraction of a second was gone. "Hi there, Miss Bowl, how you doing?"

"Did you just Joey Tribbiani me?" she asked.

"That depends, did it work?"

"Maybe a little bit, right now I think yeah Joey wants me."

"Oh well, if that's how it is, then in that case no I didn't."

"Well, in that case I'll get back to what I rang you for Mr Bronx. I was just about to go for a walk and get some fresh air, I wondered if you fancied a picnic?"

"That sounds lovely Cassie; however, I just had a mystery caller ring me about some evidence on Clarke Richards and I know he isn't the killer but I need to take a little look at it. I won't be too long though, if you don't mind making a picnic and I'll swing by after and pick you up."

"Sounds good, give me a message when you're on your way to me and I'll grab a blanket and sort some food out."

"I shall see you when I see you then."

"So you shall, bye for now."

Seth got back to his car and made the drive to Monica's house. This certainly wouldn't be the easiest conversation he would have, last time he spoke to her he assured her that her husband was innocent and now he had to check on a lead that suggested otherwise. Regardless of how annoyed she may now get, he just had to do it and rip the plaster off quickly and find out what this locker had to show him. He pulled up outside her house and as it would happen Monica was just heading out.

"Seth, this is a surprise, you seem to make a habit of doing that though."

"Yes, I guess I do, I'm sorry to bother you again unannounced but I need a favour. I can see you are on your way out so I'll make it quick. I was wondering if I could have the key for Clarke's locker?"

"Yes, of course you can, can I ask why?"

Seth was hoping she wouldn't ask why but at the same time he knew that she would.

"I stand by what I said the last time we spoke Monica, your husband is innocent, however, I have been told of something that I need to check out and I need that locker key. I don't believe it will implicate Clarke but there is only one way to find out for sure."

"You have to make me a promise, Seth. That no matter what you find, good, bad or even ugly, you won't hide it from me. Promise me that and I will give you the locker key."

"Monica, I promise you if there is anything incriminating in that locker, I will inform you, no matter what. You have my word."

"That is good enough for me, Seth, give me a few seconds to go grab it."

She headed into her house and he waited by the cars for her return.

"Here you go, Seth, one locker key. Now, I don't mean to be rude but I have a meeting at work about a promotion I'm up for, so I have to run."

"Well, I wish you good luck for that Monica, hopefully, we will both have good news to share later today, farewell."

"Bye Seth."

Seth waved off Mrs Richards and then got in his car and headed to Clarke's former employer. He had never been to the taxi company before and wasn't sure where exactly the locker storage was. It was a public unit open to everyone and was presumably near the taxi rank as apparently Clarke would walk there before or after he went to the office. Seth wanted to go in there and speak to Clarke's boss if he was in, and then go to the locker. Seth parked a few minutes away and took the last part of the journey by foot, he entered the door to the taxi office but no one was there so he rang the bell. It took only a few moments and someone arrived to greet him. "Hey buddy where do you want to go?"

A short and seemingly happy guy asked him.

"I want to go and speak to your boss please."

"Sorry, are you here for an interview?"

"No, I just need to see your boss if he's in, tell him my name's Seth Bronx and I'd like to speak about Clarke Richards."

"Oh, you're the detective guy, I've heard about you, you're going to prove Clarke is innocent."

"Well, I think I already have but I need a word with your boss if I can."

"I'll go grab him; he's in the back office."

Soon enough the same short man appeared with another, this one was towering way above him.

"You must be Seth. I have heard great things about you, Monica said you have a great moral code and if you need me, I should make myself available, for Clarke."

"Is there somewhere we could speak privately?"

"Of course."

The man disappeared out of view and reappeared next to Seth out of a door to his left.

"Just in this door opposite lad," said the tall man.

They both entered a small room which was apparently the staff room and sat down, the tall man offered Seth his hand to shake.

"Call me Derek."

"Nice to meet you, Derek, I won't keep you long just want to ask you a couple of questions."

"Fire away, Seth lad."

"Derek, can you confirm what time Clarke arrived on the day he died?"

"He arrived about ten, maybe fifteen minutes later than normal, he got here just on time. Normally, he arrives early, goes to the locker storage to put his lunch in and then comes back for a cuppa if he has time like."

"Do you know why he was late?"

"Well, technically he wasn't late to the office just later than usual so I didn't question it too much but he mentioned he had car trouble and his wife Monica jump-started him."

"Thank you, and do you know if he had any issues or problems with any of your other employees?"

"Not that I can think of, one or two may have been disgruntled as he got a big tip from some rich person, he drove the day before but I think they were just jealous, don't think anyone wanted him dead."

"His wife mentioned someone swapping shifts with him, because of a complaint."

"Oh, that guy left the company just before Clarke died, he wasn't exactly employee of the month and kept getting complaints, wasn't good for our reputation so I asked him to leave."

"OK, thank you for clearing that up. Lastly, did he act strange or give you any reason to suggest anything was wrong?"

"None at all, he was a reliable and hard-working guy, plenty of times I had the old dears ringing me saying he was a big help with the shopping etc, he always wanted to help the customers."

"That is pretty much all I needed; I was wondering where exactly the public locker storage area was? I know it's around here somewhere but I've never actually been there before."

"If you head out the front door, walkabout one minute and turn left, go to the end of the alley and when you come out, it's just on your right." Seth now offered his hand to shake.

"Well, thank you, Derek, thank you very much, enjoy the rest of the day."

"Thanks, you too, Seth lad."

Seth went out the front door and he headed off towards the locker storage, he followed Derek's directions and was soon there. He took the key out and headed for the locker numbered sixty-eight. It was an average-sized locker, no bigger than Seth's torso, he put the key in the lock and opened the door. All he could see inside was a sports bag. He took the bag out and placed it on the floor in front of him and checked again; nothing else was in the locker. He unzipped the bag and had a peek inside.

He opened his mouth wide and gasped. He didn't know how much money was in the bag but it was more than he had ever seen in one place before. What did this mean? Seth wasn't sure what his next move was. Did he take the money and hand it in to the police? Did he give it to Monica, technically it was hers now right? Should he just leave it in the locker? What if he did leave it here and someone stole it? He closed the locker, not forgetting to grab the bag of money, and headed to his car, he needed to count it, he wanted to know how much money was in his possession. Derek mentioned a big tip, surely this wasn't it. There was an easy way to clarify that, just ask Monica if Clarke brought a big tip home the day before. If he didn't then maybe it was a really big tip and Seth could just give it to her. He decided to ask Cassie her opinion before he made his next move.

"Hello Cassie, I'm on my way to you now I should be about ten minutes, I need to show you something first though before we go out."

"OK, I will see you then."

Seth raced to Cassie's; his mind was racing a lot faster than his car though. He needed to explain this money somehow, if he didn't and it got out then people might think he was being paid for something to do with Eleandra's death. He continued to think over and over again on the way to Cassie's. Once inside her house and the curtains were closed to prevent any prying eyes, he put the light on and explained what happened up to this point. He instructed Cassie to open the bag.

She gasped.

"Wow."

"I know Cassie."

"Seth, we need to count this."

"Then we better get started."

Chapter Thirteen

They divided it in two and counted their respective halves, and then they swapped and counted each other's. In the end, they both had the same figure.

"Two hundred thousand pounds!!! What the hell is going on?" said Seth.

"I wish I knew; do you think it's the tip that Derek spoke of?"

"It seems a lot of money for a tip. I'll give Monica a quick ring and ask her if he mentioned it but I'll message her first and see if she's free as she had a meeting at work."

He sent her a message and waited for a reply. Monica didn't reply, instead, she rang him.

"Seth, I got the promotion."

"Congratulations Monica, I'm really happy for you."

"So do we both have good news?"

"I don't know yet. Derek mentioned a customer giving him a rather large tip the day before he died. Did he mention it to you at all?"

"I didn't realise that was related so I didn't mention it. He brought home a big chunk of cash, yes."

"I'm sorry he brought the money home to you?"

"Yes, Seth, he brought it home the day he got it as the bank was closed. I put it in the next morning before I got the terrible news a few hours later that he had been involved in a possible murder."

"Sorry to ask, Monica but how much was it?"

"It was five thousand pounds."

"That's a large amount for a tip. Did he explain where it came from?"

"Yes, he said a rich girl gave it to him, she had loads of cash apparently and had filled the taxi up with shopping and he helped her unload it all and she gave him lots of money. I said we shouldn't accept it but he said we weren't turning it down, so we kept it."

"Did he say what her name was or where she lived?"

"No, he didn't I'm afraid."

"Well, thank you for that information, Monica, I think that clears everything up. I'll speak soon."

"Thanks, Seth and let me know if you need anything else at all."

"I will do Monica and congratulations again." Seth hung up the phone and looked at Cassie who had heard the whole conversation on loudspeaker.

"Do you think this money came from the same person that gave him the five grand?" said Seth.

"Possibly, if Clarke knew Monica would be hesitant about keeping five thousand then maybe he figured she'd never accept two hundred and five."

"That's a good shout, Cassie. I am inclined to believe that as well but…"

"But what Seth, what is it?"

"I have ruled Clarke out as a suspect, and then I get a mysterious call saying he has a big bag full of money in his locker that no one knows about. It seems forced to me, like someone is trying to steer me in another direction, steer me away from Ludlow perhaps."

"I agree, it does seem fishy, how will we know which theory is correct?"

"The man who rung me said that Clarke had a bag of cash that Mrs Richards hadn't claimed yet, he didn't actually say it had anything to do with Eleandra's murder."

"Those were his exact words?" asked Cassie.

"Yes, basically, he said he has a bag of cash that Mrs Richards hadn't taken yet, not that she knew about it though and that was it."

"I think you're right Seth, I think this is a distraction technique to take your focus away from the real killer, you worry about finding where the money came from and the real killer is under less pressure of being exposed."

"I think we should look into this at some point, Cassie, but for now I would like to leave it here hidden and go enjoy our picnic."

"I will put it in the bottom of my laundry basket, I doubt any burglars would look there."

Once Cassie returned, she picked up the bag with the food in it and Seth grabbed the blanket and they headed for his car and off for a romantic picnic just the two of them and nature. After a nice hour of just the two of them, they headed back to Dorothy's before starting off the day's tasks.

"So have you decided what you are going to do about Eshima and Lucas?" asked Dorothy.

Seth had filled Cassie in at the picnic about the meeting earlier and they had discussed it all the way back to her house. They took separate cars to his aunt's and now they were back in the kitchen when Dorothy brought it back up.

"I've actually been trying to get hold of Eshima now for a few hours but no luck," said Seth.

"Try her again, what happens when you ring?" said Cassie.

Seth rang Eshima's phone again.

"It goes straight to answer phone. I never asked her where in town she was staying, what if something's happened to her, what if Lucas is alone and she's collapsed because of her tumour?"

"Let's not panic OK, you ring the hospital and I'll research her online and see if we can find a lead on her, I'm sure she just left her phone in the car or something along those lines," said Cassie.

Seth rang the hospital but they had no record of her at all so then he tried the police station but got the same result, nothing. As he hung up his phone, Cassie was waiting for him with some potentially bad news.

"Seth, come look at this."

"Is that her Instagram account?"

"Correct, and if you scroll down what do you see, lots of?"

"Lots of bikini shots of her on beaches mainly."

"Exactly but not a single photo ever of Lucas. That's peculiar."

"Maybe she doesn't like posting photos of him online for his own protection, I know a few people who are like that."

"That could be correct but we saw photos of a boy around the age of six on her other social media accounts. Also, this account is six years old, no pregnancy photos and always on the beach or on a boat. Where is Lucas when all this is happening?"

"What are you suggesting, Cassie?"

"I am suggesting that she isn't hurt somewhere like you think, I'm thinking maybe Lucas isn't real."

"You think she made up having my children?"

"What if the Lola story was true and she had a mental breakdown or something and made Lucas up. What if she's the killer? Why did she turn up now? Right around the time you start investigating Eleandra's death?"

"I don't know Cassie; I have no answers to any of these questions but if you are right about any of that then we really need to find her."

"I agree, where do you want to start?"

"There's only one hotel in Kentsville and three B and B's, so let's start there, I'll give them a ring and you keep digging."

Cassie continued on her laptop as Seth rang each establishment in turn. Three down and only one to go with no sign of her so far. Seth was beginning to think Cassie was right and she had gone. However, the last number he called was for Lynda's B and B and it turned out after some persuasion from Seth, the little charmer, that Eshima was staying there but she had apparently decided to cut her stay short and was leaving later today. Seth told Cassie what Lynda said on the phone and then Cassie relayed some more information to Seth.

"I found two more things out while you were on the phone. Firstly, there is an arrest warrant out for Eshima in Manchester and secondly, she apparently has a serious drug problem."

"I know what to do, I'll call Chief Abraham and fill him in and get him to meet me outside with a few officers, we shall get to the bottom of this at once."

And with that, he was on the phone again.

"Seth, do you want me to come with?" she said when he finished his call.

"No, can you stay here and see if you can find out anything else, please? If you do, would you ring me?"

Cassie nodded and with a quick kiss for her and a hug for his aunt, Seth was out the door and, on his way, to face Eshima at Lynda's. Seth arrived just before the Police and waited in the car outside as Chief Abraham had asked him to on the phone. When they arrived, they all went in and the Chief let Seth lead the way. As they approached the reception desk, Seth could see a woman with long brown hair in a plait, standing behind the desk with a name badge on.

"Hi Lynda, we spoke on the phone, my name is Seth, is she in her room?"

"Yes, she's up there alright, it's room fourteen."

"You two stay here please and don't let her leave, me and Seth will go to her room," said the Chief.

"Thank you, Lynda," said Seth.

With that, they made their way up the stairs. Seth knocked on her door and Chief Abraham spoke without hesitation.

"This is the manager; I was just wondering if I could have a word about your checkout time."

A few seconds later, the door opened and there stood Eshima, she tried to close the door but both Seth and the Chief put their feet against the door as she slammed it, stopping it from moving anywhere.

"Eshima, what is going on?"

"Nothing is going on Seth, now leave."

"Then why did you try and slam the door in my face and why are you leaving and ignoring my calls?"

Eshima stood quietly with her head down and didn't respond.

"My name is Chief Abraham, I have been informed there is an arrest warrant out in your name, so this is going to play out one of two ways and you can choose which. One, you answer Seth's questions truthfully and then I take you to the station for some additional questioning. Or you can go with option two, ignore Seth's questions and I take you to the station now and arrest you for the murder of Eleandra Jacobson."

"Wait, you can't do that, I never killed her, I wasn't even living in Kentsville then."

"Then I would advise you to answer Seth's questions, now."

Eshima took a few steps backwards and sat on the bed.

"I was leaving because I was given instruction to go today without saying bye."

"You were instructed to, by who?" asked Seth.

"I don't know."

"I think you need to start from the beginning. Go," said Seth.

"I was in a cafe back home the day you started your investigation and I went to the toilet before I went to pay. I was only gone a few minutes, and when I came back out to pay for the food there was a note on the table saying check your emails ASAP. Obviously, I was intrigued, so I did."

"Please continue, Eshima." Seth wanted to know who instructed her to do this.

"I opened it and it said, 'I will pay you Fifty thousand pounds to come to Kentsville and tell Seth Bronx you have a child with him. I will be in contact again soon, please delete this email'. So I waited and a few hours later, I got an email with this whole routine of coming here and telling you about Lucas. It told me what to say and where and when to make contact with you. I'm so sorry, Seth, I was desperate for the cash; I owe some people over Forty thousand pounds and they are dangerous."

157

"Why didn't you go to the police?" asked the Chief.

"I have a warrant out for my arrest, I wasn't going anywhere near the police, plus someone was going to pay me money just to lie to someone I had sex with years ago. All I cared about was the money and getting away from the thugs after me."

"So what happened next? What did they tell you to do or say to me next?"

"They told me it would hurt you more leaving abruptly before you got to see your son and I was to leave you a letter saying I got cold feet and Lucas is gonna stay with his babysitter."

"Do you have any idea who it is telling you what to do?"

"None, I've never technically met them or spoken to them, just the emails."

"Then how do you know they will pay you?"

"They sent me travel documents and a confirmation of a hotel booking all paid for so I believed them and besides it got me away from where I was."

"So now what?" asked Seth.

"No idea, I got an email saying I had to tell the hotel I was leaving abruptly and I'd receive more information within the hour. That was two hours ago, I'm still waiting."

"It must have been the killer, keeping you pre-occupied from your investigation, Seth. Whoever killed Eleandra is a true mastermind and master manipulator. We may have our work cut out for us," said Chief Abraham.

He turned to Eshima.

"We are going to take you down to the station now, please gather up your belongings."

A few minutes later and the three of them were downstairs in reception. Eshima apologised once more to Seth and then she was put into the back of a police car. The chief said goodbye to Seth and they drove off with the other squad car following behind. Once out of sight, Seth went back in to speak to Lynda.

"Lynda, do you have the details of who paid for Eshima's room."

"I'm afraid not, I opened my mail a few days back and there was an envelope with instructions about booking a room for that young woman and the exact cash for it too. It was an unusual way of booking a room so I kept it in the safe until she turned up and then I booked it on the system and took the money."

"Well, thank you for your help and your time Lynda, bye bye."

Seth got in his car with a heavy heart, the whole thing was made up, he didn't have children, Eshima was part of a plot against him from an unknown individual, probably the same person he was after for Eleandra's murder. Whoever the killer is one thing was clear, they were an absolute monster.

Seth arrived back at Dorothy's to find the two girls in the kitchen where he left them.

"Have you even moved since I've been gone?" he asked.

"Not really," Cassie said.

"Well, Seth, what happened?" asked Dorothy. Seth filled them both in on what had just transpired and after about half an hour of discussing it, Seth stood up.

"That's enough talk about Eshima, I'm done on that subject. What's the plan for this evening?"

"Shall we go and watch a film?" said Dorothy.

"That's a great idea Dotty, anything you fancy?"

"Not really, Cassie, but nothing too scary otherwise I'll be wetting myself all night."

"Thank you for that information, Aunty," said Seth, followed by a chuckle, and a grim look on his face.

"You are very welcome, my darling."

"So ladies, what will it be?"

"Have a look at the new films section and pick one of those," Dorothy suggested.

"Oh, this looks good, I've heard it's got fantastic reviews."

"I'm fine with that, Cassie. Aunty, what do you think?"

"Rom-coms are the best. Let me get the lights and then you can press play."

Lights off and subtitles turned on because that's how Dorothy watched all TV, they all relaxed, watching the film with the intentions of having a nice evening.

Within the first thirty minutes, Dorothy got up twice to use the toilet, disturbing the once peaceful atmosphere.

"My bladder has a mind of its own this evening, sorry, press play again, Seth, please."

They continued watching their movie for roughly another ten minutes when a loud slamming noise sounded throughout the house. It was almost as if someone had used a battering ram to smash down the front door. The sound made them all jump out of their skin and Cassie even let out a small squeal. Seth picked up one of Dorothy's heavy candlesticks that she used as decoration and walked towards the front door, hushing the two women who sat shocked on the living room couch. Candlestick in hand, Seth was about to open the door when the same loud bang resounded throughout the house. He stumbled back before quickly reaching for the knob and yanking the door, candlestick raised and ready but before he could speak, a dishevelled Chelsea pushed past him with floods of tears streaming down her face.

"It's Ludlow, he went mad and attacked me, I said no and he tried to..."

She couldn't get the words out, stumbling all about the place and shaking like a leaf.

"He tried to what?" Seth said very loudly, causing Cassie and Dorothy to appear beside them.

"F...f...force himself on me," she cried.

"I'll kill him," Seth roared.

"Dorothy, why don't you take Chelsea through to the kitchen and make her a nice hot drink."

"Excellent idea, Cassie, Chelsea dear, let's go get some tea."

Chelsea walked with Dorothy leaving Cassie and Seth alone to talk.

"Seth calm down. Chelsea needs us to comfort her and give her support, so for that, we need to be calm, not plan a ruthless way to murder Ludlow."

"I am calm. I just know that he's the murderer, he has to be. This just proves it, its evil."

"There is a big difference between attempted assault, sexual assault and a murderer. We should report this to the police right away, you know as well as I that we can't blame him of committing a crime with no evidence to show he committed it."

"I know. Maybe I should just go and beat a confession out of him," Seth replied, running his hands over his face in an attempt to calm himself down.

"No Seth, you shouldn't. I get you are angry; I am too but you need to keep a calm head. We need to prove that he is the killer or if he even is, and in order to do that you need to keep yourself from being put behind bars."

"After what he has done, I want him to be the killer. I want to watch his face as I bring him down. He will get what's coming to him."

"Let's not think about that right now. We need to go and see Chelsea, I'm sure she could use our support. We also need to talk her into going to the police."

They both walked to the kitchen where Dorothy had made all four of them a drink and laid out some biscuits for them to snack on. Chelsea was sitting at the table with a blanket around her and Dorothy just across from her, neither of them speaking or making a sound, complete silence.

"I'm sorry to ruin your evening like this," Chelsea burst out once Seth approached her.

"Chelsea don't worry about that, you haven't ruined anything, just explain to me what happened so we can notify the police."

"No Seth, you can't go to the police. Eleandra's dead, my dad is dead, I told you I would be next. We can't tell them, he'll hurt my mum next. I'll tell you but not them, please you have to promise me."

"Chelsea please reconsider, I can protect you, the police can protect you."

"No, I won't risk it. I'm sorry but I can't. Promise you won't tell them."

"OK Chelsea, I won't tell them but you have to tell me everything that happened."

"Say you promise first. Please Seth please say you promise," she almost begged.

"I promise you I won't tell the police. Now you need to tell me everything that happened, I mean everything."

"I went to see him at the rowing club," she started. Cassie interjected.

"Sorry, you went to see him, if you think he may be the killer, why did you go to see him on your own?"

"Ludlow and my dad were very close when we were together. He always wanted a son, even preferred him to me. I thought I should go and see if he was OK too, see if he was hurting like I was."

"I see."

Cassie wasn't sure she entirely believed Chelsea's reasoning but decided to let it drop and hear her out.

"So what happened next?" Seth asked.

"He was alone at the rowing club, OH MY GOD…"

"What is it?" said Seth.

"I think I killed him."

She was now trembling; she was shaking from head to toe. It was so quiet again now that Seth was sure he could hear her tears hitting the kitchen floor, well not entirely but she was sobbing loud enough.

"Chelsea concentrate. What do you mean you think you killed him?"

"I…I…I…" she stuttered out.

"Take some deep breaths darling, it's going to be OK, just breath, and when you're ready, answer Seth," Dorothy said sympathetically, standing behind Chelsea and gently rubbing her shoulders.

Chelsea put one of her hands on top of Dorothy's and proceeded to give it a little squeeze. Once she managed to compose herself, she lifted her head and answered Seth.

"I was trying to fight him off, he was so strong. I saw something black on the floor so I grabbed it and hit him as hard as I could on his head near his ear. He fell on me and that's when I noticed he was bleeding. I managed to push him off and didn't know what to do so I just ran, I was scared he would get back up but he didn't move."

"OK let's stay calm. I will go to the rowing club and check on him."

"Oh god Seth, what if I killed him?"

"I'm sure Ludlow's fine and in the worst-case scenario, it was self-defence, OK Chelsea?" She nodded her head, still trembling.

"Aunt Dorothy, is it OK if Chelsea stays here tonight?"

"Yes, of course, she can have your room, it's not like you use it anymore."

"Chelsea, try and get some rest, Cassie and I will be back once we've checked everything out. I'm sure he is fine and he's off licking his wounds somewhere."

Seth and Cassie left Chelsea in Dorothy's capable hands and headed to the rowing club for the second time, the third in Cassie's case. Seth wasn't surprised that the night hadn't gone as planned; nowadays there wasn't a day that was uneventful for him. Nearly arriving at the rowing club, Seth couldn't help but notice how beautiful Cassie looked with the moonlight shining in on her through the car window. He wouldn't ever take this sight for granted as he truly knew that he was the luckiest man alive, she was a remarkable woman and she was his. Cassie saw Seth looking at her and smiled back at him.

"What's on your mind, boyfriend?"

"Right now. Just how stunning you are, girlfriend."

"You charmer, you." She blushed.

"I speak the truth, Cassie, you are so very beautiful."

"Thank you. I happen to think you are rather dashing, you know?"

"Oh, really? Do tell."

Before Cassie could speak, Seth abruptly stopped the car in the middle of the road, there was a body blocking the way. Getting out of the car, they approached

162

a heavily bleeding man. Moving his arm from his face, Seth identified him to be Ludlow.

"He's in bad shape, breathing but it's not looking good. We need to get him to the hospital now. Open the door behind the driver seat," Seth commanded, panic evident in his tone.

"OK, shall I sit with him?" Cassie asked, panic also evident in her tone too.

"No, you drive and I will keep an eye on him in case he deteriorates. His breathing is shallow at best."

"OK, I'll drive."

They put him in the back of the car as delicately as they could to ensure that no more damage was done to him. The hospital wasn't far from the rowing club, and with Cassie's driving, should take them only a few minutes. Seth concluded that Ludlow was potentially trying to make it to the hospital himself and passed out due to blood loss. He had lost a lot of it and was completely covered. Seth had called ahead to the hospital to ensure that they would be fully prepared to deal with the situation. They pulled up to the entrance of the A&E department where there was a team waiting with a crash cart.

"Where did you find him?" questioned one of the nurses.

"He was passed out on the road just in front of the rowing club. His breathing is really shallow and he has lost so much blood, it was all over the road where he lay. He must have been bleeding for a little while at least."

"Are you relatives?" asked another nurse who had stopped them at the doors to the emergency rooms.

"No. I'm actually investigating a murder of which he is a person of interest; he may know something in relation to the case. I was on my way to speak to him when we noticed him on the road."

"OK, so you know who he is then? I need a name to notify his next of kin."

"Yes, his name is Ludlow Fenston."

"Thank you. I will let you know how he is, if you could wait here please."

"Seth, will he be alright?" Cassie asked.

He noticed her face had gone from happy to concerned.

"Yes, I think so. I think I heard them say something about potentially broken ribs and they were assessing the bang to his head on the way to the emergency rooms. He will live if that's what you mean."

"That's great news. Chelsea will be relieved about that. Do you think we can get her to push charges over the attempted rape once you prove he's the killer?"

"I don't know, maybe. I think we should let her decide that and not push her too much. Let's concentrate on Ludlow for now."

"Are you going to tell the police about it?"

"I'm going to call the chief now and explain about Ludlow but I will leave the rape incident out of it as I promised her I would."

Cassie waited with Seth while he spoke to Chief Abraham.

"He is with the Doctors now. I can't tell you his condition but I think he will be OK."

Seth explained to the chief over the phone. Seth put him on loudspeaker so Cassie could hear both sides of the call.

"Seth what happened?" the Chief asked.

"Cassie and I were at my aunt's house watching a movie when Chelsea banged on the door, she was trembling and crying and in obvious distress. She was talking about being in some fight with Ludlow so I decided to go and talk to him and Cassie came with me. Before we reached the rowing club, where Chelsea left him, we saw him unconscious and bleeding profusely on the road in front of us. We had no choice but to rush him straight to the hospital."

"You didn't see anyone around?"

"Not within the vicinity no, but we never managed to make it to the rowing club."

"They should have CCTV at the rowing club, so I can pull that up tomorrow and see what happened there. Are you staying at the hospital?"

"Yes. I am going to stay until his parents turn up."

"Thank you for that. I'll send some officers over shortly to take over, so you and Cassie can go home and get some sleep."

"No worries, I'll speak to you in the morning."

Not long after the call ended, Ludlow's mother arrived.

"You must be Ludlow's mother? Mrs Fenston."

"Yes, but why are you here? You're the one investigating Eleandra's murder, right? Seth Bronx, isn't it?"

"Yes, I'm Seth and I'm sorry we had to meet under these circumstances."

"I've been told my son is in with doctors but no one will tell me what has happened to him."

"This is Cassie."

"Cassie Bowl, I know who you are."

"Cassie and I were driving to the rowing club to speak to your son, just before we arrived, we found him outside on the road, bleeding. He has a head injury and I think some bruised or broken ribs, I can't tell you any more than that I'm afraid, that's all we know."

"Is there a suspect?"

"That is something you will have to ask the police. I have spoken to Police Chief Abraham and he is sending some officers here now. We thought we would wait until you arrived, I didn't want you to be in the dark if you got here before them."

Almost like clockwork, two of the new young officers arrived; one male and one female, both looking serious.

"Seth Bronx. Could we have a chat with you alone before we talk to Mrs Fenston?"

"Yes, of course."

Cassie stayed with Mrs Fenston as Seth and the two officers disappeared around the corner.

"Seth, the Chief is currently on his way. He wants a word with you in person. He has just received a call from the doctor, Ludlow is still unconscious but alive. He has taken a hell of a beating; he was clubbed around the back of the head a few times and is lucky he didn't die. The doctor said that in her opinion, this was no accident."

"No, that can't be right, she said it was self-defence. She claimed he tried to rape her."

Chief Abraham had turned up at that very moment.

"Who said that?"

"Chelsea Chive. She came to see me at my aunt's house and said he tried to rape her, it was self-defence and she said she only hit him once."

"You left that bit out earlier, Seth, however, the doctors are saying it was more than once."

"She asked me and Cassie not to tell the police, she was really frightened. Chelsea said she did what she did to get him to stop and then she ran, she was shaken up and probably got confused about how many times she hit him, people do things in a moment of fear."

"We will question him when he wakes up but if he says differently, it's his word against hers and as it stands, she will be taken into custody for questioning on the charge of attempted murder."

"What will happen to her?"

"If we can't prove the rape allegation, Chelsea will potentially be looking at some years in prison."

Chapter Fourteen

Seth pondered what the Chief had just told him in silence for a few seconds, he decided she could do with a friend around about now.

"I'd like to go back to her and my aunty before they take her in," said Seth.

"You and Cassie can head back now then; I will speak to Ludlow's mother and I'll call you if I hear anything else."

They shook hands and Seth departed, getting Cassie up to speed on the car ride back to Dorothy's. She wasn't silent on her opinion of the current situation.

"Chelsea told us she hit him on the side of his head near his ear. The doctor is saying she hit him on the back of the head. That's not the same, Seth."

"I am aware of that but she was fighting off her ex-boyfriend who was trying to sexually assault her, are you really expecting that in that moment she would make notes of where exactly she bashed him while trying to flee?"

"No, I'm not. But again, hitting him once and hitting him three times is different. All I'm saying is maybe he wasn't trying to attack her, maybe she just misunderstood, maybe he was just consoling her on the loss of her father and she got the wrong end and lashed out. Chelsea didn't have a single mark on her when she turned up at Dorothy's, did she?"

Seth had to admit that he never saw any bruises on Chelsea when she arrived earlier.

"Not that I could see."

"Surely if he was on top of her pinning her down, she would have had some kind of bruise or abrasion," said Cassie.

Seth had to agree with her, maybe Ludlow's actions tonight were innocent, maybe it was a misunderstanding. If that's so, then Chelsea would be facing an attempted murder charge.

"Cassie, what would you do if you were in my shoes? The police will turn up right after us, maybe even before we get back. They're going to take her away and question her. Should I go with her?"

"No. From tomorrow, you will be working side by side with them, you can use that power to talk to her, maybe even sit in when they speak to her about this."

"Good idea, let's see what happens when we get there."

They pulled around the corner and could see the flashing blue lights outside Dorothy's house. The police must have arrived a few moments before them as they were still waiting at the front door. Seth and Cassie walked up behind them as Dorothy had been asked politely if they could come in, she obliged and opened the door wider, watching as they all walked in one after the other.

"Dorothy Jacobson?"

"Correct."

"And this is your house?"

"That is also correct."

"We have reason to believe Chelsea Chive is here with you. We would like to have a word with her please."

"Did you tell them, Seth?"

"Yes, Aunty Dorothy and there's something you should know too."

"That will have to wait for now, where is Miss Chive?" asked one of the officers.

"She is in the kitchen, just through here if you'd follow me."

Entering the kitchen, it was evident that Chelsea was no longer there. If the lack of her presence wasn't anything to go by, then the wide-open back door was.

"Chelsea. Chelsea, are you there?" Dorothy shouted into the garden.

There was no response. The two officers went out to have a look but nothing. She had done a runner.

"She's scared, I know she is. We were just talking about what happened earlier tonight."

The police officers were very obviously frustrated but still remained professional. One of them closed the open door whilst the other had asked Dorothy to take a seat at the table. Just like the two at the hospital, one of the officers was male whilst the other female. Seth thought they looked very similar to one another and would even go as far as to say that they were somehow related, brother and sister maybe?

"If you call this in, I will find out what has been going on."

The male officer said to the female.

"Will do."

She walked into the living room closing the kitchen door behind her.

"Miss Jacobson, if you could please tell me what Chelsea said to you before we arrived, that would be a great start?"

"Well, Chelsea started off by talking about when they dated a few years back, she said Ludlow and her father were always close and that he always wanted a son. Even after they had broken up, he would always check up on how he was doing, I think she was jealous of Ludlow and wished her father paid more attention to her, the way he did him, he was her father after all. She mentioned that when she was at college, her father told her if Ludlow ever proposes to her, that she was to tell him yes, that way he would finally have a son, someone he could be proud of. Chelsea was studying something to do with computers and her father didn't approve, always thought it was pointless."

"Did Chelsea mention anything about tonight's alleged attack?"

"Alleged? Ludlow attempted to rape her, why would she make that up? She is so scared, terrified even, she has run away for goodness sake, out there all alone. A victim that has been attacked by her ex-boyfriend and on top of that her father has just died too. Poor lass. Chelsea needs us to help her, not to go throwing accusations around."

"Ms Jacobson please, what did she say about tonight?"

"Fine! She went to see him at the rowing club to see if he had heard the news about her father, she wanted to see if he was OK because regardless of their history, Ludlow and her father were close."

"Go on Aunty," Seth encouraged.

"Ludlow tried to kiss her and she had told him no. Chelsea didn't love him like that anymore and wasn't trying to give him the wrong idea. He didn't like being told no and hit her across the face and threw her against the wall."

"Sorry to interject but may I ask my aunty something?" Seth inquired.

"Go ahead Mr Bronx."

"Did you see any marks on her face or any bumps and bruises where she supposedly was thrown against the wall?"

"Supposedly, not you too, Seth."

"Did you see any?"

"Well no, I mean I don't know. I wasn't looking at all of her face, just her sad eyes. They were red and puffy. I didn't notice any bruises or anything else."

"Do any of you know where she would have gone?" asked the officer.

"Not a clue," Seth chipped in.

"I doubt she would go home, she's smarter than that, maybe somewhere that's linked to Eleandra," Cassie suggested.

"Ms Jacobson, any ideas?"

"No, we only recently met her. I don't know her that well, I'm afraid."

The female officer returned and asked the male officer for a word in private. Once they were both out of the room, Seth spoke.

"I think they're brother and sister."

"Really?" said Cassie, eyebrows raised.

"Yes. They have a similar face shape and the same eyes. He is taller than her, yes, but I'd put money on them being siblings."

"A tenner says they're not," added Dorothy.

Cassie laughed at them.

"You two are terrible."

"Ten pounds and loser cooks a roast dinner on Sunday for us all."

"Deal."

They had to wait for the officers to return for a few minutes but when they did, Seth was quick to ask the question that they had been dying to know.

"Are the two of you related?"

"Yes, he is my little brother."

"BOOM! I knew I was right." Cassie shook her head.

"You had inside information, didn't you?" Dorothy said, unimpressed that she had lost the bet.

"No, I am just a great investigator."

"Well, Mr great investigator, Ludlow is awake, and he won't talk to anybody but you. So shall we get going?" the female officer said.

"He only wants to talk to me, that's strange, but yes, let's go."

He gave Cassie a smacker right on her ruby red lips.

"Told you so," he said to his aunt.

"You just couldn't resist, could you Seth."

He had a little smirk on his face.

"Bye Aunty, I'll call when I'm on the way back." She bid him goodbye but not before telling him that she would wait up for news on Ludlow's condition and on any sightings of Chelsea. Seth got in the back of a police car and headed to the hospital with the two officers.

"Did he say why he would only talk to me?" he asked them.

"Chief Abraham mentioned something about Eleandra telling him if he ever needed a friend to look to you. That you wouldn't let him down."

"He said that?"

"That was the message."

"Then he must have known Eleandra better than he claimed."

Seth picked up a newspaper out the back of the driver's seat. He turned a few pages and saw a news article about Chelsea Chive and read the headline.

"On this day, 14 years ago, a child hacks supermarket computers from her house."

Almost like a lightbulb going off in his head, Seth had an epiphany.

"Holy shit, I know who killed her, I know who killed Eleandra!!!"

The car swerved and there was a screech and a sudden stop with everyone whipping forward from their seats. Seth's overly loud declaration caused the officers in the front to jump. He didn't mean to shout; it just came out but the daunting realisation hit him like a ton of bricks. He heard Eleandra tell someone those exact words on the phone around 18 months ago and now seeing that article, it all made sense. He was right the first time. He got caught up with everything that had happened over the last few days and had gone along with it, he had been led the way the killer wanted him to. Now, however, the clues were all there. All the previous bits of information meant nothing to him, they didn't make sense but now, now they finally did. All he had to do was factor in the murderer, the correct murderer, and he could see it, almost as if he was finally opening his eyes for the first time. He was spot on from the start and then he had been manipulated into changing his thoughts based on lies. Seth, now noticing, that the police car had stopped and had stayed still, looked at the officers in front. Bro/sis, the sibling officers (As Seth decided to now refer to them) were both staring directly at him waiting to hear his big announcement.

"Can you get Chief Abraham on the radio?"

"Yes, why?"

"I know where Chelsea is or where she may be going."

"That can wait for a second, who is the killer that's more important, plus how do you suddenly know that? And you said you knew where she was going, how?" said the brother.

"Quickly, just get him on the radio before she kills again."

"She?"

"Yes, she, Chelsea Chive. Chelsea chive is the murderer, she killed Eleandra," Seth rushed the words out.

"If you won't call him, shall I?"

"I'll do it now," said the sister.

The brother officer wanted more information, the minimal amount that Seth had given wasn't enough to quench his thirst for the case related knowledge.

"How do you know it's her?"

"I can't prove it without Ludlow but I think she's going to the hospital to kill him, to finish the job she tried to start earlier. With him dead, I can't prove anything all I've got is theories and her lies. We need him alive."

"This is car one-two-seven to Chief Abraham, come in Chief Abraham. I repeat car one-two-seven to Chief Abraham come in."

"Chief Abraham here, go ahead."

"Don't just sit there, drive officer's bro/sis, we need to get to the hospital."

The male officer wasn't exactly sure as to why he was being called bro/sis, Seth hadn't yet explained it to them, it was a quip for his own amusement.

"I repeat Chief Abraham here."

Bro/sis accelerated turning on the blues and twos, loud blaring and flashing.

"Glenn, it's Seth, Chelsea is heading to you."

"Why on earth would she do that? Didn't she just run from us at your aunt's house?"

"She killed Eleandra."

The more he had said it out loud, the more he couldn't believe it took him this long to work it out, he suspected it could be her at the beginning, it was only her story that had changed his mind and ruled her out.

"She killed Eleandra! Are you sure, Seth?" said the Chief.

"Yes, I'll explain everything when I get there. I think Ludlow is the only one who can prove her lies, that's why she's trying to kill him."

"So he didn't attack her?"

"No, she attacked him. Thought he was dead and claimed sexual assault as a cover so it would seem like self-defence. If he was dead, he couldn't argue his case but he isn't dead and now she needs to finish the job."

"Bloody hell, Seth, I didn't expect this turn of events. Are you sure about this allegation?"

"Only Ludlow can tell me for sure but what he said about Eleandra makes me believe so and the newspaper article lends strong weight to it, I'll show you that when I arrive."

"How long till you get here, Seth?"

"If I was driving then about three minutes but with driving Miss Daisy here, maybe about five to seven."

"Oh no way, driving Miss Daisy my ass."

The car suddenly accelerated a bit more as Seth had clearly hit a nerve.

"I was driving carefully and responsibly, thank you very much."

"Well, now try driving like you want to catch a killer instead."

Seth still had the receiver pushed down on the radio and Chief Abraham heard the small interaction.

"You heard the man, put your foot down."

"I have sir."

"Good, then see you soon, I'll get officers on all the exits."

"See you shortly," Seth replied.

"I will have every other officer standing guard of Ludlow until you arrive."

The radio correspondence ended and bro/sis increased the speed again. Upon arrival, the sibling officers stood by the lift waiting to go up to Ludlow's room which was on the fourth floor. Seth decided to take the stairs, leaving them both behind, he wasn't willing to wait, this was urgent. He ran out the stairwell and down the first hallway, second left and he was there. Three officers stood outside Ludlow's room and through the window, he could see Chief Abraham talking with one of the doctors and Ludlow's mother. The Doctor went to take her leave just as Seth entered the room, however, she stopped him politely on her way out.

"Chief Abraham told us the development, please take it easy, he has had a tough ordeal tonight and he needs his rest."

"Yes, doctor. It's not like I have a murder case to solve or anything."

"I mean it, he took a beating tonight and he needs rest, not an inquisition."

"I'll be as delicate as I can be when trying to find a homicidal psychopath."

The doctor did not look impressed but decided not to mince words with Seth anymore.

"Impressive Seth, I think you should consider joining the force, you have the stuff," the chief said.

"Thank you but again, I'm OK where I am."

"I don't want to speak to anyone but Seth," Ludlow said.

"I understand that Ludlow but we need some answers, so I'm afraid I will be staying as will your mum," The chief answered back, trying to be as sensitive as he could.

"You won't be getting any answers until I talk to Seth alone. Do you understand that Chief or shall I repeat it a few more times?" Ludlow spat out in a very weak but aggressive tone.

"I understand, Seth I'll be right outside."

"Mum you need to leave as well, please."

"No Ludlow, I'm staying."

"No, Mum, I'm afraid you're not."

"Baby, I don't want to leave you."

"Mum, get out, I need to talk to Seth in private, no exceptions." Chief Abraham reluctantly left, taking Ludlow's mum with him.

The fact that Chief Abraham managed to get her to leave was impressive as she was as stubborn as Seth. Finally, Ludlow and Seth were alone. Seth stood a few metres from his bed, he thought it best to stand so he could look more professional. He wanted answers and now was not the time for Ludlow to be messing around, he was hoping for a far more serious conversation than at the rowing club.

"So now you want to talk?"

"I'm sorry I didn't before, telling you this opens up a whole can of worms for me that I just didn't want to get myself into. I was protecting myself. I realised Eleandra would have been ashamed of me, and after that psycho attacked me tonight, I want to make sure she is locked up before she hurts anyone else."

"Go on, tell me what happened."

"I was locking up the rowing club after going for my evening row. I saw a reflection in the mirror out the corner of my eye, it looked like Chelsea but I couldn't be sure. Before I could turn around to double-check, they cracked me over the head and I fell forward, then they hit me again once more. The Doctor said they hit me a third time but I was out of it after the second hit and don't remember much more."

"So why did you want to talk to me? I've heard something you said when you first woke up. What did you say? Could you repeat it for me?"

"Yes, I said I would only talk to you. Eleandra told me if I ever needed a friend that you wouldn't let me down."

174

"I heard Eleandra say that to someone on the phone a few months before she got killed. It was you she was talking to."

"Yes, she was talking to me."

"So it was you and Eleandra that were dating and Chelsea was jealous, is that why she dumped you?"

"No, at first, me and Eleandra weren't dating, we were just friends. Chelsea had a crush on Eleandra and I told her to steer clear from her, she was a needy and clingy nut job who always liked to play the victim."

Seth sighed.

"Of course she does, just like tonight when she turned up at my aunt Dorothy's house. Chelsea told us how she thought she had killed you in self-defence. She insinuated that you had tried to rape her."

"That bitch said what?"

Seth nodded.

"Seth, I never touched her, I had my suspicions and didn't even know if it was actually her until you just confirmed it."

"I believe you, don't worry. I think she made the story up to cover her trying to kill you."

"Why would she try and kill me?"

"Because Ludlow I think you were the only one who could confirm her lies about Eleandra and confirm that it was actually Chelsea who killed her."

"You think she killed Eleandra? But why?"

"I was hoping you could help me figure that one out. What happened between you and Chelsea back when you dated?"

"I was under a lot of pressure from my parents and it just got too much for me, she got too much for me. I was really down, I was suffering mentally; I needed to win a race coming up really badly, so I took performance-enhancing drugs for a rowing meet. Afterwards, I felt so guilty; I cheated my opponents, myself, but also my team and my coach. Eleandra was the only person I could talk to about it, she helped me tell my coach. I promised I'd never do it again and he gave me a second chance and promised not to report me or drop me from the team."

"What about you and Chelsea?"

"She was so controlling and on my back twenty-four seven. It made me depressed and after the whole cheating debacle, I told her it was over, I didn't like who I was when I was with her."

"You dumped her?"

"Yes, and I never really spoke to her again after that, the only downside was I was really close to her dad and talking to him was awkward when she was around."

"So after you, she had a thing for Eleandra?"

"Yes, she did and I warned Eleandra to be careful because I didn't want Chelsea having a negative effect on her the way she did on me. I didn't want her changing Eleandra; she was such a good person. That's when she told me if anything ever happened to her and if I ever needed a friend, you wouldn't let me down."

"So why did Chelsea kill her?" Seth asked himself out loud.

"Seth, if you are sure she did it, then there must be a reason."

"Yes Ludlow, I'm positive it was her. Although I don't have a reason, I know she was trying to blame you for this and I think she would have had you saddled with her dad's death too."

"You think she killed her dad too?"

"She killed him alright but again, I don't know why."

"OK, well, there was this one time when me and Eleandra got drunk and stayed up all night talking, we ended up kissing, nothing else, just kissing. Maybe she found out about that, we never got around to dating because of what happened to her but I really did have strong feelings for her, our friendship grew into something more, she made me feel good again, she made me feel on top of the world. I think we were in love, true love. That's what I wanted to tell you. I have nothing more to say I'm afraid. Is there anything else you need from me, Seth?"

"To rest, doctor's orders and mine."

"Now you agree with the doctor," Ludlow huffed.

BANG, BANG, BANG. They heard three loud bangs that sounded like gunshots, they weren't too far away either. Seth walked out of Ludlow's room and noticed that one of the three officers standing guard was no longer there; he had assumed that he went to see where the shots had come from. Seth didn't speak to the remaining two officers, instead, rushed off to find the gun wielder. He heard voices as he approached the waiting area, one of which sounded like Chief Abraham. He poked his head around the corner and the gunman had her back to him. It was Chelsea. She was face to face with the chief and a few officers, all of which were pointing their own weapons at her.

"Lower the weapon, don't do something you can't take back."

The Chief seemed in charge of the situation, he spoke softly, attempting to keep Chelsea calm.

"Who said I care about taking it all back. I killed my own father, I wouldn't take that back, he was an arsehole who got what he deserved. Now stay back or you'll get what you deserve."

"Chelsea, what happened with your dad exactly?" the Chief asked.

"If you must know then fine, I'll tell you. I sat them both down him and my mum, she wasn't exactly thrilled at it. I could tell by her face but she said she loved me and supported me in my life choices. My dad on the other hand was less than cordial. He said I was being stupid and whatever I thought I knew and felt was merely just a phase and once my head sorted everything out, I would be back to normal. Then we started roaring at each other and my mum left the room. I told him I am normal, being gay is normal but he just laughed at me and told me his dad and granddad didn't fight in the war just so his daughter could one day become a lesbian. I stormed out and later that day when I knew Mum had left the house, I snuck back in and confronted him, only this time I stabbed him. He was dying, gasping for air. His final words were 'you are no daughter of mine'. I was about to leave but then I thought about Eleandra and wrote her name on his chest, not sure why but it was fun to once again carve away at someone's flesh."

She had a nurse around the throat with a small blade in her hand and a gun in the other. Seth could only see her reflection in a vending machine that was across from them, so it wasn't perfect, he just continued to listen for now.

"Chelsea, let the nurse go, she has done you no harm, you said your father deserved it, does she?"

"No but sometimes there's collateral damage which can't be avoided."

"Chelsea, please let her go."

Chelsea pointed the gun at the nurse's head. Seth wanted to approach from behind and grab the gun but he was worried about the blade next to the nurse's throat.

"If you won't let me kill Ludlow then I shall leave, with the nurse in tow."

"Chelsea, I can't let you do that."

"Oh really?"

BANG. She fired a shot straight into Chief Abraham's knee, he went down instantly. A nurse nearby ran over to him to put pressure on the wound.

"Sorry but it doesn't look like you are in a position to stop me now, does it?"

Seth had enough of the commotion and stepped out from behind the wall to address her.

"No, it doesn't seem so, Chelsea."

She spun the nurse around to face Seth but was very aware of everyone now behind her.

"You lot move over there where I can see you. Now!"

She was getting agitated and losing her grip, Seth was worried she was going to go off like a bomb, he needed to act fast.

"Why don't you let the nurse go and I'll be your hostage. I'll come with you."

"Oh aren't we the hero, Seth, just like I pegged you to be."

"I'm not a hero, it just makes no sense taking someone hostage who you can't leverage for. You don't know her or her family but you know me, you can use me, she is worthless to you. I thought you were smarter than that."

"You do make a solid point Seth but I know you are manipulating me somehow! I know you better than you think Seth!" She bellowed at him and took him off guard a little.

"OK, maybe I am Chelsea, after all, you have spent the last few days manipulating me and those I love the most."

"I'm afraid it was necessary to keep you away from the truth."

"I know the truth. You murdered Eleandra!"

Now it was Seth's turn to bellow.

"No, it wasn't like that. It's complicated, you wouldn't understand."

"It wasn't complicated. Ludlow told her what you were really like, he warned her to stay away from you. She rejected you and you killed her, didn't you?"

"She broke my heart! So I broke hers."

"You bitch. You are going to get what's coming to you, I swear to God."

"Oh dear Seth, God won't help you, no one will. Now get on your damn knees and move slowly towards me."

Seth hesitated.

"Now! I won't ask again." She pushed the knife even harder against the nurse's neck, piercing the skin and drawing a small amount of blood.

Seth did as she had asked, slowly getting down on his knees and making his way towards her.

"I guess in the history books you'll forever be known as nurse collateral."

BANG BANG.

Chapter Fifteen

Seth couldn't believe it; he knew she was callous but Chelsea put two bullets in the nurse's back out of nowhere before anyone could react. They all watched as Chelsea smiled at the nurse as she fell hard to the floor. Seth felt numb, the sound of her body hitting the floor shook him to his core, it was a sound that he felt would haunt him. Chelsea wasted no time in pointing the gun at Seth's head now, she used him as a shield as he stood and up and they both walked slowly backwards.

"Get me that chair," Chelsea demanded, directing an officer to go and get it from behind the nurses' station.

He brought the chair around and pushed it slowly towards her and Seth.

"Sit on the chair, slowly. Anyone who attempts to follow will get the same treatment as poor little nursy collateral there."

Seth sat on the chair as Chelsea pushed him with her foot down the corridor that Seth had come from

"Move the chair with your legs and feet, any funny business and I'll put a bullet in your head and give Cassie the same fate."

"I won't try anything but tell me why you cut up Eleandra after you murdered her?"

"She ripped my heart out and stomped on it. I loved her and she spat on that love, then I saw her kissing Ludlow and I figured that I should return the favour, so I stabbed her and watched her die. I watched as the light left her eyes and her body stopped moving. I ripped out her heart and stomped on it, just like she had done to me. It felt so good to do, I would even say it was fun, so I decided to do it to a few more organs, only that I got more aggressive as I went on."

"You're sick, Chelsea."

"No, I'm very healthy. It's my diet, it's very nutritional."

"You will spend the rest of your life in jail for this, and I will make sure that you will remember her face every day for the rest of your life."

"I already remember her face every day, I loved her so much, I still do. It's a shame she listened to Ludlow, he did this, it's all his fault. He knew too much, he would have unknowingly given me up, so he had to go."

"And your father?"

"I told him I was gay. I told him I loved her. You all encouraged me to, and with your support, I decided to finally tell him, I didn't need you there, I am strong. He told me he was ashamed and that I was no daughter of his."

"So you killed him? You could have just left; you didn't have to see him again. It was wrong of him to treat you like that; you are his daughter, but to murder him as well. You need help, Chelsea."

"I don't need help; I just need to be loved. If people loved me for me, then I'd be fine."

"No, you wouldn't, you'd still be a sick and twisted monster."

Chelsea hit Seth around the back of the head with a force which caused him to stop moving the chair.

"Shut your mouth and keep moving."

He started rolling the chair again and headed towards a lift that she directed him to. She pressed the ground floor and down they went in silence. Seth was wondering whether to ram her against the lift wall but she had a knife and a gun and all he had was a notepad and pen in his pocket, so thought better of it. If only he had brought his gun from the glove compartment. They exited the lift but instead of heading for the main exit, she took them down another corridor and smashed a window.

"Climb out and step back away from the window, once I'm out lean in and pull the chair through after us."

"If I say no?"

"Do you want me to shoot you?"

"I mean, I would rather you didn't."

"Then climb out the damn window."

Seth didn't wait for her to tell him a third time; he climbed out the window and looked on as Chelsea used the chair to get herself out. Once she touched the ground outside, she pointed the gun at Seth once more and made him pull the chair through the gap, which he did but he made it look like he was having great difficulty. Seth was then made to carry the chair towards a car park which was made solely for the use of ambulances to park in. He stopped at one point, feigning dizziness but Chelsea didn't believe him and put the gun to his head once more and told him to move. They walked towards the front of one of the ambulances and she pointed her gun to the driver inside, telling him to start the vehicle and then to vacate it. He obliged, no question asked and she climbed into the driver's seat and once again turned her gun towards Seth.

"This is where we depart Seth, you will not see me again. Tell Dorothy that I will miss her and that I meant what I said about Eleandra, she just didn't feel the same as I, so she had to die. Have a good life knowing I beat you, I led you down a merry path and you bought it."

Chelsea pulled up the windows and directed the ambulance out of the car park before speeding away, leaving Seth feeling empty and stupid. How could he have believed her lies? She killed Eleandra and now she was getting away. One minute she was tearing her heart out and almost one year later to the anniversary she's singing karaoke with her family and telling fictional stories about her to us. He was so mad at himself, he wouldn't let this drop, he would find her and he would bring her down, even if it was the last thing he did. Then he remembered Cassie and Dorothy, were they OK?

Pulling out his phone, he dialled Cassie's number.

"Hello Seth, how is Ludlow?"

"He's fine. Listen to me, lock the doors and don't let anyone in, get a weapon. I'll be there as soon as possible."

"What's going on?" said Cassie.

"It's Chelsea, it was her all along she killed Eleandra."

"What? Chelsea! But why?"

"Eleandra rejected her. She said she broke her heart so she killed her, then she finished off her dad because he wouldn't accept she was gay and oh, she also shot a nurse at the hospital in the back but it's OK because according to her, there is always collateral damage in these situations."

"Wow, and she has been pretending with us all this time. How did she know the password to Eleandra's phone and email, and about her secret email account?"

"She is a computer whizz, she hacked it all. I guess she reset the passwords so she could prove to us she knew what it was, when in reality she had set it herself."

"OK, front door and back door are both locked and I've pulled the kitchen table in front of the back door. Dorothy is upstairs when she comes down, I'll tell her."

"I'll be on my way shortly. I just need to check on Glenn, he got shot in the knee, then I'll make my way to you, Chelsea said goodbye and told me to give my best to Dorothy, I think she is making a run for it to escape from Kentsville but even so be careful."

"We will see you soon, and Seth, I love you."

"I love you too Cassie."

Seth went back into the hospital and ran up the stairs to the third floor. Chief Abraham was being helped into a wheelchair by a nurse and a police officer.

"How are you doing, Chief?"

"I'm alright Seth. I won't be walking on my own for a while but looks like the bullet went straight through so shouldn't be any complications. They're going to fix me up shortly. Where's Chelsea? Tell me you got her?"

"She left in an ambulance so it shouldn't be too hard to find and unless she has more bullets on her, she should run out soon enough. We need to find her before she kills again. Broadband, put out an APB on her and the ambulance, I want every available officer looking for her," Seth commanded, adrenaline pumping through his body.

Officer Broadbank looked at Chief Abraham.

"Yes, do what he said Broadbank. Seth, I know that you will be going after her too. Just be careful and my officers will be there if you need anything, oh and take my car as we brought you here. It's the black Porsche parked in car park B. And his name is Broadbank, he's not an internet provider."

He gave Seth the keys.

"Thank you. I shall let you know the moment I hear any news on her. Sorry, Broadbank."

With that, Seth left the chief in the hospital and headed to his aunt's house. He wanted to catch her before the police did, he started this and he wanted to finish it. After all, that would be a fitting ending for her. On his way to Aunt Dorothy's, he decided to call Quinton and fill him in on the news about Chelsea, just in case she went there. As he scrolled through his call history, he received an incoming call from Cassie.

"Cassie, I'm on my way to see you and Aunt Dorothy now, I shall be about five minutes or so."

"They won't be there, Seth."

Chelsea's voice left a fearful ringing in his ears. "Chelsea, why do you have Cassie's phone? Where are you?" he shouted down the phone at her.

"I'm on my way to the place where it all ended for Eleandra. I've decided if I can't have the woman I love, then you can't have the women you love either."

"Women?"

"Yes, good old aunty Dorothy has come along for a nice ride too."

"I swear, if you hurt either of them, I will kill you, Chelsea."

BANG.

There was only one shot that rang out but it filled Seth with undeniable dread, he began racing dangerously and illegally to the warehouse, he had to get there ASAP. He decided to go to his aunt Dorothy's house as it was on the way as he needed two things first. It was three in the morning and there was no one on the road but Seth knew that even if the roads were full, he wouldn't have slowed down. This whole turbulent affair was about to come to an end, only one more question remained, who was going to survive the night?

Heart lurching, adrenaline pumping, hot blood coursing through his veins, Seth was in an almighty state of urgency to get there. He didn't have a plan of action and decided to just wing it, although, to some that may not seem like the appropriate action to take when saving the lives of the two women he loved the most, Seth knew that he would never do anything to cause them anymore danger. He may have been worried and slightly fearful for their lives but he knew that this would end here and now. He got out of his car; he had swapped into his and left the Porsche at Dorothy's.

"Seth, so nice of you to join me," Chelsea shouted as he entered what was left of the warehouse she had burnt down. She was talking through a megaphone to amplify her voice for some reason. Seth thought that she had truly lost it. Surveying the scene in front of him, he noticed that both Cassie and Dorothy were sat upstairs on one of the warehouse balconies, with Chelsea stood in the middle of them, her gun tucked into the front of her faded blue jeans. Wielding a blade in one hand and a megaphone in the other looking like a possessed movie villain, Seth still wasn't sure the best course of action.

"It's time for the big game. First you have to qualify, so here is your question. If you get it right you enter the game but get it wrong and I kill you and then

184

you'll never know what happens to your lovely Aunt Dorothy and your precious boo. Are you ready hero?"

"Ask your question, Chelsea."

"Alright Sethy boy this should be an easy one for you, what was Eleandra's favourite colour?"

"Her favourite colour was green, it always reminded her of Christmas, in particular Christmas trees, it was her favourite time of year."

"Correct answer, I'm so glad you got the first one right I'd have hated to end the game early. This is brilliant, now we can move on to round two."

"First, I have a question for you, Chelsea. What did you and Eleandra really argue about the day before you killed her?"

Seth could see she was annoyed by this interruption but she went along with it anyway and gave Seth the answer.

"We argued about her thinking she had feelings for Ludlow, I tried to tell her she was confused and that she should be with me but she didn't listen she said she wanted him. It made me angry and I shouted at her and she shouted back at me, saying she can have feelings for whoever she wants. He poisoned her against me I wanted to kill him but instead, I killed her. I know in my heart Eleandra loved me really, she just didn't realise it at the time."

"Wow, Chelsea, you are something else."

"Thanks, Seth, you are too kind, NOW, ON WITH THE GAME!!!

I'm going to ask you another question and if you get it right, I will cut dear Eleandra's mum free. If you get it wrong, I cut her the same way I did her daughter."

"Oh, I'm starting to really love this game Chelsea, what's the next question?" said Seth.

He was seething with rage but trying to remain calm for the sake of the two most important people in his life.

"Whose fault is it that Eleandra is dead?"

Seth knew the answer to this question; the fault lies solely on the blade-wielding psycho in front of him. However, he knew that if he had said it was her fault then she would not hesitate to kill Dorothy and that realisation didn't sit well with him. He thought through his answer carefully but she was becoming impatient.

"Hurry up Seth! You are wasting my time. I am becoming irritated and the clock is ticking."

"You didn't mention a clock before, kind of unfair to bring it up now, isn't it?"

"Fair point, Sethy boy! But hurry up, whose fault is it that Eleandra is dead?"

"Eleandra's death lies on her own shoulders. It's her fault she's dead," he said through gritted teeth, his reply feeling bitter in his own mouth.

It pained him to say those words out loud.

"Hooray, correct answer. If she had just loved me back, she would still be here with us today, we would have been happy and in love. But no, she was too good for the likes of me."

True to her word, Chelsea cut Dorothy free and let her walk down the fire-burnt stairs and into Seth's safe arms. Holding her tight, Seth begged her to go and wait outside but a stern shake off the head showed a refusal to this request. She wasn't going anywhere, especially not now. "No, I'm staying right here, till the end," said Dorothy, stubborn as ever.

It was no use trying to persuade her otherwise. Although kind-hearted, Dorothy was a stubborn woman and there was no reasoning with her once her mind was set on something. Seth thought it must run in the family and turned back to the madwoman holding Cassie hostage.

"What about Cassie? Are you going to let her go?"

He was desperate, he had only just gotten her into his life as the lover and partner that he had always wanted her to be, he wasn't prepared to lose her.

"Nope. IT'S TIME FOR ROUND THREEEEEEEE. Same rules apply, get it right and I let her go, get it wrong and she dies. I wouldn't mess this up if I were you Seth, we don't want your precious Cassie to die at your hands now, do we?"

"Just ask the damn question, Chelsea, I'm sick of this game now."

"Patience Seth, I'm the one in charge, I'll get to it when I'm God, damn, ready."

"What's your question?"

"Why are we all here tonight?" Compared to this question, the first was a walk in the park. He was able to give a proper answer the first time around due to everything that Chelsea had said about Eleandra earlier on in the night. She was so convinced that all of this was Eleandra's own fault, blinded by her own hatred, she was truly a psycho. Although it pained him to say anything negative against Eleandra, Seth had to give her the answer that she wanted to hear rather than the truth. It had to be something Eleandra related but what was it exactly that she had wanted him to say? He turned to his aunty for any suggestions that she may have had, and just as she was away to answer him, two loud gunshots rang out around the warehouse. Chelsea had shot the bullets on the floor next to their feet.

"No conferring with her, I want your answer and your answer alone. So what's it gonna be Sethy boy?"

"I don't know, I'm thinking, I just need a little more time."

"No, no, and no! Answer me right now or I will put a bullet in her pretty little head."

The blade was tucked into her trousers now and the gun in her hand pointed at the back of Cassie's head.

"It's Eleandra's fault again."

"Oh Seth, you disappoint me and you were doing so well. Unfortunately, you are out of luck tonight and instead of a lovely prize, you get to watch as your beautiful beloved dies."

Frozen to the spot, Seth watched as she stepped around the side of her prey and pointed the gun against the left temple of Cassie's head. He couldn't do anything to stop the flow of tears from streaming down her face as he gazed upon that of his love, Cassie. Closing his eyes, Seth felt his heart break the moment he heard her pull the trigger.

CLICK...CLICK, CLICK, CLICK.

She was out of bullets. There must have been someone watching over him because by God she was out of bullets. He had never been more grateful for anything in his entire life.

"So you think that you have gotten the better of me do you Seth? Well, thankfully, I have my trusty knife here. The same blade I ended Eleandra's life with."

Chelsea dropped the gun on the floor and took the knife from the front of her trousers.

"Shall I slit her throat or shall I stab her in the heart?"

Seth watched on completely awestruck as Cassie took matters into her own hands. Cassie wasn't going to let Chelsea bring her down, she wasn't going to suffer the same fate as Eleandra, Mr Chive or the nurse at the hospital. In a moment of both sheer panic and utter impulsiveness, Cassie rammed into Chelsea before she could get the knife out of the front of her jeans and then launched herself off of the balcony and towards Seth. It was roughly a fifteen-foot drop which caused her body to slightly bounce off of the floor, side first. Seth and Dorothy rushed to her aid while Chelsea who was getting back to her feet leaned over the balcony. She picked up her megaphone that has been knocked out of her hand.

"Well, is she dead? Or do I need to come down there and finish her off myself?"

"Sorry to upset you Chelsea but Cassie is alive, but you don't need to come down here, I'm coming up there. I'm coming to end this, now."
Before making his way up, he stooped and whispered in Cassie's ear so that even Dorothy couldn't hear what he said. She barely managed to give him the nod that showed her acceptance to what he had said, however, she was strong and gave it her best shot and slowly moved her head back and forth. Seth smiled, kissed her lips softly and moved towards the stairs.

"Come on then hero. I wanted to watch as I broke your heart but I guess I'll just stab you in it instead."

At that moment, the police showed up. One of the nearby residents must have called them when they heard the shots or so Seth concluded. Seth called over to Dorothy and asked her to stay with Cassie, she was awake but in a lot of pain. Then he ran up the stairs.

"Chelsea, give me the knife and this will all be over with quickly."

Chelsea cackled and threw the megaphone on the floor a few inches away from her feet, after all she wouldn't be needing it now that Seth was mere metres away from her.

"Seth, I'm going to kill you like I killed Eleandra and then I will go down there and finish both of them off as well. You see, Eleandra loved you all more than she loved me and I just can't be having that now, can I?"

"Stop talking and let's finish this."

Seth was never one to hit a woman and he always stood by that, to him it was wrong but just this once he was going to have to make an exception; she was trying to kill him and the ones he loved after all. Seth was never going to allow that to happen. Chelsea waved her blade around wildly before finally lunging it at him, missing his ear by millimetres. Seth swayed out the way and Chelsea's force made her go past him, they had naturally just switched places.

"You are going to feel true pain when I launch this blade through your heart. I promise you, Seth, I'll make it quick and you will feel nothing but the warmth of my steel. Well maybe you won't, you'll be dead but I'll feel the warmth of your blood on my hands."

"No Chelsea. You are going to spend the rest of your life in prison where you will never be able to hurt anyone else in this town ever again."

"You want hurt; I'll give you hurt. Dorothy's dying, your aunty has cancer and she didn't tell you, that shows how much she loves you. Bet that hurts, doesn't it? Oh wait, there's more, what about Cassie? This will sting too."

"Spit it out already."

"Cassie accepted a job in Australia two weeks ago. Apparently, she is trying to find the right time to tell you, I guess it never came up. Soon you'll have no Cassie and no Dorothy. They'll both be leaving you soon enough and you'll be all alone, it's better that I put you out of your misery now Seth, save you the pain later."

"Put me out of my misery. You are my misery, Chelsea! And all you've really been doing is giving the police time to sneak up behind you."

Chelsea spun around in panic but to her surprise, there was no one there. Seth used that moment of distraction to attempt to rush her. Jumping towards the one who had caused all this misery and pain, he managed to wrestle her to the ground and proceeded to fight with her to gain control of the blade. He was much stronger than her and had the upper hand as he was on top of her and able to minimise her upper body movement, however, that was quickly changed with a knee to his balls. Momentarily winded, Seth released his grasp on the hand which held the knife, giving Chelsea the chance to plunge the blade into his shoulder without hesitation. Using his injured state to her advantage, Chelsea kicked him in his chest with both her feet which caused him to fall onto his back. With the rolls now reversed, Chelsea jumped onto his chest and held the blade to his throat.

"My mum always said 'kick a man in the balls and he is at your mercy'. Didn't I tell you that I would kill you?"

"Yes, you did but you're missing something, Chelsea, one piece of very vital information."

"Really, Seth, and what's that?"

BANG.

He shot her straight in the chest without hesitation, surprised that she was actually still breathing due to the close proximity. She fell forward straight onto Seth, her blood running all over him and her hot breath on his face. He pushed her almost lifeless body onto the floor beside him and sat up next to her.

"You didn't know this until now but I also have a gun, I just never used it before, turns out I'm a great shot at point-blank range."

Chelsea was barely breathing but she managed to utter some defiant words about how she would soon be reunited with her one true love, Eleandra.

"No Chelsea you won't, she will never accept you. Do you think she would actually love you after what you have done to her? After what you have done to the people she loves. She would never in a million years be with you. Her heart was too kind and too and pure for someone like you. You will go to jail, and you will forever live with what you have done, forever living with the knowledge that she never loved you and that you were never good enough for her."

"I stabbed her, she deserved it, I saw her and Ludlow that morning having coffee, I wanted to be that happy with her, not him."

"You don't get to choose who makes you happy, it just happens. I hope you are never happy again, Chelsea."

Seth put his right hand over his left shoulder to apply pressure and walked away. He finally felt relief, a lot of pain but relief too. A weight had been lifted. Although he would always feel the pain of her loss, Seth knew Eleandra would be proud of him, he could practically feel it. It had been a long and painful year and a person he thought he could trust turned out to be a deceitful liar, who was actually the cause of all of this pain. Looking back at Chelsea, Seth saw her eyes flicker shut. He had never wished death on another person before and even after all she had done, he wouldn't wish it on her, Eleandra would not have wanted that. He wouldn't shed a single tear if she was to die but he wouldn't be displeased if she didn't. All that mattered to him in that moment was the closure that his family would now have, the closure that Clarke's family would have. Chelsea would suffer in death or she would suffer in life, either way, Eleandra finally got the justice that she deserved, and Seth was finally able to say, case closed.

Ambulances took everyone to the hospital for a full check-up shortly after and Chief Abraham escorted them all the way. Cassie was allowed to leave the hospital the next morning as she only suffered some severe bruising and was able to walk on her own but the doctors wanted to keep Seth in a day or two to make sure there was no infection. There was no rest for the wicked though as the following day Seth, bandaged shoulder and all, checked himself out of the hospital against doctor's orders and with Cassie by his side, he wanted to clear up the whole Eshima mess and a few other little things still bugging him. His aunty Dorothy was also in the room and he took this time to have a heart to heart with her before they all left.

"Cassie, could I just have a word with my aunt alone, please?"

"Yeah sure, I'll wait outside."

Neither of them spoke until Cassie had left.

"Everything alright, Seth?" said Dorothy.

"I want to talk to you about your cancer."

"You want to know why I didn't tell you."

"Well, yes."

"After losing Eleandra last year, I decided I would do this alone to prevent you from having to suffer again. If I lose the battle then that would be grief enough, I didn't want you to worry about me or change your daily routine just for me."

"But…"

Dorothy cut him off.

"No buts. How long have you known?" she asked.

"What do you mean?"

"When Chelsea told you I had cancer, you didn't look surprised like you did with the news about Cassie. So how long have you known?"

"I found a letter about a week ago when I opened a draw in the kitchen to look for something. I didn't mean to read it but I saw it was from the hospital and was curious."

"It's OK Seth. I wish you had come to me then but it's out now, you know and I know. You know, I stand by what I said though I don't want anything to change."

"What type of cancer do you have?"

"I have colorectal cancer, it's still early on in the process, I've only had two meetings but once I know more, I promise I will tell you."

"How bad is it?"

"Initial outlook is positive but again I won't know more until my next appointment. Please don't put in a call to anyone or start googling ways to help, let the experts deal with it. All I'll need from you is your support, Seth."

"I won't interfere but if you need anyone to go with you to any appointments then you know you only have to ask…"

She cut him off for the second time.

"I only have to ask Cassie, that's what you were going to say, right?"

"I'm sure Cassie would go with you if you asked her but I was going to say me."

"No offence darling, but you aren't the best at feelings; it's taken you how long to tell Cassie your true intentions for her, so if I want someone to go with me, I will ask Cassie, if you don't mind?"

"No, that makes sense."

"Now that's sorted and that evil woman has been dealt with too, what are your plans going forward," Dorothy asked.

"Well, me and Cassie are going to be moving in together soon and once I've spoken to her about a few things we shall see where we go from there, she's not going to Australia, she turned the job down when she found out about my feelings for her."

"That girl really loves you, you do right by her and you two will live a long and happy life together, I have no doubt."

"I believe you are correct with that assessment, now, we best get Cassie back in here, I have a few people to see."

"Hug first?" she asked.

"Sounds good to me."

They shared a hug and then Dorothy opened the door and Cassie came back in the room so Seth could talk to them both.

"I need to speak to Eshima again."

Cassie wasn't happy with this; Seth could see it written all over her face but she never tried to talk him out of it. Seth rang Chief Abraham and he said he could speak to Eshima who they still had in custody. It wasn't normal to keep someone this long without charging them but because she had connections to Seth who was investigating the murder, Chief Abraham pulled some strings and she was still in custody against her lawyer's wishes. Seth and Cassie arrived at the police station and met with the Chief, he explained that he had spoken to Eshima and her lawyer and she agreed to talk to Seth with him and her lawyer in the room, on the record.

"Really, why the sudden change of heart?" asked Seth.

"No idea, I guess we'll find out soon enough, ready to go in?"

"Oh you best believe I am! See you soon, Cassie."

Cassie took a seat in Chief Abraham's office and waited for them to come back.

Once all four of them were all in the interrogation room together, Chief Abraham started recording.

"Well Seth, I guess it's time to find out what this lying bitch, sorry I meant, what Eshima has to say."

Chapter Sixteen

"Interview with Eshima Sato, present is I, Chief Abraham and Kentsville's private investigator, Seth Bronx."

"Eshima, I heard from Chief Abraham that you wanted to talk to me. May I ask what about?"

"You know what about Seth," said Eshima.

"I may do but could you please state it for the tape."

"Fine, I wanted to talk to you about the lies I told you about us having children together."

"What did you want to say? That's rhetorical, don't answer. We already know it was a complete fabrication and we know that someone was paying you to distract me from investigating Eleandra Jacobson's murder, so you are an accomplice to a killer. What would you like to add?" said Seth.

"I think I know who was paying me, it doesn't mean they're the killer but I think I know who was paying me money to lie to you "

"Really? Well before you give us that information, can I ask why you are coming forward with it now?"

"I just want this to be over, I need the money but I don't want to spend too much time in jail, I was hoping if I help you, then maybe I would not go to jail."

"What is it exactly that you know?"

"I followed a woman when she dropped off an envelope to me when I first got to town; I wanted to know who I was dealing with, so as she left, I followed. I found out she had loads of money, I was actually considering blackmailing her for more money when she told me I had to leave."

"What's this woman's name?"

"Chelsea Chive," said Eshima.

Seth looked at the Chief and he nodded at him; it was like he could read his mind.

"Chelsea Chive," repeated Seth.

"Yes, that's her name, she paid me to lie to you, she must be helping the killer."

"You mean the same Chelsea Chive who was arrested yesterday after she tried to kill me and my family, the same Chelsea Chive who in fact committed the murder of Eleandra Jacobson and Clarke Richards."

"Oh my god! I knew she was in on it but I didn't think she was a killer. Is everyone OK?"

"Eshima, I don't know about Chief Abraham but I am done here."

"No, please Seth, I had no idea she killed anyone, you have to help me."

"Chief, I understand that Eshima has a serious drug addiction and some serious debts too. I suggest we drop the charges and she be checked in to a rehabilitation centre to sort herself out and hopefully for her, turn her life around."

"For now I guess, interview terminated at fourteen hundred hours."

"Goodbye Eshima, I hope to never speak to you again."

With that remark, Seth left the room and hoped he never did cross paths with her again.

"Thank you, Chief. If only she had done the right thing and came forward before she was arrested, we might have saved Mr Chive's life and that poor nurse too."

"I know Seth, it seems some people are only willing to help when it's their last resort or they think it will help them in some way."

"Sad state of affairs."

"Very true. Anyway, I'll be in touch, have a good day Seth and you Cassie."

They had just entered the chief's office and Cassie was now, back in their company again.

"I really need the toilet, are you two OK seeing yourselves out?"

"Of course, when nature calls you must answer. Speak soon, Glenn."

"Where to next then, Seth?" Cassie asked when they had got back into the car.

"Chelsea is alive and I am going to visit her as there are a few things I want to know. I know you probably think that it is a mistake but just let me finish. I spoke to Chief Abraham and he told me she has been patched up and, in a few days, she will be transferred to her new home at Castle prison on the island."

"Do you think that's a good idea? She can't hurt us anymore and everyone knows who really killed Eleandra now, shouldn't we just leave it at that?"

"I just want to keep my promise to Monica, I cleared Clarke's name but I want to know why she killed him. Then it's over and I can put her behind me for good."

"I don't like it Seth but I won't stand in your way if you need this closure then go and get it and let's move on."

"Do you want me to come with you again, Seth?" Cassie asked.

"I was wondering if you would but I want to do this alone."

"I understand, and of course, I will drive you to the Psychiatric ward."

"Thank you, let's get going then, the Chief has got me in and I want to make a few other stops too but I don't imagine I'll be staying at any of them for too long."

The whole way there Seth sat quietly in the car staring out the windows; he had a pensive look on his face and was wondering if Chelsea would tell him what he wanted to know. He only had one way to find out, ask.

"Thank you, Cassie, I won't be long."

Cassie put her hand on top of his and kissed him on the cheek.

"Take as long as you need to get the closure you want."

He went through security and waited in a padded room with chains and handcuffs on one side of the table. He waited there for ten minutes and then Chief Abraham limped in with the use of his new cane.

"Chief, what are you doing here?"

"I will be in the room through there when you speak to her, it's double-sided glass so I can see and hear everything she says I just want to see if she tells you anything and if she does, I will get it all on tape so it's official. I hope that you don't mind?"

"No, not at all."

"I'll head out and then they'll bring her in, don't let her know anyone is in there or she might not say what you want her to."

"Understood."

Two men led Chelsea into the room a minute after Chief Abraham left, the last time he saw her she was on death's door, a few days later and she didn't look much better now. They sat her down and handcuffed her to the table which Seth noted was now bolted to the floor as well.

"So you lived?" said Seth.

"Obviously."

Chelsea was defiant but Seth noticed she wasn't as confident as a few days prior when she thought she was in control.

"That's a shame."

"If I had died you wouldn't be able to come and gloat now, would you?"

"I'm not here to gloat, I'm here to tie up some loose ends."

"You come to finish me off, did you?" said Chelsea.

"No, I don't want to kill you, I want you to spend every day locked away, miserable and alone."

"Then what do you want Seth, I'm chained to the desk so I have to listen to you but please, at least make this interesting."

"Sorry, I'm not here to make this interesting for you, I just want you to clear a few things up for me."

"What exactly do you want to know, I'm pretty sure I told you most things."

"No, you didn't. First, why did you frame Clarke?"

"That idiot was an easy mark that's why."

"So how did you pick him to take the fall?"

"I got a taxi home with him a few days before I killed Eleandra and I thought to myself this guy is so basic and boring, he would be perfect, it would be the most exciting thing to ever happen to him, I'd basically be doing him a favour."

"You're insane."

"Let's agree to disagree, Seth."

"So what next?" he asked.

"I decided to get a taxi home with him the day before and give him five thousand pounds to enlist his help."

"What kind of help?"

"Don't worry Seth, you were right about one thing, which did surprise me. Clarke was innocent, he wasn't involved in killing anyone. I asked him to hide my bag for me. I told him to meet me in the morning and I'd give him another five thousand and then if he dropped my bag off the next day at the same time, I'd give him a further ten thousand."

"Instead, what you did was kill him and pin Eleandra's murder on him."

"I know what you're thinking Seth, I'm a genius."

"No, not even close to how I would describe you, Chelsea. Why did you put so much money in the bag? Why not just fill it with clothes or paper?"

"I said he was boring, not stupid, if I gave him that much money to hide clothes, he might have got suspicious or not bothered turning up. If he knew I had money, he'd turn up to get more."

"And you got someone to tip me off. It was still in his locker as a distraction, to get my attention away from you."

"I wanted to pin it on Ludlow, that was the main aim but anyone but me would do in the end."

Seth got up and made to leave. He had heard enough; he didn't want to look at her anymore.

"That's it? I thought there was more you wanted to know Sethy boy."

Seth hesitated, he took a deep breath and turned back around to face her, still standing by the door.

"There were a few little things but I despise you, I don't want to be near you another second. I have the information I needed to tell Mrs Richards, I'm done with you, Chelsea. You can rot in whatever hole they put you in."

He turned to leave for the second time but she wasn't finished with him just yet.

"So you don't wanna know about poor Lucas then?" Seth stopped dead in his tracks again. "It was you; I already knew you paid Eshima, is that what you're trying to tell me?"

"Of course it was me, I wanted more than one distraction to keep your head on a swivel and not zoned into the real killer, who was right under your nose the whole time."

"You fabricated the death of a child that didn't really exist. Do you not see that you are in serious need of psychiatric help?"

"All I need is to fully recover from my gunshot wound and then get out of here and finish the job," said Chelsea.

There was pure evil in her eyes Seth could almost feel her hate burning into him.

"Finish what job?"

"I'm gonna reunite Eleandra and her family real soon."

"No Chelsea, the only thing you are going to be doing real soon or in fact anytime going forward is enjoying the view of your four walls. We are done here. Oh and for the record, Eshima never left, she confessed everything to me and we are going to get her some help to fight her demons. I hope you get that too. I'll make sure Mrs Richards spends your money well."

He got up to leave again, for the third time. This time he wouldn't turn back, no matter what the venomous witch said.

"Seth, that's my money, Seth, get back here now. Seth. Seth. I'm gonna kill you, Seth Bronx, I swear it. I'm gonna kill you dead."

Seth had a smile on his face as he walked out the front gate and saw his beautiful Cassie waiting for him.

"I love you, Cassie Bowl," he said.

"I love you too, Mr Bronx. Why are you smiling?"

"I'm smiling because the hate and poison that infected our lives, is gone, from now on we will all live happy lives, Chelsea Chive free."

"That sounds good to me, so where to now?" Cassie asked.

"Let's go to see Ludlow and then after, I'll go tell Monica what I found out about Clarke, meanwhile, this is what she had to say."

They drove to Ludlow's house, he had moved into the apartment next to the rowing club yesterday according to Dorothy, she had been meeting with his mum for the last few days since he came out of the hospital and they had become friendly. They parked outside and could see Ludlow through the window to the left of the front door, Cassie gave a little wave and he waved back. Seth got out of the car and waited for Cassie who never exited, she must have thought he was going in alone again, so he ducked his head back in the car.

"You coming?" said Seth.

"Yeah, sure."

They both walked towards Ludlow's new front door together and he opened it to greet them.

"This is a nice surprise, please come in."

Ludlow led them into the living room in which they had waved at him upon arrival. There was a leather two-seater recliner sofa, a corner unit and eight boxes. It was clear he hadn't had time to unpack yet and Seth offered him a hand to do so.

"No, you're very kind to offer but I will get around to it, I just want to get back into competition shape ASAP, unpacking can wait, plus you were hurt too, Seth. I'm sure you got the same take it easy speech too. I've decided that not unpacking is, me taking it easy and working out is rehab," said Ludlow.

"I like that, it's smart, wouldn't you agree Cassie?" asked Seth.

"I agree with the doctors, you should both be taking it easy, not going rowing."

"Well, I will row slower then to make you and the doctors happy."

Seth and Ludlow laughed and Cassie gave them a sarcastic smile.

"So to what do I owe this visit?"

"I wanted to ask you about the day Eleandra died. I have the bigger picture but I'm just trying to dot the i's and cross the t's."

"What do you want to know?"

"You saw her that morning, why?"

"We had started going running together, no one knew except us, it wasn't a secret or anything we just hadn't told anyone. We had only been out twice before that day I believe."

"So you went running together and then went your separate ways?"

"No, I got there in my running gear and then remembered she had asked if we could do coffee instead that morning as she wanted to just chill out before a busy day. We had coffee, then I went for a run alone, that was the last time I ever saw her. I think about it all the time, I used to beat myself up about it all the time, blamed myself for most of the last year."

"It wasn't your fault Ludlow, I guess you know that though as you said used to," said Cassie.

"Yes, although I will never forgive myself for leaving her that day, I know it wasn't my fault she died, I just miss her so much, there's no one else like her."

"We know, we get it. We were lucky to be in the small group who really knew her, I for one know I am so proud to be her cousin and she will always live on in my heart."

"Well said, Seth," added Cassie.

Ludlow who had stood for this conversation as he had insisted Seth and Cassie sit on the sofa, now pulled one of the many boxes over and sat down.

"What else did you want to ask?" said Ludlow.

"So you left her where?"

"I left her in the cafe; it was full of people so I figured she was safe and sound."

"I guess Chelsea found her somewhere between the cafe and the warehouse. I'm glad the warehouse is gone, I didn't feel anything when I first saw it burning but after our recent encounter there, on top of Eleandra's murder, I say good riddance to the place."

"I agree, Seth, I'm glad I never have to see that place again," said Cassie.

"Yes, I heard what happened there after the hospital, it must have been awful."

"It was terrifying but I guess getting your head smashed in isn't nice either?" said Cassie.

"No, I can attest it is not but thankfully, it's over and you put her away, Seth."

"Well, I didn't do it alone Ludlow. What we did, together, was get justice for Eleandra and everyone else in Kentsville she has ever hurt, hopefully, we never see her evil face ever again."

"Amen to that," Ludlow said.

"I guess we should be off then, we are going to see Clarke's wife."

"I bet she is over the moon with the outcome."

"I bet she is too. Don't be a stranger, Ludlow."

"Thank you, Seth, and it was an honour to be a part of Eleandra's life."

"Like I said, don't be a stranger, you are family now."

Ludlow hugged Seth and then Cassie with tears in his eyes.

"Right, well you two should go now as it's getting really steamy in here and I need to open a window," Ludlow said.

"God, you men are all the same, Seth is always making excuses when he tears up, some rubbish about someone cutting onions nearby or his make-believe hay fever kicking in," said Cassie.

"I don't know what you mean Cassie, I never tear up."

"Bye Ludlow, see you soon."

"Bye Cassie, Bye Seth."

Seth shook Ludlow's hand and they headed off for Monica's.

"Last stop Cassie and then I'd love it if we could go for a walk by the river."

"That sounds nice Seth."

Upon arriving at her house, she opened the door to welcome them with floods of tears.

"You did it, Seth, you officially proved my husband was innocent, you cleared Clarke's name."

She threw her arms around him and squeezed him tightly once more.

"Monica, I appreciate the hug but my shoulder is still kind of sore."

"Sorry, I'm just so happy. Do you want to come in for a cuppa?"

"No, we won't be staying. I just wanted to come and say sorry that Clarke was killed for nothing. Seems Chelsea thought she was doing him a favour; she really is sick and twisted. I spoke to the Chief and I understand if you don't want it but this is yours technically, so here."

Cassie handed over the bag with the two hundred thousand pounds in it.

"Chelsea paid your husband that, he didn't know he was getting paid to die and be framed for murder but still it technically was his and now it's yours," said Seth.

"How much is here?"

"Two hundred thousand pounds. If you want to keep it, please do, if not then I'd understand and we can donate it to charity but like I say if you decide to keep it, spend it well, maybe a family holiday."

"Seth, I'm so glad you cleared his name, my boys will be so happy when I show them this, we will forever be indebted to you."

"Monica, you and your boys owe me nothing, besides, I didn't do all the work myself, Cassie helped me a lot, she was by my side through it all. I couldn't have done this without her." Mrs Richards threw her arms around Cassie now and squeezed her too.

"I was just helping Seth to do what was right, nothing more," said Cassie.

"Well, I thank you both for your hard work, if you ever need anything let me know."

"We will, goodbye Monica."

"Goodbye Seth, goodbye Cassie."

Monica waved them off and Cassie drove them both towards the river for a romantic walk.

"I'd forgotten how beautiful this place is, and it's so peaceful too. We should come here more often," said Cassie.

"I came here a few days ago, it was the first time I'd been here in years and I couldn't agree with you more Cassie, it's beautiful. I came here to clear my head and just think."

"Did it work?"

"Not really. I got a couple of phone calls, there were families everywhere making memories that I used to make with my parents, memories I thought I'd be making with Lucas around about now."

"How are you feeling about that? We've been so preoccupied with Chelsea that we haven't really had a chance to talk about it, do you want to now?"

"Not really, what's done is done, it was all lies, Eshima hurt me but it's in the past now I want to look to the future, our future, Cassie. So let's start with when you're moving in, officially."

"How does tomorrow sound, Mr Bronx?"

"Tomorrow seems as good a day as any."

"Then that's when it'll be. I'll speak to Adam at the estate agents and get him to come price up my old place for me and get the ball rolling, and then afterwards, I'll start packing."

"How about I cook us a nice dinner as well, a welcome to your new home."

"That would be great. I've got you trained already."

"Trained, really? You honestly think you could ever train this wild beast you see before you?"

"Yes, it'd be easy in my opinion."

"Oh please, like you could train me, I've got you in the palm of my hand already Cassie, you just don't realise it yet."

They both smiled and looked out at the river.

"How about we bring our children here in the future, teach them to ride their bikes, feed the ducks, ride the miniature railway etc. If you want children that is?"

"It's probably one of the very few things we have never discussed. I want three though, just so you know."

"Three, what's wrong with one?"

"Fine we can compromise and have two," she said.

"Still too many for my liking. How about one and a half?"

"How do you have half a child? And that's not a rhetorical question I actually want to hear your answer."

"I don't know, maybe give birth to two, pick our favourite and hire the other one as our butler."

"So two it is then?"

"If we get that far, we can negotiate nearer the time, I'm a good negotiator so I'm sure we will stick to one."

"Seth, on a serious note, are you really wanting children or is this a knee jerk reaction to what happened with Eshima?"

"No Cassie, I'm sure. If the last week has taught me anything it's to stop wasting time, if you know what you want and have the means to get it or make it, then get on with it, before it's too late."

"Well, I like this go and get 'em attitude Seth. So what's next on your list?"

"First, we get you moved into our house and then, well I seem to recall you nodding your head in the warehouse just after you jumped off the balcony to my suggestion."

"Well, go on then Mr Bronx, spit it out."

"When we get married, will we stay living there or buy a new house?"

"Well you see Seth, when you whispered that question in my ear, I was half out of it so I'm not really sure it counts, plus you never even gave me a ring."

"Really? Right, let's get that straightened out right now then."

"What do you mean, Seth?"

Seth took a small jewellery box out of his pocket. He stood directly in front of Cassie and smiled at her for a few seconds but didn't say anything.

"What's this?" she asked.

He opened the box away from her so she couldn't see inside it and then took her left hand with his right.

"I have already asked for your dad's approval and he was happy to oblige, so now Cassie it's your turn. Apparently, the first time didn't count, so I guess I have to do this properly, don't I?"

"I guess you do."

"Cassie Angela Bowl, it would be my distinguished honour if yo..."

"Sorry Seth, you got shot in the shoulder, I didn't think that affected your legs."

"I can take a hint, Cassie."

Seth got down on one knee and continued.

"It would be my distinguished honour if you would make me the luckiest and the happiest man in the world."

He spun the box around so she could see the beautiful engagement ring he had chosen for this special moment.

"Oh, my God! Seth, that's stunning."

"As you approve of the ring, I guess I only have one more thing to ask.
Will you marry me?"